MY LAST MOVIE STAR

RANDOM HOUSE

NEW YORK

MY LAST MOVIE STAR

A NOVEL OF HOLLYWOOD

MARTHA SHERRILL

This is a work of fiction. All of the incidents described, and all of the characters with the exception of a few well-known public and historical figures, are products of the author's imagination and are not to be construed as real. Where real-life figures appear, the words attributed to them in dialogue are in certain cases adapted or quoted from memoirs and interviews. However, the situations and events concerning those persons are entirely fictional and are not intended to depict actual incidents or to change the entirely fictional nature of the work.

Copyright © 2002 Martha Sherrill

Owing to limitations of space, acknowledgments of permission to quote from previously published materials will be found on page 355.

Library of Congress Cataloging-in-Publication Data
Sherrill, Martha.
My last movie star : a novel of Hollywood / Martha Sherrill.
p.   cm.
ISBN 0-375-50769-8
1. Motion picture actors and actresses—Fiction.
2. Hollywood (Los Angeles, Calif.)—Fiction. 3. Women
journalists—Fiction. 4. Traffic accidents—Fiction. 5. Missing
persons—Fiction. 6. Actresses—Fiction. I. Title.
PS3619.H469 M9   2003   813'.6—dc21   2002069707

Random House website address: www.atrandom.com
Printed in the United States of America on acid-free paper
98765432
First Edition

Book design by J. K. Lambert

TO BILL

One curses and calls her fickle, inconstant and immodest; a second condemns her credulity and lightness of behaviour; a third acquits and forgives her, while she is arraigned and reproached by a fourth; some celebrate her beauty; others find fault with her disposition: in short, she is censured and adored by them all; nay, to such a pitch hath their extravagance risen, that some of them complain of her disdain, tho' they never spoke to her; and others, in their lamentations, pretend to feel the rage of jealousy, which is a passion she never inspired; for, as I have already mentioned, her fault was known before her inclination was suspected: there is not a hollow of a rock, the margin of a rill, nor the shade of a tree, that is not occupied by some shepherd, recounting his misfortune to the winds; wherever an echo can be formed, it repeats the name of Leandra; the hills resound with Leandra; the rivulets murmur Leandra: in short, Leandra keeps us all enchanted and perplexed, hoping we know not how, and dreading we know not what.

Miguel de Cervantes, Don Quixote, *Vol. 1, Book IV*
(translated by Tobias Smollett)

MY LAST MOVIE STAR

t didn't feel like a lark anymore. We had started out in Palm Springs that morning and now found ourselves on an empty stretch of Interstate 5 pointed north, still inland but edging slowly toward the coast. It was hot—strange Christmas weather. Allegra had insisted on driving. "It'll be more fun," she said. But she was dopey behind the wheel, was paying half attention, grinding gears, and swerving abruptly. The top was down and her blond hair kept blowing into her eyes and she'd leave it there. Knots had formed on the windward side of her head. She kept touching her bottom lip, nibbling it, and scratching her neck.

I could hear the engine behind us, its low baritone growl. The old white Porsche sat so low to the ground that the heat-cracked highway was a blur of gray cement beside me. Allegra had borrowed the car from an old boyfriend, a recently dumped boyfriend, a TV star who looked like he wanted to be more than that but never would. He lacked the necessary depth, or mystery, or pain. He was probably wondering where the car was. He was probably wondering all kinds of things. Allegra had almost married him—a grotesquely large ring had been designed—but now she never mentioned him, not even to tell me this was his car. I had come across his name and address on a white registration stub in the glove box while searching for a tire-pressure gauge the day before: Tom Swimmer, 1147 El Cabron Drive, Hollywood, CA.

He lived in one of the canyons, probably gazed foggily out his windows every morning, at the dry brush and brown hills and the smog line coming and going, and told himself life was good. The only problem was, he had to keep reminding himself. He'd been left behind—Allegra moved quickly—discarded, relinquished. "Isn't it amazing how you can forget a person exists?" I could still hear her saying. "They just slip from your mind." And I wondered how many days after we'd parted, after I'd done my work, asked my questions, taken my notes at night in the bathroom with the door closed while she watched TV on the hotel bed, comforted her through an ordeal or two— a temporary girlfriend, an extemporaneous yes-man— before she'd forget that I'd ever existed too. Or perhaps that process had already begun.

Way off ahead, a big white box of an RV was taking up a

point of road on the horizon. It was either stopped or going so slowly it looked stopped. I noticed it just as Allegra veered again, more dramatically than before, as though she'd seen the RV too and had been startled or awakened by it. She looked over at me and laughed. It's what she did when she didn't have another idea. My eyes met hers, then returned quickly to the road in a demonstration of serious-ness. I had learned that prolonged eye contact with Allegra would initiate more eye contact, more talking, and then gesturing. She had to connect when she talked. She needed to meet another gaze even while driving.

As we approached the RV, the Porsche's tires played with the center line, moved over the white slashes then back. Over and back again. It seemed deliberate, at a regular rhythm, as though Allegra was paying attention after all—toying with the RV, teasing it. And me.

"It's weird how there's no traffic," she said as we roared past the camper.

"Oh, somebody will turn up," I said, "when you don't expect it."

"No cars for, like, miles."

"It's Monday."

"Oh yeah."

She sped up. Her legs were stretched out in front of her, and I could see her bare feet in the shadows under the dashboard. When she pressed on the pedals, the blood left her toes, made them turn whiter, and I could see her new coat of reddish-purple toenail polish glistening in the dark.

San Simeon was today's destination. Allegra insisted I
see it before returning east. It was her "favorite place on
earth," as she put it, "haunted and scary and full of ghosts."
What would we do there? "Talk about the old days," she
said. I went along. I was older, certainly smarter, had been
picking up the tab for meals, the syrupy pancakes she ate almost every morning for breakfast, the Cobb salads and chef
salads and wilted-spinach numbers with the hot bacon
dressing she had for lunch (my wallet was bulging with re-
ceipts from Coco's), but this was Allegra's show entirely. It
felt like a slightly dated road-trip picture. Everything was a
little false and too laughy. The old white bathtub roaring
toward a hilltop castle. Two gals roaring into the future.
The journalist and the rising star—young, alive, learning
from each other, writing in their respective diaries at
night—except, I'm afraid, that fantasy was part of Allegra's
show too. She was full of shows. Her handwriting was
loopy and cutesy. She bought secondhand dresses at thrift
stores. She washed her face with water and uncooked oat-
meal. Everywhere she went, she left behind piles of old
clothes and half-empty cardboard canisters of Quaker
Oats. She was dreaming she was free, pretending she was
still a girl, pretending she wasn't levelheaded, or a hard
worker, or ambitious, or doing a sky dive toward some
bull's-eye of fame. It was hard to remember whether she
was sixteen or twenty-six or somewhere in between. She
had been on her own for years, already been married and
divorced, raised her younger half brothers, driven her

semifamous parents and stepparents to drug-treatment centers and dry-out tanks. Her mother, the sometime B actress Kay Blyth, had eventually dried out so much she turned to ashes. Allegra drove to Big Bear Lake to scatter them.

She was probably going to see a few million this year, now that *Sphinxa* was looking like it might be a hit, a controversy, something. The offers of more movies and more money were coming in every day, people wanting her, needing her, hoping to make some cash off her, gambling that she'd be golden and lucky and hardworking forever— that somehow she'd keep that thing about her, the girlishness, the irresistible careless-idiot thing that made you want her around, want what she had, and think, while you watched her and desired her, that you could get some too. Get some of that . . . what? Joy? Insousiance? *Tendency to forget?*

"Do you ever worry, when you're sitting in a car, that there's something alive under your seat?" She was looking at me with a puzzled expression. She waved her hand around and finally pointed to the shiny wooden hump between us. "Like things stabbing you from underneath? I have that feeling sometimes, like there's something alive under the car, sort of lying in wait for me. You know, like a snake or a poison frog, a knife . . . some kind of long pipe. Do you have that?"

Her voice was floaty and ethereal. She whispered, really, and her thoughts emerged in thin little bubbles that drifted out of her mouth and blew into the wind, bouncing down the long stretch of gray highway behind us and melting in the waves of heat. I could hardly hear her, barely caught the spume as it floated past me. The wind was whirring in my ears, and her blond hair was flying. Her lips moved as though in a silent picture. They were large lips—outlined by gravy-colored lipstick—and when they parted, shadows hit a small gap between her front teeth. At the Erawan and Two Bunch Palms, hotels in the desert, she had stretched out by the pool in a white polyester bikini that looked as old and dated as the car. The bottoms looked like wrestling briefs. The cups of the bra were dented, old plastic and foam, and several sizes too small. "It used to be my mom's," she said. "Truly." When she talked about her mother, she grew neutral, quieter—seemed tired. And in the sun, she turned light pink, then deep rose, and by the end of the week she'd roasted to an oaky golden brown. As she grew dark, her teeth had become improbably white. "I've never had a tan before," she'd said, and I suppose I believed her. On the screen she was luminescent but almost translucent too. You saw her skin but felt you were seeing more, the insides of her. I wondered how a tan would change that, how differently she might refract the light. She had a movie to make soon—or rather, a movie she was under contract to make. But that was a commitment she appeared to be avoiding, a subject she didn't seem to want to discuss or had forgotten about already. Like Tom Swimmer.

"I did it once on the beach in the pouring rain," she said by the pool one late afternoon when the sun was slipping behind the wall of the hotel and nobody else was around. On the subject of sex, she was open in the way women never are after they've become very famous, unless they happen to be crazy too. "It was nighttime," she said, "and I was all wet and cold but hot and sweating, if you know what I mean, and the waves were amazing. The dark sky was so moody. The guy was so amazing—some surfer dude from Newport Beach.

"My luck changed after that. I got *Vices,* and things started really happening. You know, the Buddhists—or maybe it's Hindus?—believe that your karma changes with every person you're with, like, every new acquaintance and meeting, but it intensifies if you have sex, obviously. You take on another person's load, karmically, even in subtle ways, and it changes your fate."

I pulled from my purse the small black microcassette recorder I'd bought at the beginning of the trip. Allegra watched me, kept looking over as I loaded in a tape. It was time I started asking questions. Although not asking them usually worked better.

"Can you hear me okay with the top down?" Allegra asked rather formally.

"I'm not sure," I said, looking at the recorder. "Probably not."

She pressed the brake pedal, slowly pulling over to the

side of the highway. She twisted around in her seat and grabbed her black crocheted Mexican tote bag that was resting on the little half seat in back and dragged it between us. She dug around, pulled out a purple cell phone, some lip gloss, her little black journal. Finally, she extracted a pair of backless shoes and shimmied her feet into them. Together we got out and stood on either side of the old Porsche and unrolled the graying vinyl top, yanking it into place. A car slowly drove up beside us, a high quiet whine, a big car, American. Behind its smoky windshield, I saw the faces of two men, middle-aged and white, staring at Allegra in her cutoffs and mules. Rather than looking menacing the way two men in a front seat can sometimes, they looked helpless, defenseless. They were L.A. nerds—sharpies in suits who were trying too hard.

"Need anything?" they said at once, both of them, over-lapping dialogue, competing desire. "Can we take you somewhere?" "Can I help you with that?"

"We're fine," I said, and their heads suddenly shifted to my direction, meeting my face with disappointment.

Allegra was looking at the ground. Her clownishly large sunglasses had dropped down on her face, and she was coughing a deep-lung cough. Her face flushed.

"We're completely fine," I said. "Thank you."

As she bent over to snap the corner into place, the men watched. And as they pulled away, they were watching still.

"You okay?" I asked her.

"Yeah, I think so."

She walked around the car, coughed again, and tripped. The Indian print on her T-shirt didn't entirely hide the moons of wetness under her arms.

"Want me to drive?"

"Nope," she said. "I'm loving it."

For the past six days, she'd been vacantly outgoing with strangers. I'd seen her blow a kiss to a young cashier at Tower Records, embrace a saleslady at Aida Grey, and sign, easily, several dozen autographs. She was unafraid of foreign attention, the gaping mouths and long stares. She wore a tight dress the day we met, the day she won the exacta at Santa Anita, and there was an ensuing series of tight dresses and tight cutoffs and tight tops. She sat in booths at coffee shops and clomped down the commercial strip in Palm Springs and went largely unrecognized. Oh, people noticed her and gawked, but she was just a beautiful girl in tight clothes, an empty vessel for men to dump their dreams into. Bertolucci's remake of *L'Avventura* was being cut. *Sphinxa* had only just been released—rushed into theaters at the end of the year so Allegra's performance could be considered for an Oscar in a couple of months. Timing was everything—timing and talk. In Hollywood, she was like a racehorse that you heard about while you were standing around the paddock. But here, out in the other world, she was only another sort of perfect creature, something to stare at, something your eyes wanted.

———

The Porsche made its way through hay-colored hillsides and green alfalfa fields kept green by ceaseless watering, by the long spidery sprinklers with their graceful arcs of spray. In the distance, the mountains were bald and brown. We were approaching Buttonwillow and the exit for Highway 58, where we would be approaching cooler winds and the sea. Allegra took a slug of Volvic, swallowed four or five green capsules—some kind of herbal remedy for her lingering smog cough. She steadied the car's speed to something well over the limit, then produced her left foot from under the dash and stuck it out the window. She pushed her polished toes up against the chrome edge of the wind wing, and the wind blew up the leg of her cutoffs. She grew chatty again, nervously so. Her tendency was to discuss whatever was happening in the moment, as though the past and the future were miles away. The subject shifted from driving—what it felt like to sit low in a sportscar versus up high in a truck—to a discussion of the interview process itself. She asked me about *Flame* magazine. "Is this story about me or the *idea* of me?" she asked a little hopefully. Her eyes were open, sadly earnest. She looked at me as though I were unknowable, a giant redwood or the Arches National Park. Like I wasn't entirely human: a religious relic, a rabbit's foot, a comet in the sky. I had the power to do something for her, but whatever that was seemed vague and slightly mystical. I had arrived in L.A. just a week before, a gray-faced writer embarking on the last celebrity profile assignment of her life, a New Yorker with small patches of psoriasis from a vitamin A deficiency caused by—one nutritionist told me—too much time under fluorescent lights. Now I was brown and barefoot like Allegra. And I had power. Allegra needed me, depended on me. Somehow I liked that, but it also made me uneasy. Like I'd let in a stray cat.

Originally, we were to spend two days together, mostly on business. I had been scheduled for a few hours with her, getting acquainted, a lunch, interviewing her with my tape recorder running; then seeing her once again, participating with her in some "activity" like shopping or walking on the beach or betting on the horses. Then I'd attend to the writing of a five-thousand-word piece about who she was—or about the show, at least, the Allegra Show. I was supposed to be insightful. I was supposed to be a bit jaded too, though surprisingly impressed by this young star's talent and presence. That's how it usually worked, anyway. I was critical and hard to please—perhaps because I had been trapped for the last few years in small hotel rooms and forced to listen, very carefully, to the lofty musings of movie stars. Their stories, their memories, their self-absorption. I nodded. I said little. (The less I said, in fact, the more they talked.) And then I sat in front of my computer trying to devise ways of bringing them to life.

But I was done with all that. I'd quit, left celebrity reporting and Hollywood shilling behind me—in a blast of fury and faith in myself. Some weeks later, though, right before Christmas, I got a call from Ed Nostrum, my old editor at *Flame*. He needed a quick profile, a cover piece. Last-minute, rushed. He was proud, but he begged. He humiliated himself. Allegra Coleman was suddenly being offered up, exclusively his, exclusively mine. She was suddenly an Oscar contender, for her performance in a small, disturbing picture that was coming out in limited release. ("It sounds like *sphincter*," I said to Ed.) It was supposed to take two days, three at the most. I'd be home for Christmas. The dead week afterward to write the piece . . . But then the *Sphinxa* criticism, explosion, whatever you want to call it, happened. Suddenly her name was everywhere, and stills from the movie. The breakup with Swimmer was hitting the tabloids. Unauthorized photographs of Allegra naked (doing difficult yoga postures) on Catalina Island appeared in *Celebrity Sleuth*. She was ascending, bursting. She stood on the edge of being a star like it was a stage of dying.

"It's out of control," she had said the day before, sitting in a 108-degree mudbath at Two Bunch with a white towel twisted over her head. "I can tell. I can feel something's different. It's how people look at me. Before, it was a fascination, like they were exploring me visually. Enjoying me. It was about my skin, my surface. There was a generosity to it. Now it feels like I'm being robbed of something."

Paranoia didn't really suit her. It didn't fit easily into

her overall worldview, and you could feel her trying to jam it in. Usually, the various instincts and emotions she relied on to get herself through an average day were upbeat, hyperpositive. Her general epistemological model was a hybrid of pop Buddhism and a can-do Norman Vincent Peale Californianism. She believed in both karma and self-empowerment, and as she felt her way through the dark alley between fate and will, she came up with self-serving explanations of the universe. She believed she was *meant to be an actor,* for example. Obstacles had been eliminated for her, magically, by something she referred to as *the spheres* or *the energy of the universe.* She also thought she was *creating her stardom* herself. She did not seem aware, in any way, that she might be an illusion created by carefully positioned lights and smart writers and directors who were in love with her, or that she was an expensive commodity or a cheap blowup doll or, perhaps worse, the football that a team of men was tossing to complete an end run.

She was being robbed. That's how she saw things at present. It was hilarious to hear her expound on this while she sat on the toilet seat, trimming her pubic hair into a perfect V. Things had changed. The vibe was different. She'd turned angry. She was being robbed, and she was going to make somebody pay. But who? This was a piece of the fame puzzle Allegra wasn't accepting: that at first it required her utter compliance and now survived entirely on her resistance.

In unseen hotel-lobby phone booths and dank highway bathrooms, I called Ed Nostrum seeking guidance. "Do I turn her in?"

"Turn her in?" Ed said to me. "*To whom,* darling?"

"People must be looking for her."

"People people or *People* magazine? No. I think you must hang on."

We'd been quietly on the lam for days now, drifting into places, checking into hotels and then never quite checking out. As the days progressed, Allegra remained cheerful—her daffiness was almost a bad habit—but I wondered if there wasn't some rage behind her mindlessness and rootlessness. We started at the W in Westwood, then switched to the Sunset Marquis in Hollywood, then to Shutters on the Beach. We drove to Erawan in Indian Wells, then relocated to Two Bunch Palms. Over breakfast the day before, we'd read an L.A. *Times* Calendar column questioning her decision to appear in *Sphinxa*'s comic gang-rape scene—"unsettling that an intelligent young actress would agree to participate in this kind of exploitation"—and later, after lunch, she came across a *Daily Variety* story, reporting her as "officially AWOL" from Cosmos Studios, absent from meetings and rehearsals for *Apache.* The delays had already cost the production an estimated $150,000. The Michaels—the movie's producer, Michael Tibbs, and its director, Michael Minor—had both refused to comment.

Allegra found me lying beside the swirling pond at Two

Bunch a couple of hours later. She appeared with an odd expression, her voice hollow and distant. "We'll be leaving in the morning—early," she said. "Have you been to the Post Ranch?"

By the time we got near Buttonwillow, she was talking a blue streak, a giddy wild streak of nonsense. After days of sporadic chattiness, she was now unstoppable—on the mostly tedious subject of acting. "My nature is the nature of change," she said. "Do you know what I mean?"

I nodded.

"At my deepest point, my still point, I am water," she said. "And I can make that water be different temperatures. I can make the water drip out, seep out slowly, or be like Niagara. It can be hard or frozen. It can be soft. It's like I have perfect control over my essence. That's all acting is."

She began coughing again, a phlegmy, bronchially infected kind of sound. And on my tape player now, listening to it again, it seems violent, too loud—like she's coughing up her guts. Right afterward, she wiped her mouth. As I looked down at her hands on the worn wooden steering wheel, I noticed a bit of red-purple nail polish on her thumb, the same as the color on her toes. A few seconds passed—and I realized it was blood.

Later on, of course, I heard the rest of it on my tape: the horrible screaming of brakes, the resistance, the rubber. It was like the tires were laughing at her, laughing at me. There was a loud crushing sound, the compacting of metal, the breaking of glass, then nothing. Silence. The Porsche's final hour. Toward the tape's end, sounds reemerge. The howling sirens, the terrible drawing nearer of the sirens, louder, louder still, the slamming of doors, so many doors, the voices of my rescuers, the Jaws of Life, then more silence, long, long stretches of no sounds at all. Then the tape runs out.

y body was floating. It rode in one ambulance and then another. It was in Bakersfield, then helicoptered to San Luis Obispo. People pushed me, wheeled me. I smelled the sea, but I also remember nothing. My world was dark, veiled. My eyes were covered and throbbing. My head was throbbing and hot, as if my skull were pressurized, volcanic, and about to burst molten lava.

My mind was in New York. The fluidity of the city stayed with me, perhaps the thing that kept me alive. Sometimes I was walking down Broadway on my way to *Flame.* I was stopping to buy soup or a smoked-turkey sandwich at a deli, picking out a piece of fruit from an outdoor stand. Sometimes I was in my apartment, squeezed into my closet-size "office" and working on a story. I was on deadline. I was always on deadline. It was endless, re-curring, one after another, a hamster wheel of celebrities. Sometimes I was a doctor in a white lab coat and the movie stars were my patients. They were stretched out on exam-ining tables. They were nude and cold and wearing thin paper jackets or thin paper robes, and I was very serious. I had a reserved manner. I arrived in the examining room and closed the door quietly. I sat down on a small stool with aloof professionalism and began to ask questions, calmly and with chilly dignity.

"Your head injury is severe," I would say.

And: "Please lift up your robe."

And then one day, I sensed the world again, as though it were dancing on a surface of the water above me. Faint glimmers of people, snippets of talk. Shimmering lights, dark corners. I could smell flowers in my room—and ripening fruit. Somehow I knew that I wasn't a doctor any-more, and that there was no waiting area of famous people needing to be examined. That nightmare was over. It had melted into something else, another sort of dream. I felt relief and tranquillity—the hospital had centered me, or perhaps the liquid drugs had. I felt light, almost breezy, spiritually nonchalant. And the air on my skin felt cool.

There were no more stars to be examined. The words skidded through my mind. *There are no more celebrities in the waiting room.* They were all gone. Soon my life could go on, my own life—quiet, obscure, bookish—overshadowed by nothing and nobody else.

"I'm busy, Ed. I'm moving," I said in my half sleep.

"I'm busy, Ed."

"No, I'm busy."

———

He had called the week before Christmas. I was bending over a box when the phone rang. My arms and hands were sore from all the books, from carrying and packing and taping. Ed wanted me to stop by for a talk.

"I'm moving, Ed," I said. "I'm busy."

"Thank God you found a bigger place."

"I did," I said. "Five bedrooms. Eat-in kitchen."

"In Brooklyn?" He seemed too interested.

"Farther away."

"God, not Montclair."

"Paris," I said.

"Very funny."

"I'm serious," I said. "Paris, Virginia."

Christmas decorations were up all over New York City—waving Santas, plastic reindeer, dying wreaths that lost needles or left clumps of synthetic snow on the shoulder of your coat. Everybody at Conglom had gone retro with vintage ornaments that year, fifties designs, swirls, triangles, atomic modern. Those big, old-timey colored Christmas lights were strung up inside the cavernous Conglom lobby too—a thematic touch conceived, no doubt, by one of Conglom's genius art directors. Gone were those tasteful little white lights except in Ed's office at *Flame*. It was a zone of whiteness, spareness, fabulous good fortune and feng shui. In the corner was an enormous ficus tree smothered in white twinkles.

Ed jumped up from his chair as I entered—an unprecedented, almost theatrical display of respect—and rushed to me, leaning down from his great height. Two kisses actually met my cheek. There was a handshake that extended into hand-holding.

"Darling, terribly sorry about everything," he said.

His suit jacket was off. He'd just had his weekly haircut and his dark forelock of hair looked perfectly on the verge of too long. His thin cotton shirt was starched to an elegant smoothness. His sleeves were rolled up above his elbows. Bach was playing in the background, a swirl of repetitions and digressions. As he sat down behind his burled-wood partner's desk, I looked at his Signet Society coffee mug, his big hands and tanned skin, his toothy ironic boarding-school smile. There were framed pictures of his weedy kids, his unhappy ex-wife, his exotic new girlfriend, the King Charles spaniels.

"Ed, your office looks like Tavern on the Green."

He grimaced in a captivating sort of way. "Clementine, I want you to come back."

The music swirled to a crescendo and began backing

down. Over his shoulder, his computer's screensaver blinked on—an architectural rendering of Blenheim. Ed's father, John Wyndham Nostrum, had been ambassador to India but had always longed for the Court of St. James's.

"The movers are scheduled to come in two days," I said. "And last night there was a going-away party that I would have invited you to if you weren't such a dick."

"I was a dick," he said. "I am a dick. So sorry about the Von Stroheim piece. I never should have assigned it."

"It's too late to apologize."

"People love it, Clem. Heard lots of good things . . ."

I looked out the window. On the twenty-second floor, we were far above the streams of yellow cabs and hard mounds of brown snow. We were in the sky, up in the weather. A thick layer of dark clouds was drifting apart, and there were patches of blue in the west, in time for a sunset that nobody would talk about because nobody had seen it. When Conglom bought the building five years ago and announced plans to restore the deco masterpiece, there was a loud public outcry, but it quickly subsided. And when Conglom renamed its piece of the Manhattan skyline the Conglom Building, there was another passionate but brief public wail. People soon started to forget the building had housed anything but Conglom and its interlacing subsidiaries— its publications, satellites, cable outlets, movie studio and video-rental chain. Conglom owned Cosmos and C-Sat and C-Web and everything in between. And, until recently, me.

"Let's call a truce," Ed said.

"But it's been so much fun hating you."

Ed chuckled with the sort of effort that would have exhausted him if he'd had to do much more of it. "Go to Rome and be with your dog trainer if you want. Just keep writing for us."

"Paris," I said. "And he's not training dogs. He's—"

"Listen, I have a great story for you."

"Not interested."

"Clementine. Listen, it's perfect for you. You can be as morbid and philosophical as you like—Freudian, Baudrillardian, Neoplatonist—whatever you want."

He was patronizing me, but I was feeling immune. Looking out the window again, I wondered what a view like that—so steep, so world-at-your-feet—did to the human psyche. Since the late twenties, the building had drawn great photographers, inspired coffee-table books and calendars and kitschy key chains. It had inspired a lot of suicides too, most of them leaping from its sleek Machine Age tower.

"Allegra Coleman," he said. "We've been offered an interview for a cover."

"Who?"

"She's in *Vices.* She's in *Sphinxa.* Oh, don't pretend you don't know her. Bertolucci's remake of *L'Avventura.* She's the one who looks like a blond Indian."

"Nope. Sorry."

"Margaux Clarke called this morning."

Silence.

"It's about the need for newness, the addiction to fresh. It's not a profile, really. It would be more of a think piece— an essay—about the idolization of youth in Hollywood."

"No, it wouldn't."

"It will be so quick you won't know you wrote it. Really. She's a wild girl—doesn't have a home, lives on the road. Don't forget, her father is Max Coleman, the op-art drag queen. And she's apparently breaking up with Tom Swimmer."

"That's all super-fascinating. But I'm moving in two days."

"You go to L.A.—tomorrow, if you want. Delay the move a week. You turn the piece around before you leave for Virginia. The girl is so hot and so wide open it will write itself."

"I'm sick of hot. I'm sick of girls."

"Want anything to drink?" Ed swiveled around in his space-age chair and opened the door of his little white refrigerator. He found a Badoit and handed it to me. He was trying to calm me down, or himself. He needed to get back in touch with his charm. His instinct, his ability to know exactly what was achievable—what he could persuade somebody to do—tended to be infallible. I always enjoyed trying to be the exception.

He twisted the cap off a water bottle for himself, and I watched him take a slow elegant guzzle while he stared at the ceiling. He was calculating his odds, strategizing.

At the *Journal,* he had gotten me to spend weeks on assignment in dismal end-of-the-road towns where madmen lived—kidnappers, bombers, molesters. He had talked me into two funeral parlors, an operating room, and six federal prisons. I wrote about mobsters, serial killers, and plastic surgeons; graduated to profiles of tennis stars and fashion designers. When he took over *Flame* a few years ago, Ed somehow convinced me to apply my lifelong ardor for movies—and a wasted film degree—to the strange work of profiling movie stars and the occasional director, an embarrassing undertaking that was now thankfully over. His bludgeoning of my twenty-thousand-word Erich von Stroheim piece—by far the best thing I'd ever done—had been the final straw.

Ed gazed at me in a disconnected way, and then he smiled. The look in his eyes was desperate, like something out of *The Treasure of the Sierra Madre.*

"I'll double your rate."

I said nothing at first. I couldn't.

"Clementine, did you hear me?"

Ned was so different, so direct. No affectation, no manipulations, no games. His days were mostly about the dogs and getting his throng of old horses from pasture to their stalls. He smelled like beer. He looked a little like Leslie Howard and a little like Sam Shepard. Lanky, a fragile smile. He didn't have a screensaver or e-mail. He didn't seem to like the telephone much. He drove a Volvo station wagon that was so old and rotted that you could watch the road through holes in the floorboard.

Ned was an animal trainer—not exotics, mostly dogs—when we met four or five years ago on the location of *Scout,* a Rin Tin Tin derivative with Mel Gibson and an Australian shepherd. We were just friends at first—sardonic exchanges, colluding against the suits, conversations after dinner that kept getting longer. He was renting a house in Calabasas, a split-level ranch with fly strips and dog hair and a spare bedroom that he reserved for "The Twins"—identical one-hundred-pound deerhounds who had starred in everything from car commercials to *Father of the Bride IV*—but it didn't take me long to figure out that they slept in Ned's room. Sometimes when I called late at night, I could hear them whining and snorting in the bed.

Ned and I quit smoking together, propping each other up when the patches didn't work, confessing when we'd slipped—deciding alcohol wasn't such a bad replacement. We were just friends, until one night the summer before, when his blue jeans rubbed up against my bare legs under the table at a diner where Lucinda Williams was playing on the jukebox. He was living in Virginia by then, cleaning up his dead aunt's collapsing horse farm in order to sell it. And by the fall, everything had changed. It wasn't just him and me. It was something else. The East had flushed the apathy and lassitude out of him. He was bursting with ideas, full of plans—for solar panels, renovations to the barn, for a new life entirely. He called one night to say he was staying. He was done with movies and Milk-Bone commercials. He was done with making the Twins walk across the Golden Gate Bridge or forge rivers with small kittens in their mouths. He was going to take his great-uncle out of an assisted-living place in Leesburg. He and Bram were going to start some kind of animal-rescue thing together, he said. Wild dogs, neurotic dogs, lame dogs, stray dogs—and they wanted to take in old horses too.

Ned was cool, reserved, and generally not given to drama or great sweeps of feeling. I liked that too. He minded his own life—left me to my own decisions. (So much so that I had begun to think of him as the negation of Ed, as Not Ed or N'ed.) It was last fall, in the middle of the Von Stroheim ordeal, that I was on the phone giving him the tedious blow-by-blow of my dealings with *Flame*—the intricacies of Ed's betrayal, the dreary chronology of souring office politics—when I realized that at least fifteen minutes had gone by and he hadn't uttered a word. I heard the throbbing cricket sounds outside his open window, the screaming of tree frogs. I heard a beer bottle being uncapped with a metal opener.

"Ned?"

"Yeah?"

"Are you still there?"

I heard him take a drink and swallow. "Oh, yeah. I'm still here. And here's what I'm thinking: *Fuck Ed.* Okay?

He's a creep, and the magazine's beneath you. So why do you keep working there?"

When I couldn't find an answer, he suggested, in a few words, that I leave New York and join him in Paris—the kind of romantic offer I'd been waiting for him to make. "You can write about horses, write about dogs," Ned said. And when I laughed, he said, "Okay, write about suburban sprawl. Christ, you could write about Washington—it can't be that bad." I imagined myself knocking on doors of real people, ordinary men and women without face-lifts and Franck Muller watches. I imagined lobbing my Filofax of film-industry phone numbers into Ned's bonfire.

As soon as I moved down to the farm, we planned to bring Bram home for Christmas—another thing that complicated my taking an assignment, not that I was close to considering it yet.

Ed tossed me a small tangerine from a bowl on his desk, then took one for himself and began to peel the skin.

"She'll probably get the Oscar for *Sphinxa,*" he said. "You won't believe her performance."

I said nothing.

"Incredible. Magical."

"Sorry," I said. "Get somebody else."

Ed looked at me. His right eye was twitching. He was angry but trying hard not to be. "Triple. I'll triple it," he said.

I felt the waxy tangerine in my palm. A hundred and

fifty thousand dollars. How much time would that buy me on the farm? For one profile. One more hot, wide-open girl.

"She's exclusive to us," Ed said. "An exclusive cover."

"You said that."

"But with one stipulation."

"What?"

"That you write it."

CHAPTER 3

t was sunny when I woke up. There'd been a rainy spell, the nurses told me, three days of low clouds and wetness, but I had missed it. A new year had come, and the L.A. weather wasn't stopping. A dry wind blew in from the desert; the sky was clear for miles. The sun beat down on the windows of the hospital room and the curtains had to be drawn. But even so, the light forced its way around the thick coral-colored fabric and seemed to be setting its edges on fire.

Cool air-conditioning was blowing on me from somewhere, a vent in the ceiling. I could feel it on the parts of my face that weren't bandaged.

"Can I make you more comfortable?" Ruthie, my daytime nurse, asked in her Irish accent. "How are those sheets? Any smoother?"

I had complained about the sheets, apparently. Now I was feeling more agreeable.

"Very smooth, thank you."

An enormous television was perched near the ceiling and looking down on me and my room and broadcasting its shows, its news, its talk and lights and canned laughter. The TV seemed to turn itself on. It was always on, always having its way. Sometimes it seemed like a hateful presence, a consciousness lowerer—an enemy of healing, of all good things—and sometimes I enjoyed the movement, the feeling of going somewhere when I wasn't. The sense of traveling, of adventures, of things happening around me, the whirl of activity and drama. I was amused, made joyful. Sometimes I laughed, even at the news. And in the afternoons I was following Erica again, after many years, Erica on *All My Children*. She was coy with police when they came to her mansion. She flirted with a loan manager at the bank, brushed up against him with her little body, her fleshy upper arms. And when she didn't get her way, she stomped her feet like Shirley Temple. She was ageless, timeless—her dark hair, her dimples, those pointy canine teeth. She looked twenty-nine and vaguely orange, like she'd been using sunless tanning creams.

From my bed, I had seen the fireworks over the Thames. I had seen the ball drop in Times Square. The Tournament of Roses parade had come and gone, and the endless succession of football games was over. Meanwhile an after-party looked like it was still going on in my room. The place was cluttered with sympathy debris, potted plants and flowers, gift baskets and tissue paper and raffia. The staff of *Flame* had sent a banana tree and a refrigerator for the room. Michael Tibbs and Michael Minor, who had halted production of *Apache,* sent a Nightingale's hamper so colossal that two nurses struggled to carry it in. Margaux Clarke was in a state of perpetual activity and apology, always dropping by, always dragging in some too-large floral arrangement or bag of goodies. She was guilt-ridden, hand-wringy—she was Allegra's publicist, the one who had insisted that I write her client's profile. She mothered me, she sistered me. I was drugged and tolerated it.

She was a slim silhouette against my sunny windows, forever gesturing and fidgeting in her tight black clothes, her short blond hair in a different kind of mess every visit.

"How's the girl reporter today?" she'd ask with practiced breeziness.

"Lousy."

In New York, the packing of my apartment had been finished by strangers, handlers, Ed's assistants, and—after Ned had wrangled with *Flame* over logistics and control—my boxes and furniture had been moved into storage. Money was wired into my checking account. My bills were opened and paid. Ned had tried to fly out to be with me, but a small blizzard hit Virginia and he found himself stuck on the farm, wondering what to do about the Twins and Bram, who had slipped while getting out of the truck and was grumpy and belligerent, refusing treatment or doctors or even much in the way of help: He had holed himself up in the first-floor library and was sleeping on the sofa. "He's being such an ass," Ned said. "And he's drinking too much. Are you sure you're okay?"

He sounded calmer a couple of days later, but I could tell he was tired, probably wished I was there to help. He'd never wanted me to come to California in the first place. There was a faint I-told-you-so in his voice that bothered me a little but which I decided to ignore. I suppose I could have been mad, but it was hard to feel neglected in a roomful of food baskets and a banana tree and *All My Children.*

"Don't come," I said to him. "Don't. Really. I'm fine. But if I ever tell you that I'm writing another movie-star profile, you have permission—maybe I should put this in writing—to shoot me in the head."

Ed was far away in those days, in New York running the magazine, but also in my ear, running my life. He found experts, surgeons, and trauma specialists and had secured a spacious room for me at Cedars-Sinai, the "hospital of the stars."

"Frank Sinatra and Michael Landon were both here at the end," one of the nurses told me. Before his babies were born, Jack Nicholson came with his own cleaning supplies and rubber gloves and swabbed down the delivery room himself. Annette Bening had made a memorable entrance,

I heard. "She was so pregnant—out to here—and surrounded by fifteen bodyguards," whispered Ruthie. "They put her in a wheelchair and threw a blanket over her head."

Ed was a distant voice on the phone, and then suddenly, before the surgery, he was at my bedside—loaded down with concerned looks and thoughtless gifts. He brought chocolates that I didn't eat. He brought an armload of entertainment magazines that I didn't want to read, as well as half a dozen books, bad Hollywood memoirs full of earnest musings and pedestrian insights and self-promotion—indeed, the very last thing I wanted near my wounded body. ("You have to be kidding," I said.) Ed towered over me in his enormously long black coat with the collar upturned, his New & Lingwood shirts, his nervous assurances. He looked like a gigantic black crow of death. And he talked too loud.

"It's such a lousy business, I know, darling," he said. "But we've got the best, absolutely the best."

It was sad, almost insulting, how easily an eye can be removed—an eye you were born with, that you'd been seeing your life with for thirty-three years. An eye that couldn't be replicated or cloned. It was a matter of forty-five minutes, perhaps an hour. The nurses wore blue smocks, plastic shower caps, rubber gloves. The doctor wore clear goggles. I was draped in green sheets and given local anesthesia.

I heard sounds of snipping, like a beautiful piece of thick velvet being cut with scissors. I heard suctioning, like the sound of an espresso machine inside my nose. Afterward, there was a piercing smell, the burning of flesh. A temporary eye was installed—not an eye, actually, but a small egg of glass that was as clear as a fortune-teller's ball. It would hold everything in place, keep the socket from collapsing while an artificial eye was being custom-made. My new eye. It would come in eight weeks.

"The Bio-eye is amazing," Ed enthused. "And it will be gorgeously hazel and flecked, just like your other one. A perfect match." Ed knew everything about Bio-eyes, even seemed a bit downcast that he couldn't have one too. When I blinked my left eye, he told me, my right eyelid would blink almost as quickly—only a brief delay. When I moved my left eye, the Bio-eye would follow along. It was attached to a little rudder, a cable, in turn attached to a nerve that directed the Bio-eye to shadow the movements of my real one. If my left eye looked up at something, my right eye would follow along, blindly, dumbly, like a signature machine.

At night, after Ed and Margaux and everybody else had gone, I lay in the dark with the television flickering and thought about Allegra. We were in the car again, driving. She was talking about her life, about her mother, about acting. I was always quiet, and she was always talking. My mind went over everything—looking for a way to simplify, to process, wanting a way to digest her and move on. But the ride hadn't ended. We were playing Skee-Ball on the Santa Monica Pier. We were sitting on the swing sets at Will

Rogers Beach. We were sharing a small dressing room and trying on tube tops at Canyon Beachwear. Even when I was groggy, drugged up on Percocet and whatever else the nurses gave me, Allegra and I took our final drive again and again in my head, like a movie I couldn't stop renting. Lots of things didn't add up, lots of small and quiet things that were hard to explain. In my dreams, we were passing by the Mulholland Fountain at night, and she was laughing. She was always laughing and lifting up her face to the night sky.

The story went that the Michaels came and dragged her away. That's the way the story went inside my head, at any rate. (Sometimes she was alive. Sometimes she was dead. Sometimes screaming. Sometimes limp.) The official police report said I'd been found in a 1956 Porsche Spider that I was driving alone. The report was amended later on, of course. Allegra had been in the vehicle too. And she'd left the scene before the fire and rescue team had arrived.

—

Detectives turned up at Cedars—despite Ed's string pulling and delays—two guys from the Kern County sheriff's office. They wore khaki uniforms with wide belt loops. Their hair was shaggy, to their collars, and one of them had a mustache. I wish I could tell you they were like Steve McQueen in *Bullitt* or even Dana Andrews in *Laura,* but they were Western guys, country guys, Dennis Weavers. At first they were friendly, made jokes. Then the officers,

Manny and Moe—as I came to think of them—grew serious.

"Ma'am, what was your relationship to Allegra Coleman?" one of them asked. Moe, I think.

"I was writing about her. We drove around and talked."

He looked at me, puzzled.

"That's what I do for a living—or used to."

"Oh," Manny interrupted, "I'm sure that you're going to be fine."

"It's not that."

Moe shifted his feet restlessly, like he had to go the bathroom. "You drive around with movie stars?"

"I talk to them. Or actually, they talk to me."

"Like who?" he asked.

"Ralph Fiennes, most recently. Before Allegra."

"Who?" asked Manny.

"Nicole Kidman before that."

"Really?" said Moe.

"Really?" said Manny. "What was she like?"

"All business," I said. "And also very tall and pale."

The officers looked a little dreamy and disoriented. Manny's head seemed to clear first. He asked his questions like he'd memorized them beforehand.

"What was the last meal you ate before the accident?"

"We stopped at Coco's."

"Do you remember what Miss Coleman ate, ma'am?"

"Pancakes."

"Did you know Miss Coleman previously?" Manny asked.

"No."

"Would you describe yourself as a friend of Miss Coleman?"

"No. Yes. Well, I don't know, exactly. I was working. She drove. I sat in the car. It lasted a week, and then she was gone—the accident."

There was a pause while Moe wrote things down. He held a big notebook, like a kid would use in school.

"Were you involved with her romantically or sexually?" Manny asked. He scratched his face.

"No," I said. "Not really."

Moe looked up from his big notebook.

"Well," I said, "it wasn't romantic or sexual in the way that you mean."

"And what way is that?" Manny asked.

"Do you guys have a romantic or sexual relationship with me?"

"Nope," Manny said.

"No, ma'am," Moe said a bit more forcefully. His face was turning the color of poached salmon.

"Well, I'm lying in bed in my nightie and robe and no underwear while two men in elegant khaki uniforms are intensely interested in every word I speak. To me, there's something romantic and sexual about it. You, me, us . . ."

They looked at each other.

"Am I right?"

—

That night the lights in my room were turned low, and I thought of a Buddhist exercise Allegra had told me about. It was an exercise that was supposed to tell you the state of your karma. You look at yourself in the mirror, Allegra told me. You look for an hour, or longer, without blinking. After a few minutes of staring, your face becomes a blur, she said, and your eyes get dry and start burning. Tears begin pouring down your cheeks. But you keep staring. And then, according to Allegra, things come to you. Visions come, nightmares come. "You can go insane doing this," she warned me. "Students have been dragged from meditation centers in India wrapped in straitjackets and tied up in their own bedsheets."

Maybe some things weren't worth knowing, I speculated. Then I asked if she had tried it herself.

"Many times," she said.

"And what did you learn?"

She laughed. The Mulholland Fountain was changing colors as we were driving by. The spray of water was turning green, then blue, then purple. The top of the car was down, and Allegra kept laughing, and it was as though the sound of it enclosed us. I could feel the vibration echoing around my chest. There were rainbows in Allegra's laugh, baskets of ripening fruit, truckloads of September corn, maternity wards full of babies, altars ablaze with candles, the Alhambra at dusk. She was careless. She was a fool, a distraction, a gloss, a sheen, a piece of candy. But her laugh seemed to say something more.

I shifted around in the hospital bed. I felt a wrinkle under the sheet, down by my legs. The wrinkle was lying there like a snake under the mattress cover. The sheets were nubby, pilled, worn by many chapped bodies, many sicknesses and miseries. I thought about Cedars, all the others who had been there—the long unbroken chain of dying famous people. Their bodies, aged, decaying, sick. The sheets, the surgeries, the gurneys, the scalpels, the medications.

I walked unsteadily to the bathroom. Under the fluorescent tubes of light, I looked swollen and chalky. My glass eye was weeping a kind of thick goo, a honey that was sticky on my thumb when I wiped it away. I stared into the mirror and, after awhile, felt myself, my face, my body, falling away, melting away, and suddenly birds were flying out of my left eye, black birds, flying and flying, more and more of them, waves of blackness, crows and ravens, dark jays, clouds of them around me, filling the room, pressing up against the ceiling.

awoke in darkness. I was alone in bed and the lights were off, the bathroom door was closed, and the television was finally silent, euthanized by some decent nurse. It was beautifully quiet. I felt a dream just leaving my mind, vanishing somewhere—receding, the passing parade of ghost thoughts that made up everything I don't know about myself, the wellspring of life. I tried to hold on to them. And then I sensed something on the side of my bed. It was in the corner, hovering in the dark.

It was very close. Something was breathing on me. It was only inches from my face. I felt it—a warm sensation, faint, spidery, on the side of my face where my eye used to be.

A face was pressing up next to mine. I felt the energy of

the thing. I felt its incandescence, a flickering, then movement, a vibration, like waves breaking on a shore that you can feel with your feet. I was afraid to turn my head. I smelled something powdery, a light dusky scent.

"Hey there," she said.

A small soft hand touched my forehead.

"Hello," she said. "Aloha."

Her hair was brown and wavy and cascaded down to her waist in wisps at the end. Her face was a perfect oval. Her eyes were dark blue, little eyes surrounded by a wet, fresh kind of puffiness.

She was staring at me, standing over me. Her sarong was soft and printed with red and green tropical flowers. She had a white flower behind her ear. She was wearing a lei heavy with white plumeria, and it smelled sweet, faint, like a song I couldn't quite hear.

"Are you feeling okay?" she asked.

I nodded.

"You look a little pale."

"I'm okay."

She looked at me skeptically.

"I had a funny pain in my side once," she said. "Right after I made *The Hurricane*."

She paused, looking into my face. She was trying to see how the story was registering, trying to figure out if I was following her, if I knew who she was. But she didn't want to come right out and ask.

"Did you like working with John Ford?" I finally asked.

"I did," she said, and seemed relieved. "Pappy. We called him Pappy."

I nodded.

"Anyway, I had this pain in my side. It started when we were shooting the tree sequence, and I was holding on to this big collapsed tree for dear life. Wind machines and tidal-wave machines and you can't imagine what all we went through. If I'd known how hard it was going to be, I'm not sure . . ."

She fiddled with her sarong, adjusted the pin. She had a smallpox vaccination dent on her left upper arm.

"You know, Pappy never said one thing about my performance. Not for thirty years."

"Really? For *The Hurricane*? That's kind of crappy," I said.

She giggled. "Crappy Pappy." She covered her mouth, embarrassed. Her fingers were slim sticks. Then she bent down and held the right side of my head. "It's true," she whispered. "Pappy Ford calls me up one afternoon in 1971 and says he's been watching TV—*The Hurricane* had come on television—and that it was the first time he'd seen the movie all the way through. Isn't that queer? He'd had a big fight with Sam Goldwyn over the final cut, he tells me. And he figured that Goldwyn had ruined it. 'Dottie,' he says, 'I was never able to watch it until now, and you know what? It's a damn fine picture. And you did a beautiful job.'"

She looked at me, waiting again.

"You did, Dorothy. You did a beautiful job," I said.

Her eyes softened. Her eyebrows were skinny, barely existent, a thin arch of dark hair. Her forehead was a bit crinkled. She couldn't have been over eighteen. Nobody was ever so smooth and sweet and beautifully puffy under the eyes. She was a New Orleans girl, born in a charity ward, never knew her father, never finished high school. She played the saxophone, became a Girl Scout, was devoted to her mother. When her best friend became a beauty queen, she decided maybe she should do that too. She was disqualified from a Miss USA competition for wearing lipstick at a time when none was allowed. And Dorothy Lamour became a film star on her own. By 1939, when the first road picture was made, she was big already, had played exotic native girls in *The Jungle Princess* and *Her Jungle Love* and *Tropic Holiday*. She was a sure thing, and Bing Crosby and Bob Hope were a gamble. I knew all that. And something in her eyes said she knew I knew.

"I'm sorry about your mother," she said.

"My—?"

She brushed the hair away from my face. "Anyway," she said, "I was telling you my hospital story. I think it's exhaustion and hard work that's causing this funny pain in my side, so I go right off to do an NBC radio show I'm supposed to sing in, and then one night I'm having dinner with Singapore Joe—that's what everybody called Joe Fisher, he owned lots of theaters and a distribution company—and we are at Lucy's near Paramount, and the pain in my side becomes worse and worse. Dr. Branch removes my appendix that very night. I could have died from peritonitis . . ."

She was standing on one bare foot and shifted her weight to the other. I looked down. Her feet were skinny and long, looked almost boneless, like they were melting into the hospital floor. She caught me looking. "I hate my feet," she said.

"They're not so bad."

"They're too skinny."

"No, they aren't," I said.

"Let me see yours."

She walked to the end of my bed and moved her hands under the sheets. "You know, in *The Jungle Princess,* I was so ashamed about showing my feet on-screen that I complained to the studio, and they had a pair of rubber ones made. Prosthetics—beautiful fake rubber feet that I put on like gloves. But during a scene where I had to climb up a waterfall, climbing and climbing, they started slipping off! I almost died. I really did. Anyway, I think I was on the eighth floor of Cedars when my appendix was taken out."

I shifted in my bed, rolled over on my left side. I wasn't trying to get away from her, just trying to get more comfortable.

"You should get yourself moved down there, to the eighth floor," she said. "Isn't that where the rooms are extra big, with sitting-room suites?"

"I'm not sure. This is Cedars-Sinai, you know, not Cedars of Lebanon."

This didn't seem to register. "I had marvelous flowers, like yours. The studio was really trying to build me up in those days. My illness got so much publicity that my room was filled with flowers, and the corridors crowded with people wanting my autograph. 'This girl is sick, she's not a monkey in a cage!' I heard Dr. Branch telling everybody out in the hallway, and I started to laugh so hard that I broke my stitches."

She was still laughing quietly to herself when I fell asleep for a time, and when I woke again, she was in the corner of my room watering the banana tree and singing a number I recognized from *Road to Utopia*.

> *Welcome to my dream*
> *And how are you?*
> *Will you be here long*
> *Or just passing through?*
> *Brush off that stardust.*
> *Where have you been?*
> *Don't tell me your rainbow*
> *Was late getting in.*

Then she began dancing a little. I rolled onto my back again and closed my eyes.

"Are you falling asleep on me?" she asked, coming around to the side of the bed.

"I guess I am."

"Wait, I have a question," she said. "I was embarrassed to ask it before. You've got all those books, those biographies."

I looked over to the bookshelf and the volumes that Ed had brought—lives of the stars—which had been sitting there untouched. I'd forgotten to give them away.

"Memoirs."

"Autobiographies?"

"Something like that."

"But . . . those other actresses, their books. Why not mine?"

She was serious. Her face was dead serious. "How come I didn't make your list? D'ya think I'm kind of third-rate?"

CHAPTER 5

he phenomenon was a phenomenon, a feeling more than anything else. It felt primitive. It felt animal. We were a herd again, a flock. We became beasts, giant lumbering beasts. We were insects—ants, moths, midges—flying after her, trailing her, hunting in mobs and swarming en masse. We praised, we anointed, we adored. We waded in the opacity of her skin, we tanned in her radiance, and we lazed, imagined her, and nestled in the warm sands that she had heated. And when the sun went away, there was only madness. Her pouty face was everywhere, the sides of buses, billboards, papers, magazines, TV news, and when you signed on to the Internet.

The world was in a panic, a frenzy, an Allegra-or-nothing frame of mind. She held sway, kept us captive with her absence. The longer she was lost, the more it seemed people found her—figured out who she was, made her theirs. There were ripples upon ripples. She ascended, seemed to crest, and then ascended again. From the moment I first awoke in the hospital with a throbbing head, from the first time I became aware of the flickering cyclops suspended from the ceiling of my room, it was Allegra who dominated, who rose to the top of the news like the softest, lightest suds. She stayed there, floating above the fray of news stories—the turns in the stock market, the president's winter vacation in Deer Valley, the thoroughbred that died in a race at Hollywood Park, the cute boy who was buried alive in El Monte, and the war, of course. She floated over the endless record-breaking sunshine too—day in, day out, impossible blinding light—and the people who were shown time and time again on the local news playing volleyball in bathing suits at Zuma Beach.

The appetite was insatiable. There were pictures of the wrecked Porsche, interviews with hotel clerks and garage attendants. There was footage of her childhood home in Riverside; of the convent in the South of France where Kay Blyth dried out and died; and of Max Coleman waving away the cameras as he came and went from his enormous brownstone in Greenwich Village.

Occasionally my own face would appear on *Entertainment Tomorrow* or E! or *Extra! Extra!*—the recuperating reporter, the tragically maimed sidekick. It was an okay picture, a couple of years old, released by *Flame,* but next to Allegra's blondness, my own hair looked dull, lacking light. I was flat and she was round. I seemed wan. She seemed young and kicking and exploding. Even in the stills from *Vices,* she was so vibrant, so fully alive, poised to say something you had to hear. In trailers for *Sphinxa*—an all-network, prime-time Cosmos Studios promo campaign was in full swing—she was a diabolical mongrel. She held her head regally, but her walk was vulgar, everything generating from her pelvis. You could feel her body. You could almost smell her. Except that you couldn't and that seemed worse.

Experts were assembled—people who theorized and pontificated about Allegra or at least the idea of her, about the Allegra phenomenon, and about the phenomenon of a phenomenon. Louis Armstrong Hartley, a Harvard professor and author of *Murderous Beauty,* talked about the "social manipulation of icons by the media." Two feminists, Nancy Gilley and Fay Dominico, who'd written *The Face That Launched a Thousand Ads* (about the use of images of Marilyn Monroe in advertisements), discussed how the existence of film stars stripped the self-worth of everyday women, diminishing real life rather than enhancing it. "Celebrities overpower and overshadow us," said Gilley, "and trap women in social stereotypes that are no longer useful." Dominico expounded "the disastrous results of objectification"—despite the fact that, at present, there was no object at all.

Meanwhile, there were the knock-knock jokes, conspiracy theories, and an idiotic mysticism, a Paul-is-dead kind of thing. She was a mythical creature—a unicorn, a goddess. There were nuttiness, group misery, and a hundred new Internet sites devoted to solving the mystery of the missing star. Grief makes fools and nonsense-sayers and blubberers of us all, I guess, for people were talking about installing a quickie bronze star in the sidewalk of Hollywood Boulevard, talking about an HBO biopic of her life. A rumor began that Allegra had never existed in the first place, that she was computer-generated—and this became a concept for a movie deal starring an Allegra lookalike. On Interstate 5, where the Porsche had crashed, white crosses staple-gunned with Allegra's photograph were set up alongside the road, near a grouping of seated Buddhas. There were piles of flowers, baskets of fruit, notes, postcards, letters. Somebody had left a pair of men's plaid boxer shorts.

Voices came at me, phones were handed to me. I was in demand, and you'd think this would be a good feeling, but it often wasn't. People had a way of tracking me down anywhere—the eye clinic, the toilet, rehab. Television producers left dire voice-mail messages for me, talking so fast that I couldn't understand what they were saying. They were smart and frantic. And they needed me. I was Allegra by proxy, her amanuensis, her stand-in. They wanted me to dish, to be a town gossip and confiding betrayer like Gladys Kravitz on *Bewitched*. They asked if I thought Allegra was an ecstasy addict, a pot-head, a nymphomaniac (this was the latest suspicion in an ongoing assembly line). I said I didn't know. They asked if I thought she was alive. I said I didn't know. They were insistent and thick-skinned. I said I didn't know, didn't know, didn't know.

Tom Swimmer called every day, like clockwork, and left dreary, unimaginative messages as if he'd forgotten Allegra had dumped him a month before. ("Hey Clem—I mean *Clementine*—this is Tom Swimmer again, hoping you're feeling okay. Wow. *What an ordeal.* Give me a call sometime.") Max Coleman called from New York and managed to exude a mesmerizing blend of queenly and cloying charm: "Call me, would you, dear, whenever she turns up?"

Ed's bizarre obsession with the story seemed to overtake his life. He was lobbying the higher-ups at Conglom for a special all-Allegra issue. He was making almost daily appearances on TV (the stand-in for the stand-in). And he had begun encouraging me, very gently but persistently, to write an on-the-road account—partly, I felt, to answer the questions that preyed on his restless mind. ("You didn't see her naked, by any chance?" he asked me nonchalantly one day. "I think so," I said.)

Margaux, with her bony shoulders and straw hair and bloodshot eyes, came every morning. She slunk in without knocking, and acted proprietary, nurturing. Sometimes she brought me outfits, slippers and pajamas from Dejeuner sur les Herbes, hair combs from Saks, the CDs of whatever musician she was currently promoting. (I had a stack of them, unopened: Placido Domingo, Mel Torme, Baggy "The Creeper" Billy. A new Latino folk group called Fizz.)

The morning Ed was on *Good Morning America,* Margaux arrived with a blue shopping bag full of Evian for me and a heart-shaped red satin purse.

"Is it Valentine's Day?" I said.

"Do you like it? I thought it would be cute for a couple weeks, leading up to the fourteenth."

"Sweet. It looks like a Whitman sampler."

Margaux faked a scowl—she was oblivious to all manner of insult—then changed the subject. "Hey, did you hear from her?"

"Who?"

"I got a funny call last night," she said. "Actually, it was, like, five hang-ups. And then early this morning, I got another call with weird buzzing sounds in the background, like somebody mowing a lawn. I had a feeling it was Allegra."

I sat up in bed and threw back the sheets. "Mowing? You sure it wasn't your gardener?"

"I'm serious," said Margaux.

"I know you are," I said, wrapping myself in the waffle-weave robe that Margaux had brought the week before. "And if my head weren't so full of drugs, I could probably take you seriously. But the only movie stars I'm getting strange calls from are dead."

"What do you mean?" asked Margaux. "Like dreams?"

"Something like that."

"Oh, don't tell me," she said. "Dreams that Allegra's dead?"

"No, not Allegra," I said, growing irritated. "Like Bette Davis dead. Like Grace Kelly dead."

"Poor Allegra," she said. "You don't think that's a sign, do you?"

"A sign?"

"God, I hope she doesn't wind up that way."

"What way?"

"Dead."

On TV, Ed was sitting in a lime-green chair and wearing a dark blue double-breasted pin-striped suit. His forelock kept swinging into his eyes. ("Wow," Margaux exclaimed, "he looks fabulous.") He was a poet, an intellectual, a ponderer of the great vagaries of fame. The backdrop was a throbbing sky-blue, and it seemed as though he'd been pushed out of an airplane and was doing a free fall.

"I think she's a bit spooked," Ed was saying. "I'm not sure I believe the reports of drug addiction, or any other kind of addiction. She's just a very talented, brilliant, sensitive girl—young woman—who got spooked."

Margaux nodded in utter agreement. Ed seemed sure that Allegra was not only alive but healthy, and that seemed to excite her. When he mentioned the likelihood of an Academy Award nomination for *Sphinxa,* Margaux pumped her fist and shouted out, "Yessss!" When Ed said that Allegra was "already legendary," she sang out, "Very nice!"

And when it was over, she blew a kiss to the TV screen and waved goodbye to me.

Ridiculous, pandering fanzine . . . but it was hard to blame Ed. He was a promoter, a catalyst, not somebody who practiced actual journalism. *Flame* wanted to belong, to be cool and hip and know things. It sought out novelty and linked it to progress, to openness, to discovery. We were supposed to read *Flame* and become infected with desire, infused with the sense of an expanding world—but expanding, unfortunately, without us. It was a meal we were supposed to crave yet also find inadequate, part of a diet of more hunger.

Later that morning, I called the farm looking for a break from insanity, and Bram answered the phone. I hadn't really known him well before, but the last month—both of us confined and irritable—had changed that. Bram was reading books about the Spanish Civil War while waiting for his ankle sprain to mend, but twice a day, in the morning and again at night, the eighty-eight-year-old retired horse breeder watched the news on a small, ancient television in the library. Ned had climbed up on the roof to adjust the antenna so a few channels came in.

"We saw your boss on TV this morning," Bram said. "Jesus, he really needs a haircut. He could stand a wash too. Ahh, are you looking for Neddy?"

"I am," I said. "Is he in the barn?"

"Nope," Bram said. "Right here. Working on my lunch. I'm being waited upon like Cleopatra. You know, I'd ask how you're doing, Clem, but Neddy's told me not to fuss over you too much. Says you hate that."

"That's right," I said. "No fussing—"

"Hey, I got a new nickname for your starlet." Bram had a way of changing the subject when he couldn't hear something you'd said. "Happy Camper. *Happy Camper.* Get it? Allegra—happy. Coleman, like the lantern. I think that's pretty goddamn funny. Although Neddy doesn't. Oh, here he is—" He apparently passed the phone.

"You saw Ed?" I asked.

"Ohhh," Ned said with a burst of disgust that I wasn't sure I'd heard in his voice before. "What a complete *megalomaniac.* Bram and I were beside ourselves. He's so pompous. Thank God he'll be out of our lives soon. Just another week. I'm almost done cleaning out the caretaker's cottage—it's going to make a great office. With any luck, the back road will be open soon. That will make everything easier. God, listening to Ed, you'd think Allegra's disappearance was actually important."

He was right, of course. Ned was always a calm voice of balance and perspective. Allegra was a fabrication, a product, and the excitement about her was without significance, cultural or otherwise. Except . . . and this is almost too embarrassing to admit . . . why did I find myself still thinking about her? Why did I hope that she'd call and say hello, or just cough into the phone? It was hard to fathom, even harder to put into words. And it was this, and more, that made it exceptionally hard to find a way to explain to Ned two days later that my homecoming plans had been delayed.

"I have some news," I said.

"What's that?"

"Looks like I'll be staying here for a while."

"In the hospital?" I heard a bark in the background and then the clicking of dog's nails on the old linoleum floor of his kitchen.

"No, in L.A. Just a few weeks longer. I'm moving to the Noguchi—down the block. A hotel. A month at most. Until the Bio-eye is ready."

There was a long pause. "How did he manage that?" Ned said finally. His voice was slipping away from me, drifting out the open window and into the winter sky.

"Who?"

"Ed."

"Ed? He says he'll send an assistant—researcher— whatever I need. Somebody who'll help out, do the driving, make my life easy. Of course, he's bugging me to write something about Allegra, but that won't happen."

"I'm stunned," Ned said. "I'm really— Well, I'm not sure what to say."

"I know."

"You were out. It was behind you."

"I know."

"You even got paid for a piece you didn't have to write. So you can't say you're being practical. You can't say it's the money."

"No, it's not money."

"What, then?"

"I'm not totally better, you know."

"But you're miserable there, aren't you? You hate all those fucking movie people. Picture Land. Woo-Woo World. You hate dealing with Ed."

I didn't know what to say.

"Don't you?"

The dog in the kitchen barked. Then two dogs.

"Everything's easy here. It's easy to stay. No snow. No weather, really. I've got room service, a rental car. Now I've got an assistant—all that. And . . ."

"What?"

"I don't know. Weird stuff is going on. That's all. I'm besieged by weirdness. It's . . ."

"What?"

"This will sound ridiculous, I know, but I have a weird feeling that Allegra might try to get in touch."

CHAPTER 6

M y room at the Noguchi was spare because it was too small to be otherwise. In any case, I didn't stay long. I had thought originally that the black marble and shoji screens, the timeless Zen touches and other subtleties of the Japanese hotel might bring me serenity and a certain peace of mind, but just the opposite happened.

In the heart of Beverly Hills, down the way from Cedars, I found myself in the company of other journalists—colleagues, friends, and rivals—on various birth and death watches of the stars, and on various Allegra missions for their magazines and news channels. On Valentine's Day, the Oscar nominations had come out and spiked interest in her again. And as I waited for the elevator, picked up mail at the front desk, or waited for the parking valet to produce the silver Luscus convertible that Ed had rented for me, I was approached again and again—hounded, intruded upon, interrupted by desperate reporters who sometimes pretended they cared about me and how I was doing before slipping into an endless well of Allegra questions. Did I have a good number for Max Coleman? Had I seen Allegra's old ballet instructor in Riverside? Where was Mike Mumy, Allegra's ex-husband? (And what about the nymphomania?) At the same time I felt stalked, I also began to feel a certain pressure. Pressure to know things, to be an authority. To have her, to own her. She was public domain, public property . . . everybody's girl . . . and, at the same time, it became surprisingly painful to see her name attached to somebody else's byline, somebody else's work and not mine.

"Don't get caught up," Ned cautioned me—the sort of advice I'd never needed before. So after three days at the Noguchi, right as a strange humidity arrived in Southern California, I loaded my suitcases in the Luscus and headed west down Pico Boulevard toward the beach.

A warm rain began—almost tropical, almost Hawaiian— by the time I got to the coast and Shutters. A blazing fireplace was the centerpiece of the spacious hotel lobby. The atmosphere was clubby, old-worldish. The staff wore white shorts and khaki shirts with too many pockets, in keeping with the raj decor. And when it appeared that there were no other journalists around, I checked in. My large suite had a balcony that faced an endless expanse of gray ocean. I unpacked. I left a message for Ned. Afterward, when a bout of ambition began to overtake me, I walked out to the edge of my rented quarters and leaned against the rail. I looked to the right, to the north, toward the Santa Monica Pier—to the spinning Ferris wheel with its red-orange buckets in the sky.

———

Mornings, I sat on my narrow balcony and drank tea. I read the paper while it blew around in the cold ocean air. I waited for calls. I wore my white terry-cloth hotel robe. I ordered more hot water. Church bells rang in the far-off distance, and below me, four floors down in the hollow courtyard, people swam laps in the swimming pool. The sound of arms slapping the surface of the water echoed up to me. It was rhythmic and a bit forlorn. The sound of hypnotic effort, of delusion, of ritual. Somebody trying to stave off age and decay. Slap, slap. Stave off time. But hours passed, days, weeks. Slap, slap. March would be coming soon, nonetheless. Not really winter, not really spring. More rain, I was told. Slap slap slap.

Franklin Warren, my new assistant, knocked softly at the door—so softly that he was left standing in the hallway for five minutes before he knocked again and I heard him. He was a Brit, unfailingly polite, a young guy from the suburbs of Manchester who had gotten a job in the research department of *Flame* not long after finishing college. He arrived

each morning looking fresh in his jeans and black turtle-
necks and small gold loop earring. He was witty, warm, and
conspiratorial, and it didn't take us long to bond over our
ambivalence about Lucille Ball and our love of Lee Marvin.
It also didn't take Franklin long to confess that Ed had sent
him to L.A. indefinitely—to help me write a piece, possibly
a book, about Allegra.

"A book? That's a new one," I said.

"Is it?"

"Ed is amazing."

"Really?"

"His shamelessness is almost inspiring. If at first you fail,
shoot even higher."

Franklin looked a bit lost for words, but I sensed his loy-
alty to Ed was tentative. "I'm not writing a book about Allegra," I said.

"You aren't?"

"I'm uncertain about many things but not that."

"You're serious?"

I nodded.

"Can you come up with something, then?" he asked,
locking his hands in front of his face in a posture of prayer.
"Just don't send me back to New York."

"You like it here?"

"It's rather nice, don't you think?"

Oh, I'd keep him busy, I said. There would be interviews to conduct, calls to make, and meetings to arrange. I
didn't expect Franklin to track down Allegra—everybody

else on the planet was trying to do that—but there would be a fair amount of research for a nebulous project that I had dreamed up, an essay on the vagaries of fame. Maybe we'd never see Allegra again, and maybe we'd eventually see too much of her, but wasn't there some way to write the larger, grander piece—one that would be able, perhaps, to uncover a more generic yet eternal truth? On the first day, I sent him out for *My Side of the Road,* Dorothy Lamour's as-told-to memoir, as well as a few movie rentals.

"My evening was very depressing," Franklin called to report the next morning. "I watched *The Greatest Show on Earth* and then fell asleep to *Road to Hong Kong.*"

"You found them?"

"Indeed. At WaxWorks Video in the Valley. Terrific oldies section. Huge adult section too, lots of pervs."

"Men with trench coats?"

"No, I'm afraid. Horny bastards in L.A. just wear gym clothes like everybody else."

"How's Dorothy?"

"Rather okay. She was thirty-eight when she made *Greatest Show.* She plays a circus performer who latches on to a rope with her teeth and hangs in the air. She does all right, considering."

"Considering what?"

"Thickening middle. Heavy face, as though the tissue has unfastened from her bones. You wouldn't want to see her in a sarong."

"The freshness is gone."

"Oh yes," he said.

"I had a feeling that would happen."

"Inevitable, I suppose. You're not sure whether you feel worse for yourself or for her. She was so beautiful in *Typhoon*."

"You mean *The Hurricane*," I offered.

"Actually, *The Hurricane* was 1937, and *Typhoon* was 1940."

"Extreme typecasting. I guess she specialized in tropical disasters."

"Let's see." Franklin paused a bit. "There's *The Jungle Princess, The Hurricane, Her Jungle Love, Road to Singapore, Tropic Holiday, Typhoon, Road to Zanzibar, Aloma of the South Seas* . . ."

"Wait. Are you doing that from memory?"

"I'm a hopeless show-off," he said. "I pray that doesn't bother you."

Franklin had a far worse case of moviemania than I— a childhood spent scouring video stores and sitting in art houses. He was only twenty-five or so, but his mind seemed to have been steeping in cinema lore for centuries. He'd seen everything but had a penchant for darkness, for old noir and new noir, for *The Grifters,* and for epic extravaganzas and costume dramas—for swords and sandals and anything with Charlton Heston. He'd read everything by Kael and Tynan and was devoted to Edelstein on *Slate*. Franklin's command of movie trivia was both awe-inspiring and irritating (he could list all of Truffaut's movies in chronological order and then again in order of brilliance). And his eye for the depressing anecdote was flawless.

"So she plays a circus performer in *The Greatest Show* when she's thirty-eight," he said over tea on the balcony, "and then can't get work." He picked up *My Side of the Road* and began reading. "This is the part I was talking about: 'Sometimes show business associates can be very cruel. It was suddenly difficult for me to reach certain Hollywood people by phone—the same people for whom I had done so many favors when I was "box office magic." You know the routine: Someone would be in a meeting and simply couldn't be disturbed. Or out of town . . .

"'Real friends stuck by me, but Bill's emphysema wasn't good and we worried about raising the boys in Hollywood. After a long walk, we decided it might be best to move. We went back to where Bill Howard grew up, where his family had a long distinguished history . . . to a suburb called Towson. One of our neighbors was Spiro Agnew.'"

"Towson?"

"It's a suburb of Baltimore. If that's possible."

"Poor Dorothy."

"Then what happens?"

"'I kept a very low profile. I wanted the boys to be known as the Howard boys and not the Lamour boys. I attended each PTA meeting and joined some committees. I was beginning to get my self-respect back: I hadn't realized just how much that rejection in Hollywood had affected me.'"

"At least she's honest," I said.

"Wretched, I'd say. Hold on, here's the really pathetic part: 'During the ten years that we lived in Maryland, I kept my hand in show biz, so to speak . . . Occasionally I came to Hollywood to do a television show, such as *I Spy* or *The Joey Bishop Show* but I could never seem to get on *The Tonight Show* . . . I had met Johnny Carson on one of my trips to New York. Totally charming . . . He said he was coming to Baltimore and I promised that Bill and I would take him out for a real Maryland dinner. When I called his hotel, his secretary answered and was quite rude; I never heard from him again . . .'"

"I can't take much more, Franklin."

"Isn't this what you wanted?"

"I suppose."

She made six pictures with Bing Crosby and Bob Hope before retiring in the late fifties. And then, five years into retirement, at the age of forty-eight, she discovered from reading the trade papers that a new picture, *Road to Hong Kong,* was being made. Gina Lollobrigida and Sophia Loren were being considered for the lead female role.

It hurt Dorothy that nobody called to tell her—not the producer or director, not her old friends Bing or Bob. But finally, after a little behind-the-scenes maneuvering, she was offered a part in the picture, a sentimental gesture more than anything else. But Dorothy became difficult when she received the script and realized the part was little more than a walk-on. "I stuck to my guns," she writes. "I'd do it if they built up the part. Finally I discovered that a girl had been signed to play the female lead: Joan Collins . . . She told the London papers we were having a 'feud.'

" 'I never have a feud with anyone,' I told the press, 'but if I considered having a feud, it would be with the stars of the film.' "

I thought about the girl in *The Jungle Princess* and *Road to Zanzibar*. The sweetness of her face—the way her slim arms moved as she adjusted her sarong and fixed the hibiscus behind her ear. The way her eyes always looked like she'd just been crying. Her face was so open. The innocence, the trust—youth's companions into the abyss. All passing. All gone. Perhaps it was better to disappear. To make a few good movies and give up. To leave as you were cresting. In ten years, Allegra would be considering a facelift. In fifteen, we'd feel sorry for her when the lighting wasn't right. And after that, we'd begin to feel sorry for ourselves too.

———

Ed kept tabs on me through Franklin, dropped hints that they'd spoken. But I pretended not to notice.

"You might be coming here to see Max Coleman?" Ed asked. "I'd love to see you."

"Oh, I've postponed that."

"Any sense of when you might have something?"

"Something?"

"Something for me to look at."

"Oh," I said. "Not soon."

"Any chance of making the All-Allegra Issue? We close in March."

"Nope."

"Well, tell me one thing: Is this 'Vagaries of Fame' thing, or whatever it is, going to be at least pegged to Allegra somehow?"

"Goes without saying."

"Okay. I promise to leave you alone—"

"I'd love that, Ed."

"—if you do one thing."

"What?"

"Let me send Gary La Grange to do your picture."

"For what?"

"The Allegra issue."

"Forget it."

"Darling," he said, after a frustrated exhalation, "if you haven't noticed, all we've got is that one head shot of you with the keyboard in the blurry background. We gave it out when the story hit. It's so old now. The *Enquirer* ran it three times already, doctored in three different ways. You're so much prettier than that. And the way your hand is curled up next to your chin makes it look like a claw."

"Hey, don't make fun of my claw." I was standing on the balcony and looking out to sea. "Promise you'll use Gary?" I asked.

"Absolutely."

"And he can do it quickly? One morning?"

"I'll insist."

"And here in the hotel. Not a studio."

"Whatever you say."

"Okay," I said. "But no eye patch in the photo, Ed. I don't want to look like a freak."

"No patch shots, I promise," he said. "Franklin tells me you're looking great, by the way, very healthy and rested. Like a dream."

CHAPTER 7

The hairstylist came and put in hot rollers, pinched them in place with steel clips. The rollers went from hot, almost burning my scalp, to cold. They went from pulled too tight and giving me an ache at the roots to loose and falling out. A makeup girl arrived. I'm not sure why they're always called "girls," but they are. And they're usually young, painfully lovely, and wear no makeup at all.

Paula, I think her name was. Without any direction, she began setting up in the hotel bathroom—unpacking her black duffel, withdrawing small squares and circles of black plastic, compacts of foundation, highlights, powder, eye shadow. She stood up a handful of skinny brushes inside the hotel water glass.

"Are you ready to start?" she asked in a little voice.

"I don't usually wear makeup," I said.

"Oh, but you'll need something to fight the lights," said Paula. "Otherwise all your features will just fade away." She closed the top of the toilet seat and motioned for me to sit down. She had brown hair and small intense eyes and studied my face from the edge of the tub. I could feel her breath on my cheeks and smell her lemon-mint Ricola cough lozenges.

She picked up a white sponge, and I felt a cool glaze of paint being spread over my face. A milky pink foundation.

"I want to look natural," I said.

Paula nodded and smiled. She seemed so tender and young, I believed she knew what natural meant. She began rubbing my face with a clean sponge, then picked up a small red pencil and drew around my mouth. She took a black pencil and began drawing around my left eye. Then she started with the brushes and wands. She had remedies and a little wand for everything. She had colors for brows, lids, mascara for lashes. She had concealers, highlights, lowlights, darker tones for making bones where bones weren't.

She picked up a brush with short dense bristles and dabbed it into an oily blood color. She began lacquering my mouth with great care and focus, as though restoring the edge of God's robe on the Sistine Chapel.

"Open up," she said, staring at my lips.

And: "Soften."

Gary La Grange knocked on the hallway wall and poked his head in the bathroom. He was tall and skinny, and his hair was cropped down to a half inch except for a rather bushy goatee. He wore bell-bottoms and a chartreuse baseball cap with big black letters that spelled out THERMO-NUCLEAR. He spoke calmly, sweetly, humbly—like he wasn't the sort of photographer who owned an old mansion in the hills or was followed by an entourage of assistants and two vans full of equipment. His stylist, Frankie McWelch, stood next to him in blue velvet jodhpurs and a sleeveless T-shirt.

"Hello, my dear," said Gary.

"Clem," said Frankie, blowing a kiss.

Paula put down her brush.

"Hey guys," I said. "Glad to see you."

"It's been so long," said Gary, leaning against the door-frame.

"Too long," I said.

"It's been since Robert Goulet," said Frankie.

"Wasn't it Melanie Griffith?" asked Gary.

"Cher," I said. "You guys dressed her up like a school-marm."

"She looked fab-u-lous," said Frankie. "Just amazing."

"Your piece was wicked," Gary said.

"No, it wasn't. I was nice to Cher," I said. "You're thinking of Goulet."

"Oh, it had some moments," said Frankie.

"Well, Cher can deal," said Gary. "She's a grown-up."

"She's a grandmother," said Frankie.

"Is she?" asked Gary.

"I think so," said Frankie.

La Grange and McWelch had a light, courtly way about them—never dull, never too catty—which probably accounted for their ability to get famous people to do almost anything for the camera. Celebrities swam in ponds with carp. They were painted as Hindu gods. They were airlifted by helicopter, dropped from ledges. They were naked and sitting on the john. Gary, as nice as he was, seemed to enjoy humiliating fame a little bit. And somehow the famous went along. They trusted him—or maybe trusted his reputation, or thought of it as a rite of passage—and let go. For an hour or two, he owned you, whoever you were, and somehow you wanted to be his. The arrangement worked for everybody in the end. Gary got his pictures. The magazine got its artful newness. And dressed up as Krishna, even a guy like William Hurt looked like he could laugh at himself.

"Ed wants something sensational," said Gary.

"Going to be very glam," said Frankie.

"Not too glam, I hope," I said.

"No," said Gary. "Not too—"

"Aren't you going to dress me up as Blackbeard? I already have the eye patch."

Both Gary and Frankie let out an awkward laugh, then gestured to Paula that she should join them in the hallway. There they confabbed about lighting, angles. They mentioned something about the glare of my white robe. The hairstylist joined in. They moved farther down the hall, and their voices grew faint.

I stood up and looked at myself in the mirror. Pink curlers were still lodged around my head. My face was boldly streaked with color. It was a stranger's face, a Fellini grotesque from *Amarcord* or *Roma*. I stepped toward the mirror and looked closely at my skin. It was as though I were driving over my face in a small car, passing the pale landscape of a desert, a foreign place, a new place, dry and cracking, then finding my nose, my cheek, my eye, my mouth—a fire-engine red.

A strange panic began to descend on me, a wild rage and madness—a sense of maiming far worse, somehow, than the loss of my eye. Sweat began to explode from my pores, tingling and itching. I heard the pounding of blood in my ears.

"Close the door," a voice whispered.

I thought it was my own voice, the voice of my panic, my hysteria. But it came from the bathtub.

"Close the door!"

I reached for the bathroom door and shut it. A noise came from behind the white shower curtain, a rustling. I heard the sound of a half-empty shampoo bottle being opened and squeezed.

"Gardenia . . . *Awful.*"

The curtain was flung open suddenly—with great drama and extravagance—and a small woman, not quite five feet tall and dressed entirely in black, stood before me in the tub.

"What do you need with *them*?" she said. It was a hiss, a stage whisper that echoed around the marble tiles.

I stood, stunned and speechless.

"Darling," said Gloria Swanson, "you look like a circus clown. That makeup girl has no idea what she's doing. She's getting a lecture right now."

She motioned me to sit down. She took off her gloves and threw them beside the sink. She began looking at the brushes and sponges, acquainting herself with Paula's assortment of tubes and compacts and other plastic containers.

She was fairly young, I thought, but no girl. Her outfit was so elaborate, so complicated—a frightening conjuration entirely for the screen. She wore a black velvet riding jacket with satin lapels, a long fringed skirt, suede lace-up boots, and a black top hat with a veil that dropped down to her lips, just short of the mole on the left side of her chin.

It was something from *Zaza* or *Queen Kelly,* something from one of her last splashy silents—movies that were lost or that nobody cared about anymore, nobody watched, nobody ever saw.

She began rubbing a new liquid color on my chin and cheeks. Then she moved on to the powders. The darks and lights, the shadows and highlights. After rummaging through all the lipsticks and gloss pots, she came across a pale pink lipstick and sighed with relief. "We need something frosted and pale. Modern! Sort of a seventies look. Jet set. Riviera. Faux innocence. You know . . ."

Her small head bent down as she worked. Her dark hair was swept up under the top hat, which I could see was some kind of sheared animal pelt.

"Don't let them photograph you in the hotel robe, for God's sake," she said, after a while. "Or by the pool, with a towel wrapped around your head. Such a cliché. And don't let them use the Jackie O sunglasses. Make them work!"

Paula knocked at the door. "Clementine?"

"Need a few minutes."

"Oh. I thought you called me."

"I'll be done soon."

"Can I get you some ice water or anything? Can I order you some lunch?"

"No thanks. I'll eat later."

I looked up at the face in front of me—in 1926, the most famous face in the world. Through her ridiculous veil, I caught her eyes. They were intense, mesmerizing, bright blue and flecked with gold.

"I know, darling," she said. "You've always wanted to meet me. Of course you have. But let's dispense with adoration for now. Have you seen the tweezers?"

After the shoot, Gary left me with curling Polaroids— his test runs. My hair looked big, teased up and messy and existing on a plane separate from the rest of me. It was magazine hair, TV hair, the hair of a celebrity profiler. It was Jacqueline Susann or Kitty Kelley hair. But it went with the clothes, I guess. When I had refused the robe, Frankie gave me a green silk Moda Matta pantsuit to wear, and Gary charitably turned my head to profile. "Your makeup," he said. "Sensational. It's like you read my mind."

In one shot—that Ed would eventually run—I was sitting sideways in a magnificent orange leather Mies van der Rohe chair, with my bare feet dangling over the edge.

—

She joined me outside later on, settling into a white plastic chair. She'd removed the top hat and veil. The wind was blowing—misty and wet. A storm was coming in. Black clouds and more gray skies. Maybe it was the time of year, the low-hanging gloom of late winter, but the stretch of sand and sea in front of Shutters looked lonely. There was an empty lifeguard stand—wooden, rickety, painted aqua— that seemed very much in need of a man with broad shoulders and red lifesaving gear.

Between the hotel and the shoreline was a pond of runoff, a little estuary of sorts where the gulls descended and plunged for trash.

"Darling," she said, "you were smart to pick the seaside for recuperation, but I do think some sunshine would be an improvement. Costa del Sol? Acapulco?"

"I'm working, Gloria."

"You're not *working*," she said with a laugh. "You're mending. You're healing. What is this place—this Shutters on the Beach? The Bel Air Hotel has such nice bungalows and those lovely little pink cement pathways and banana leaves spilling out all over. Wouldn't that be more fun?"

I had washed my hair and face and changed into a pair of jeans. I was eating a roast-beef sandwich while I watched her pore over the Polaroids as though planning to edit the April issue of *Flame* herself.

"Well, this is a lousy shot," she said.

"You look drugged," she said.

"What are you sitting in, anyway—some kind of dentist's chair?" she asked.

A few minutes later she had moved on, picking up an issue of *People*. "Very powerful," she said, her eyes soaking up a picture of Allegra like it was the fountain of youth. "Very animal."

"Yes," I said. Looking down on the Venice boardwalk, I could see the tops of streetlights and palms, fat, thick date palms. The rain began to start.

"She changes. She becomes what she has to," Gloria said.

"But somehow remains utterly herself."

"Well, that's the trick, isn't it?" Gloria asked.

"She has it, doesn't she? Whatever that is."

Gloria barely heard me. She was turning pages, examining every image, every nuance, every gesture and moment and recorded inch of Allegra.

"You know why I'm here," she said. "You know, don't you?"

"To do my makeup."

She laughed. "Very funny, my friend."

"To scare away the seagulls."

She smiled this time, but her eyes were serious. "We're worried about her," she said. "This wasn't supposed to happen."

he rain lasted less than an hour. My lunch tray was taken out. A dinner tray brought in. And she was still there, a smoldering, gigantic presence that swallowed up the whole room. I didn't say much. Maybe I forgot I existed, or maybe it was just habit, but around movie stars I find the more incurious I seem, the more they have to say.

The room grew dark, the sky cleared, and a dry wind erased all traces of wetness. The moon rose above the sea, floated over us, stayed with us, like a companion to her story. It was a long story, about her third marriage to the marquis. It was also about her life in pictures and the price of some things.

"Fame? What did it mean to me? Oh darling, so many

things—it's all the attention you could ever want in life and yet somehow never enough. You picture it differently in your mind, so when it comes, it doesn't seem like the thing you wanted in the first place. I am settled with my fame now. It was a marriage that lasted, unlike my other marriages. It stayed with me, enduring, taking new forms. A part of me, for better or worse. Fame gave, and then it took away. I was a sensation at twenty-one. A has-been at thirty-three. Then I made a comeback at forty-nine, playing a washed-up star. In every victory, there is a defeat. I mean that, my friend. It's true.

"I want to tell you about the day I married my gorgeous marquis. The pinnacle of joy. Followed by the most terrifying descent I have ever known. One moment I had everything I had ever wanted—and the next I was more wretched than I had ever been before. I blamed all this on the movies. What they did to me. What I had become. I still do.

"My marquis? I met him in Paris when I was making *Madame Sans-Gêne.* He was my translator. Henri de la Falaise de la Coudraye. So handsome! The most superb suits! Irresistible manners and friends! He wanted to give me châteaus, but he couldn't. He didn't have a dime. None of my husbands did. But I said, 'What do I need with castles, darling?' I had houses in the East, houses in the West, a fabulous mansion across from the Beverly Hills Hotel on Crescent Drive—park-size lawns, a private elevator, the grandest staircase built by King Gillette for his sister.

"I had my cars, my staff, my two children. I had my career that I had built myself, all alone—no agent, no manager, no man supporting me. In Hollywood, they called me the mortgage lifter, the gold mine. I made money for everybody. And with the possible exception of Mary Pickford—quite a sweet lady, I must say, although the whole world thinks I detest her—I was the most popular woman in the world. Everything Henri had to give me—love, sophistication, a certain dignity—were the only things I needed.

"And so we married, blissfully, on a bright morning in Passy in 1925. I became the Marquise de la Falaise de la Coudraye. A mouthful, isn't it? And on my wedding day, standing in the sunlight and holding my beloved's hand, I tried not to think about the days to come. We were so in love, Henri and I. Deliriously, hysterically, madly in love. But I was pregnant, you see. Henri did not know. Only I knew. And I also knew if I returned home to Hollywood and had a baby in seven months, my career would be finished.

"I can see by the look on your face that you don't believe me."

I shrugged.

"You think I've made up this excuse to tell myself, to feel better about how things turned out—to blame Hollywood, to blame movies and not me. But I'm not a victim, darling. If my life was ruined, then I ruined it—nobody else. Let all the other girls carry on about their sad lives, let them take pills and drink booze and kill themselves off because they can't face the truth. They sold themselves as playthings for the rabble. And one day, as everybody knows, the rabble won't want you anymore.

"But let me get to the point. Let me get to Fatty Arbuckle. Pictures were smart when we first started making them, you see. They were adult. They were subtle. And they stayed that way until Virginia Rappe was murdered by Fatty at some drunken orgy in San Francisco over Labor Day weekend in 1921. That's when everything changed, when every church group and ladies' club in America got a taste of blood, and the newspapers began getting into the act too. A trend was born. Newspapers had new things to write about. Suddenly Hollywood was populated by murderers and drug addicts. Suddenly we were criminals, degenerates.

"That's when we realized that the public got as big a thrill watching stars fall as it did watching them shine. One weekend in 1921, Fatty was the most beloved comedian in this country after Chaplin. By the next Monday, everybody was screaming for his head. And everything changed. Francis X. Bushman divorced his old wife and married Beverly Bayne, and his public dropped him. Hot potato. I wanted to divorce Herbert Sonborn, my second husband, less than a year after having his baby, and my studio boss, Jesse Lasky, flew into a panic.

"This sort of nonsense continued for years. I know this

probably seems silly now, but nobody had any idea that movies were a sure thing and a sure investment. In Hollywood, we always felt like we were tricking people. But as long as we were making a bundle, we wanted to keep on.

"And that's where Mr. Hays comes in. At the beginning of 1922, there were quite a few Hollywood scandals brewing, so Mr. Lasky and other movie executives set up their own internal censorship bureau. They hired Will H. Hays—he seemed like an okay chap, he'd served as postmaster general under Warren Harding—and they brought him to Hollywood to create the Hays Office, supposedly to enforce a standard of 'decency' in Hollywood films. It was entirely public relations, of course. If Hollywood had to become prudish to keep making money, then it would. Hollywood wanted to make sure that Mr. and Mrs. America didn't go burning down all the movie theaters. I'm not joking. Truly. We used to worry about that.

"So what did Mr. Hays decide? First of all, he decided that no kisses should run longer than ten feet of film. So we shot each kissing scene twice. Once for the American version and once for the Europeans. In our picture *Beyond the Rocks,* poor Rudy Valentino could barely get his nostrils flaring in ten feet. There were to be no double beds, no sheer clothing, no hints of sex.

"And all at once the gossip columnists began to gain power. Why do you think that happened, darling? The studios handed them that power—just the way they handed

Hays his paycheck. It was about controlling talent, keeping the artists in line. It was about PR and image. We all knew that, and anybody who tells you they didn't is a liar.

"Marion Davies was the only star in those days who could breathe easily. It was even a joke at parties. We all better watch what we do—meanwhile, Marion Davies kept guzzling champagne and living in sin. She was free of stain, you see. Hearst made sure nothing nasty was written about her . . . But I wasn't free of stain. This is what I've been driving at. You see, the studio hadn't approved completely of my divorce from Herbert, and I was known to be having an affair with Mickey Neilan, a married man, so my contract with Mr. Lasky had a morals clause in it. If anything unattractive came out about me in the papers, that was it. They could cut off everything. And what if I came home from France and had Henri's baby seven months later?

"Can you imagine what it's like to have all that fame and money and power over your future—and risk losing it? Can you imagine working as hard as I did for ten years and knowing that one small thing could cause everything to stop?

"So I became convinced I had no choice. The very idea of abortion horrified me, but . . . I had no choice. I told myself this over and over. I had no choice.

"I confided in André Daven, my close friend, and he arranged everything. He made an appointment for me to see a doctor in Paris on the day following my wedding. 'You mustn't blame yourself,' he kept saying. 'Leave everything to me. There's no other way.'

"His voice was reassuring, and I remember smiling feebly at him in gratitude. I tried to carry on with wedding plans, with calls and festivities. Henri must never know, I decided. We were both young. We could have other children.

"Then, one night when I was reading, I heard a voice inside me. It was speaking clearly.

"'Don't do this,' the voice was saying. And I tried not to listen.

"'I know you hear me,' the voice said. 'Listen to me. I want to live. I am frightened.'

"How big was this child? Perhaps no larger than my fist. Perhaps the size of a chestnut. But can you promise me it wasn't the voice of my child I heard?

"If the operation had gone well, I suppose I might have continued my life as usual. As the golden girl, the party girl—all the laughter and gaiety, the fun, the carelessness. I could have gone on living that way, secluded from any inner reality for years to come—oh, twinges of guilt, perhaps, a moment here and there when I remembered and felt a tiny bit sad. But would my proper feelings have surfaced?

"However, the operation was bungled, you see. The doctor was incompetent. By the next day, I had an infection, was unconscious with a fever. The day after that, I was dying. For weeks I lay between life and death in a Paris hospital having nightmares.

"The child would come to me. The child spoke to me. I prayed to be dead. So many times I prayed for that.

"My public grew more ardent and more fascinated. Day after day the newspapers in the States published accounts of my fever. This was all they knew: I was mortally ill. My fans prayed for me. I was dying, and they loved me more than they ever had before. There was a steady stream of cablegrams, flowers, gifts. And when I recovered, I was still more loved than ever. I was Sleeping Beauty. I was Lazarus risen from the dead. I was truly immortal. The studio bosses begged me to return to the States for the opening of my new movie. My illness had given them millions in free publicity, and they wanted to keep the excitement going. So I played along. Why not? I sent Adolph Zukor a cablegram: 'Am arriving with the marquis tomorrow. Please arrange ovation.'

"I stepped off the ocean liner *Paris* in New York Harbor, and crowds nearly trampled me. Wherever Henri and I went, we were followed. Reporters and photographers ambushed us in the lobby of the Ritz. Fans cheered behind barricades. The notes never stopped arriving, nor the flowers and welcome-home presents, and the hotel switchboard was so swamped with incoming calls that it took me a few hours to call little Gloria and Brother, my children, at the house in Croton-on-Hudson.

"At the hotel, the reporters wanted to know what color

Henri's pajamas were, how many flowers were in my room, what food we ordered, and they printed it up. The newspaper reporters wrote that my hair was short because I was following the latest trend in Paris—not because the nurses in Paris had shaved my head during the fever—and their readers started cutting their hair short too.

"We took the train to Los Angeles. There were thousands of fans at the train station, two bands playing, policemen on horseback, red carpets, and more flowers. A platform had been erected, and there were faces on it—the mayor and city officials and everybody I'd ever known and anybody who was anybody in Hollywood: D. W. Griffith, Rudolph Valentino, Mary Pickford, Norma Talmadge, Bebe Daniels, Hoot Gibson, Charlie Chaplin, Rod LaRocque. A platoon of motorcycle cops was clearing traffic for me, for our parade of limousines to Hollywood. The studio had shut down for the morning, and hundreds of Paramount employees were in the street throwing flowers into my car. There were placards and signs all over the streets, but the biggest banner of all was at the corner of Sunset and Vine: WELCOME GLORIA.

"That night, at the Hollywood premiere of *Madame Sans-Gêne,* we caused a traffic jam near the tunnel on Third Street. We stopped our limousine several blocks from Sid Grauman's Million Dollar Theatre and the police cleared a path amid the mob, cheering in unison for me like it was a football game. Then I emerged from the car, twenty pounds thinner than they'd last seen me. I was wearing a gown of clinging silver lamé and my hair oiled close to my skull. Henri wore his white tie and tails and Croix de Guerre across his chest.

"Inside the theater, the audience threw orchids and gardenias in the aisles and everyone was singing 'Home Sweet Home.' All the stars were there too, and all the directors and studio heads. I sat next to Mr. DeMille. The din was impossible. The ushers were insane. And just a few minutes after the speeches were made, after the picture had started, a man came up to my seat—an usher—to say that the police couldn't hold the crowds any longer. Our car was being brought around to the alley, and the police wanted us to leave immediately through the orchestra pit and backstage.

"I didn't want to go. I wanted to stay and watch. Mr. DeMille turned to me and said, 'They're right. Hollywood has paid you a tribute tonight, young fellow'—he always called me that—'and that tribute has never been equaled. Every star, every director, every head of every studio and film company in town is here. Everyone wants you to survive, young fellow. And now it's time for you to go home to bed.'

"So Henri and Mother and I crept out like thieves to the alley, to our car, and the police escorted us for the entire slow drive home, back to my house in Beverly Hills.

"It was quiet in the car. The first quiet I'd known in hours, days, weeks.

"Mother finally said, 'Glory, you're so quiet! This should be the happiest night of your life.'

"We were so different, you see. She never really understood.

"I shook my head. I was thinking about all the glamorous people back there in the theater, sitting in their dark red velvet seats on either side of those orchid-strewn aisles. And I was thinking about the price I had paid to walk down that aisle. What if I spelled it out for them—stood up and shushed them and told them my story, that in order to stand there before them, adored, in order not to break my contract or create a scandal, I had to sneak to a French surgeon like a criminal and kill my child, silence the voice inside me.

"'No, Mother,' I said. 'It is the saddest night.' I still remember how heavy and warm the tears felt as they ran down my face. 'That cheering you heard tonight had nothing to do with me. It wasn't for me as a human being. Nor for me as an actress. They were cheering a mirage. They were cheering PR. They were cheering Will Hays. They were cheering the victory of the studio, the industry. I am just the mortgage lifter, the gold mine. I'm only twenty-six. Where do I go from here?'"

CHAPTER 9

'*Avventura* arrived in town quietly, without word of mouth, without a murmur, without even a faint hush-hush swirl. Margaux let it slip one afternoon that she'd seen a rough cut. We were at Lucques, sunken into an olive-green booth next to the window. The day was ending, and the sky was turning a screaming pink and orange and violet—the Popsicle hues, air-pollution colors, that L.A. natives think are natural, even beautiful. I was staring at the sporadic foot traffic on Melrose, at the rosy faces and messy hair. Margaux was summoning the waiter, ordering a second glass of wine. Franklin was rolling the paper from a straw wrapper between two fingers and talking about Monica Vitti, the Italian film star— obsessing over Monica Vitti, actually. After we'd watched a slew of silent movies—the arched eyebrows and winks and sultry exotica of Gloria Swanson and Pola Negri and Alla Nazimova—he'd decompressed by going on a sixties binge, done two straight nights of alienation, Godard and Antonioni films rented from an on-line art house.

"Monica's so amazing. So tough," he said. "And from certain angles, she looks uncannily like Princess Di."

"Really?" I said. "To me, she's sort of an Athena Parthenos type. Broad shoulders, big nose, kind of mannish. Like Vanessa Redgrave in *Blowup*. Maybe Antonioni goes for that."

"Androgyny," Franklin said excitedly. "Confusion, interplay of opposites. A sleeping sexuality. Monica is so exquisitely numb. She's floating through her pictures as if in a dream."

"Remote," I said. "Deadpan. She's the queen of incommunicability."

"Well, there's deadpan," said Franklin, "and there's sleepwalking. Terribly big difference. Monica isn't deadpan. You sense her despair."

"I've always wondered if that's acting," I said, "or just the shape of her eyes."

"She wrote a book, didn't she?"

"I wonder if it's been translated."

"Who?" Margaux asked.

Franklin and I shared a look.

"Monica Vitti," he said.

Margaux looked blank, then stared down at her wineglass. A wounded look came over Franklin's face.

"The actress in *Red Desert*," I said, trying to be helpful.

"She's in lots of Antonioni pictures," Franklin added.

Margaux remained silent.

"*L'Avventura*?" I said.

"Oh!" Margaux brightened but quickly grew muddled again. "Wait—you mean you guys saw it already?"

Franklin shot me another look.

"Oh, I know. You're talking about the old one," she said. "The original. Right?"

Franklin was shaken out of his sullen mood. "We were," he said. "But what's happening with the remake?"

Bertolucci had brought the film to L.A. himself, Margaux told us after a certain amount of prodding, so the sound and score could be finished. The director was showing it to friends informally and keeping it from the papers, not wanting to seem to be capitalizing on Allegra's disappearance. "And besides," Margaux said, "*Sphinxa* is still hot and bringing in good numbers. No reason to discourage that. We don't want people to get sick of her."

"Oops," said Franklin.

"It might be too late," I said.

"Even in Allegra's absence," Franklin said, "she's everywhere."

It was true. *Sphinxa* hadn't gone away, even after Cosmos had finished promoting it to death. The numbers were stunning, miraculous, particularly for a semiserious movie about rape and revenge. Teens had turned it into a cult movie, buying up the soundtrack and posters of Allegra in her *Sphinxa* garb, a see-through chiffon peasant top and polka-dot skirt. Darkness didn't usually sell unless it came dressed up as a horror show or cop thriller. But ten weeks had passed since *Sphinxa*'s release, nine weeks since Swimmer's Porsche had been totaled, and the movie was still holding—topping out at number two during the height of the craze, when the Kern County sheriff gave his news conference, when the Oscar nominations were announced, and when Allegra was on the cover of *Time* with a bare midriff and a cryptic smile. (TWINKLE, TWINKLE, MISSING STAR, the headline said.)

In subsequent weeks, *Sphinxa* had been overtaken by three new releases, two gruesome action pictures—*St. Valentine's Day Massacre III* and *Cannibal Night*—and *Goose Creek,* a Tom Cessna Western with jokes and cowgirls and just enough raunchy language to get a desirable PG-13 rating. (Westerns were iffy. Cessna wasn't. A small gamble had paid off.) Studios were never sure what worked but kept trying, grafting the head of one film onto the body of another. Who could predict the fate of an art film like *L'Avventura*? The original was highbrow, an existential journey to magnificent despair. But who cared about that sort of thing anymore? It was a movie for intellectuals, film buffs—people with pretensions. And it reminded me of that old saw about foreign films: Nobody liked them over there, so they shipped them here.

Franklin called later that night, when I was stretched out in bed with the laptop on my stomach. He sounded worked up. He wanted to put the squeeze on Margaux, to see if she could get us into Bertolucci's remake. "I can't wait," he said. "I can't wait another day."

"Wait another day, Franklin."

"Aren't you dying to see it? She can't be as good as Monica Vitti. Nobody can."

"I'm torn," I said. "Remakes are so tricky. What if Allegra's painfully bad? What if she ruins all memory of Monica—and ruins all memory of what Monica and Antonioni created together, even *La Notte* and *The Eclipse* and *Red Desert* too. What if the considerable gifts of Bertolucci can't compensate? It's possible."

"Bertolucci is God."

"I thought Charlton Heston was God."

"What's Margaux's home number?"

"It's late. It's eleven-thirty. *The Tonight Show*'s coming on."

"Oh, she's still up. She's gulping down her fifth glass of syrupy chardonnay."

"You've gotten so mean, Franklin. Los Angeles has done that to you. Everybody else comes here and gets foggy. The English just get crueler."

"Uh? Antonioni? I'm not in the mood for pasta." Franklin's falsetto impression of Margaux was deadly.

"Call her in the morning. Don't seem so desperate."

"I'm exceedingly desperate. I'm aching. Won't be able to sleep. We need to see it soon. Tomorrow. This weekend. Particularly if Miss Coleman does a face plant. I'm obsessed."

"Okay. Fine. Call her. Just don't say I'm writing a piece

about Allegra when you put the pressure on. I don't want her breathing down my neck any more than necessary."

"PR people are encouraged so easily."

"They're just optimists."

"Well, it won't matter," said Franklin, "whatever I say."

"What?"

"It won't matter, I said. Nobody cares what you say or I say. It only matters what Ed tells them."

It was easy, anyway. One midnight call to Margaux and a lumbering basket of mangoes arrived in my hotel room the next afternoon, along with two passes to an eight A.M. screening the following day on the Cosmos lot. There was a note too: "Very quiet. Mum's the word. Please don't share passes."

The screening room was empty when we got there. Dark and empty, aside from a weird smell that Franklin identified as the smoke from clove cigarettes. We waited ten minutes or so, an eternity to spend in a small dark room without popcorn or Coke or a box of Hot Tamales, and then a projectionist appeared. She wore a tie-dyed T-shirt and suede hip huggers and white shoes. She had a chipmunk face and a chipper little smile. Did we need water, anything to drink? She returned with icy bottles of Evian and then asked if we were ready.

Franklin sank down into his seat.

"Oh yes," I said. "Fire away."

ranklin dropped me at the hotel after the screening, and I went for a drive. It wasn't even noon. *L'Avventura* stayed with me, clung to me like a smell I couldn't get out of my clothes. I felt a pull northward, to the cold and the sea. I needed a breeze. I wanted to see clouds. Antonioni and wind, and the sound of wind. Antonioni and the sea, the waves, the spray. Bertolucci's remake was an homage, of course. But there were glimpses of other movies, *Rebecca* and *Ryan's Daughter,* maybe *Local Hero* too. Isolation, beautiful despair. Quiet mysteries of the deep. People adrift, unmoored.

"Let's not talk about it now," Franklin had said as we walked across the Cosmos lot to visitors' parking.

"Wait, you mean you don't want to talk it to death right

now? Analyze the mise-en-scène? Tell me how awful Allegra was?"

He kept his head down as he walked, wouldn't make eye contact. "But she wasn't awful, was she?"

"I thought we weren't talking about it."

It was a warm day. I pulled away from Shutters, the top down on the Luscus. I drove up Ocean Avenue with its grassy green palisades and huge white apartment buildings, past the Oceana, where, Franklin told me, Stan Laurel had lived in retirement. On this stretch of Highway 1, the coastline wasn't what you'd expect—if you'd only dreamed about Southern California or stared at pictures in travel magazines. The moments of transcendent scenery were infrequent. It was mostly stretches of seediness, abandoned bits of the dream, and bad architecture. The landscape was shabby and ramshackle or, even worse, too perfect and naive—color-coordinated shopping centers and housing developments that looked like synchronized swimmers in a high school pool. I passed Malibu and its mammoth seafood restaurants and vast gas stations and off-kilter houses that looked reconfigured by storms. On the beach, dark clumps of seaweed and plastic water bottles had come ashore.

The March rains had stopped, perhaps for good. Tractors would come to rake the sand. Film crews and the cast of *Baywatch: The Next Generation* would return to Paradise Cove. The hills were turning a faint emerald green in places, a wash of jubilant color.

At a stoplight, a group of teenagers crossed the highway in front of my car. They wore baggy trunks and carried surfboards. They teased one another and dawdled. A boy with kinky red hair and a tan that was really a gathering of freckles, like dots of brown and pink that seemed, if you stood far enough away, to make up a tan, caught sight of my face and his gaze lingered. He stared at my eye patch. He said something to his friends—something I couldn't quite hear—and their faces turned my way.

I dialed Ned's number on my cell phone, wanting to hear his voice but at the same time dreading his voice. Spring was a month away in Virginia. A month before the bare shrubs would start to leaf out. Before tulips would pop out of the beds along the main drag in Middleburg and Upperville and in the window boxes of the Ashby Inn in Paris. Before the earth would warm again. Perhaps winter would pass for Ned too. Since I'd gotten out of Cedars, a chill had whistled through his voice, hesitancy that hadn't been there before. He seemed anxious to ring off. He let his dogs bark, and I could barely hear. Our conversations had started to feel awkward and Bergmanesque; misunderstandings, efforts plagued by echoes and static.

Sometimes I was relieved when he didn't answer. Talking to Bram was more fun. "Oh, it's *you* again," he'd always say. "Have you found the Happy Camper yet?"

"No," I said. "What makes you think I'm looking?"

This time nobody answered. The line rang and rang. Finally a scratchy tape machine picked up. "Hey," I said. "I'm in the car. Give me a call."

The remake of *L'Avventura* was in color. At first the warmth of the Bertolucci hues—the deep reds, the vibrant oranges—seemed to undermine the wistful end-of-the-world mood of the black-and-white original but then added to it. In the original story, a group of rich Italians are yachting off the humid sleepy waters of Sardinia. In Bertolucci's version, a group of rich Moroccans and Swedes are sailing to the seventieth birthday party of a rich American industrialist. There's a celebrated architect on the boat. A real estate developer. A couple of fashion models. And an assortment of jaded hangers-on.

The quarters are cramped. The heat is a problem. The boat is moored off a small uninhabited island.

There's a lover's quarrel—between Sandro, the architect, and his girlfriend Anna. Afterward, Anna stands on the edge of the deck and dives into the water. She swims away. When Anna doesn't come back, her best friend, Claudia, goes looking for her—but winds up with Anna's boyfriend instead.

The original made Monica Vitti an international sensation in 1960. As Claudia, she was fresh, powerful, a descendant of Marlene Dietrich—a tough antiheroine who was angry or alienated or both. In *L'Avventura,* her hair is shoulder-length and honey-blond, her face serious and chiseled. She walks with her shoulders—she's all shoulders and toughness. The wind is always blowing her hair in her eyes. She doesn't seem to care. She's unflappable and emotionally unavailable, until she falls for Sandro.

It's hard to say how Allegra does in the remake. Hard to be completely objective. She's more womanly and vulnerable than Monica Vitti. Her Claudia is more about breasts than shoulders. She's spoiled and indecisive rather than remote. It's only when she catches Sandro sleeping with an American journalist that she shows her feelings. She cries with her mouth open—a string of spit stretching between her top and bottom lip—and her face is full of sorrow and resignation.

"Acting is mostly about being still," Allegra had told me. "It's about having the balls to stay still and not move and letting the camera stare at you like some kind of pervert."

She'd hammered bottle caps into the walls of studios where she practiced, and pretended each one was a camera lens. She practiced seeing herself from different vantage points, different angles. If there was a bottle cap behind her, her awareness would shift. She began to act with the back of her head or the side of her face. She felt the lens on her as though it were a narrow pinpoint of heat. Robert De Niro had worked with bottle caps, she said, before he made *Mean Streets.*

"People think acting takes a giant ego," she said. "But it's more about knowing where to put it, where to store it. You're shifting consciousness to different parts of you. It's really all about energy."

Her lips are frosted in *L'Avventura*. Her hair is ratted and swept back, held by a small gold clip. The sea is splashing. The wind is blowing. For her first sixty minutes on-screen, she wears only a small string bikini and a damp sarong.

I found an entrance ramp for Highway 101 in Oxnard and continued north. I stopped for lunch at an outdoor terrace on the shady grounds of the old Biltmore in Montecito. When I checked my cell phone later, there was a choppy message from Ned. "Hey," he said, "been trying to install the solar panels all morning. I'll try you again after dinner."

Franklin had called too, wondering if I had made a decision about the Allegra Vigil. And Margaux had been looking for me, wanting feedback. "*Adventure* is fabulous, isn't it? Beyond words. How did you like the love scene on the moving train? Blows *Risky Business* out of the water. Bertolucci says it's the best thing he's done since *Last Tango*."

She was right, of course. Margaux was going to be busy all spring, all year, the rest of her life if things played out a certain way. *L'Avventura* had the smell of a hit—the pace and light and darkness and love and loss and magic of a hit. It was a movie that transcended itself, moved beyond the framework of its own conceit. It wasn't about alienation anymore, or existential despair. It lost that—or carried it heavenward, to a more bankable place. *L'Avventura* became a church where we wanted to pray, a mood we wanted to feel, a feeling we were having but hadn't quite acknowledged. It was *The English Patient* without the airplane or the burn victim or any of the rest of the extraneous story lines—only the sand, the cave, the lonely mood.

———

I drove and kept driving. Santa Maria . . . Pismo Beach . . . Arroyo Grande. I passed plowed fields of strawberries and alfalfa and grapes, billboards for shell shops and whale-watching boat tours. I flew by scenery that I was supposed to notice but didn't. I drove too fast and lost track of time. Sometimes I thought about things Ned had said. Some-times I thought about Allegra. But mostly I just drove—as though away from something and toward something else. The sunshine disappeared behind loose clumps of clouds. The fog came in. I watched the road ahead carefully—the white dashes, the curves, the reflector buttons—but it was getting hard to see.

I reached Morro Bay. It seemed like an unspoiled place: mudflats, dunes, a few streets of quiet shops. The village was settled around a bay, and in the middle of that bay was a strange solitary mass that rose up. Morro Rock. It seemed spooky, even though it happened to be shaped like the Matterhorn at Disneyland.

I followed the signs for Morro Dunes, some kind of na-ture preserve, drove through a wet grove of trees, and parked at the end of a sandy road. There were no other cars. I opened the car door, and the wind brought the smell of mint and salt, eucalyptus and fresh brine.

The cell phone rang. It was Ned. "Hey," he said.

"Hey. How are you?"

"Okay."

I waited for him to say something else, but he didn't.

"I heard on the news that it snowed again," I said. "The weather report—"

"Yeah, kind of like rain that froze on its way down to the ground. The Twins had a crust of ice on their backs when I brought them in. Then the power went out for six hours."

"Sounds bad."

"Not really," he said. His voice went low, and I could barely hear him. "Not as bad as going to screenings and driving around L.A."

I paused for a few seconds. He'd rattled me. "Are you trying to make me feel bad?"

"Didn't think that was possible. Hey," he went on, changing the subject, "where are you?"

"The dogs are always barking when I call. And if I talk about what I'm doing, you cut me off."

"Because you aren't doing anything. You're not even writing. Maybe you're mad about your eye. But you just drive around and tell me how nice the weather is."

"Of course I'm mad about my eye."

"Thank God you said it."

"Oh, I guess I should be crying on the phone—feeling sorry for myself so you wouldn't think I'm a sellout. It's like I've betrayed you in some way. Or betrayed our plans, our dreams. Such as they were."

"I didn't say that," he said. "Listen. I've retired from

bullshit for the rest of my life and I'm waiting for you to re-
tire too. I don't want to be mad. I'm trying hard not to be
mad. Okay? But you were supposed to be here already. I
thought you wanted to be here."

Two seagulls flew overhead, squawking.

"Where are you?" he asked again.

"Morro Bay."

"North of San Luis Obispo?"

"I just felt like seeing something new."

"If you want to drive so much, why don't you get yourself to Bakersfield, then pick up I-40 to Needles and keep
going until you reach Tucumcari. You could be here by Fri-
day if you don't stop to piss too often."

"I wish I could."

"And when people come to the door and ask questions about Clementine James, you could answer them
yourself."

"Somebody came?"

"Oh yeah. Round two. Round three. *The Philadelphia In-
quirer.* The FBI again. I told them to call *Flame.* That fucking magazine still owns you."

"No, it doesn't."

"You know, I had a feeling when you quit last fall that it
wasn't over. You stayed so angry at Ed."

"I guess you'd like it better if I were angry at you."

"Oh yeah," he said. "Oh definitely. I'd still be in your
universe . . . Look, maybe I should leave you alone for a

while—let you do whatever you're doing. You sort things out."

"Sounds good," I said. "You leave me alone. And I'll leave you alone."

He paused. "I thought you already were."

Nobody really hung up on the other, exactly, but it had the feeling of that—mutual disgust, a standoff, the kind of disagreement that can't be solved with words over the phone. I took off my shoes and started to walk toward the beach. There were mounds of windswept sand between me and the water. At the top of a high knoll, I sat down. The wind was damp and cold. It came through the holes in my sweater and found my skin. I put my head down on the warm sand and curled my body into the dune.

Ned was wrong about all kinds of things. And he didn't get movies. That was the main thing, wasn't it? He didn't see the beauty—only the effort, the artifice, the marketing. The natural world provided all the solace that he needed. And he was drawn to old things that needed his care. Old dogs, old horses, old cars, and old barns. Bram. I'd be old someday. But until then I wasn't sure where I fit in.

I watched the water move in and out—the rhythmic sway. The clouds began to lift, and the sunlight grew sharp. Birds drifted down to the shining ground.

I covered my face with my hands and listened to the waves. When I took my hands away, I noticed a dark figure walking along the water's edge.

She was about fifty yards away, moving with hazy dis-affection, without a sense that she was being watched. Her shoulders were broad. Her face was long. Her dress was billowy, an enormous half-open parachute of fabric that dropped to her feet. She was tossing small bits in the water, pebbles or shells or coins. Her head was turned away, toward the sea. When she looked overhead, to follow the flight of a bird, she saw me. She stared for a while. And then she began to walk toward me—a determined walk, quickening, like she was rushing to meet up with an old friend.

As she drew closer, I could see that she was tall, almost gangly. Her costume was golden, voluminous, made of silk, a shimmering sunset of a dress with a bell-shaped skirt. The sleeves were big and puffy, round as balloons. There were clouds and clouds of ruffles—more ruffles than it was possible to imagine any person wearing at one time. Her hair was not blond or brown but something in between. It was done up in two braids and coiled like two oval cinna-mon buns on either side of her head. She looked like a cocker spaniel.

And she was certainly not Monica Vitti, as I had half hoped. Her walk was neither physical nor from her shoul-ders. No, the opposite. It was unearthly. She hovered off the sand, gliding toward my dune as though pulled along by a camera dolly.

"Greetings!" Loretta Young called out. "And how are you today!"

Her voice was low-toned, balanced. I felt her presence immediately. She had an atmosphere all her own—an earnestness, a sympathy; a warm focused gaze that tried to drag you in.

"Not great," I said.

She stretched out a rustling silky arm toward the sand and balanced herself as she sat down with as much grace as anyone could wearing forty yards of fabric. Then she looked out to the water. "So magical," she said. "Such a lovely sunset."

The light was melting away. A smear of lavender was rising up from the sea.

"The salt air!" She made a dramatic inhalation. "So invigorating! So restful too! God's splendid work. His promise. His restoration!"

A tattered, one-legged seagull landed nearby. It began pecking at a pebble. "Hey, little fella!" she said in a creamy voice, as though it were the most enchanting bird she'd ever seen. The seagull hopped around her big golden slippers and flew off.

"You seem upset," she said.

I watched the horizon line, said nothing.

"Are you hungry?" she asked.

I shook my head. "Not really."

"Well, when you get hungry, there's a wonderful little place with fresh fish—a cozy restaurant. Dornan's. Looks right out over the bay. You could find an early dinner there. And then I really do think you must stay. Your vision . . .

depth perception . . . you shouldn't be driving at night. There's really no choice. But I know a splendid inn nearby, tucked right into a cliff. Come."

Her long arm lifted up gently, slowly, gracefully—like a ballerina's—and gestured north, to a bluff above the beach.

CHAPTER 11

A side from a faint moldy smell, my suite at the Morro Bay Inn was okay—king-size bed, cozy sitting room, fireplace, views out to the quiet, dusky harbor. Walking back from the beach, Loretta had vanished somewhere between sand dunes, and then—just after I'd showered, robed, and begun to study the room-service menu—she reappeared, newly attired. This time, she was wearing her costume from *Come to the Stable*. As Sister Margaret from the Order of Holy Endeavor, her hair was covered completely by a black wimple and a starched white inner collar. Her black habit draped rather dramatically to the floor. The look on her face was positively beatific—oceans of love emanating from her eyes alone.

"What's so funny?" she asked.

I shook my head.

"Oh, but these robes are wonderfully comfortable," she said with a smile. "One feels so protected and safe."

Framed by black and white fabric, her cheekbones appeared monstrous and her lips impossibly huge. She almost defined the concept of *too beautiful*—a face so extreme in its grandeur it could never be overshadowed by outrageous costumes, by corny ringlets or ruffles or bad hats. Not even by a wimple. "Oh, look!" she exclaimed. "A fireplace!"

She turned toward the hearth and began to study it. And then, quite nimbly, she crouched down on all fours with her head inside the cool hearth.

"Tell me about your fella," she said. All I could see was her rump and the cascading black drapery. Her voice was echo-y, as if she were talking inside a tomb. She lit a match.

"There's nothing to tell," I said.

"You had a fight, didn't you?"

"I hope those robes are flame-retardant."

She lit another match and held it, as she had the first, under the bottom of a cement log.

"I think it's gas, Loretta."

"Gas?" She backed up.

"The fireplace."

She stood up quickly, brushed off her robes, and soon began examining the walls around the mantel. Her fingers searched the surfaces. Her long arms floated like a marionette's. In her movies, she is fluid, flowing. She is always sweeping in and out of rooms, always accompanied by the sound of feminine rustling. Or she is pouring hot coffee or lighting a fire and it's always snowing outside. It snows in *The Bishop's Wife, The Farmer's Daughter,* and *Come to the Stable.* I'm pretty sure it snows in *The Story of Alexander Graham Bell* too. She is always skating on ponds, wearing huge mufflers and fur-trimmed hats. She is always so fiercely warm, her own furnace of womanly love and compassion and great human understanding, that it seems the ice might melt beneath her.

"He's lonely," she said. "He misses you."

I said nothing.

"A man needs to feel loved," she said, turning around to face me again. She was smiling her nonjudgmental smile. It was a movie smile—a confection, a super-pleasing expression of demure complacency—but for some reason, it was hard to dismiss. It was just there, hanging in the room like the Shroud of Turin.

"I'm sure that's true," I said. "But how come everything seems to go better if he's worried you might slip away?"

"Your poor fella," she sighed. "Is that why you stayed in L.A.?"

"I'm waiting for a new eye."

"It's more than that."

"No, I don't think so." I felt as if I were in a confessional, or therapy—or worse, being interviewed.

"You're waiting for her," Loretta said. "You want to see

her again. Don't you?" She reached up and pressed a small beige button on the mantel. And the gas jets inside the fire-place ignited in a blast.

Then she came closer—reaching out to grab my shoulders with her hands. Her huge blue eyes glommed on to mine.

"I know where she is," she said.

"You do?"

A knock at the door interrupted us. It was a man in a black vest and white shirt holding a round tray high over his head. I signed the chit, sat down on the bed, pulled the cellophane off the top of the martini glass, and studied the olives at the bottom of the foggy glass. I looked around. Loretta had gone. And then I took a sip.

——

When she returned, her brown hair was down, loose and wavy around her shoulders. She wore a golden brown sweater with the sleeves pushed up, and a matching slim skirt. She was tapping out a cigarette from a pack of Chesterfields. The sound alone made me want one.

"Do you mind?" she asked.

I shook my head.

She walked quickly from window to window and lifted up the sashes. "This will help," she said. The night air blew in. The curtains flapped. The fire bounced. She bent down and dragged an ottoman closer to the bed, where I was sitting, then produced a small silver lighter and snapped her thumb on the rough wheel. She put a cigarette in her mouth and leaned in to the flame. Her hair dropped over one eye.

She took an inhumanly long inhalation and blew the smoke out very slowly with a pursing of her enormous lips.

"I can't say exactly *where* she is," Loretta said, snapping the lighter closed. "But I can hear her."

"You—"

"Our souls fluttered toward each other. We met. We bonded. You see, she's been praying a great deal. Praying to Jesus and his Sacred Heart."

"Praying?"

Loretta looked around for an ashtray, and suddenly there was a small silver cup—shaped like a seashell—on the ottoman. She tapped an ash into it.

"And what's she praying for?" I asked.

"There aren't words, really. It's a current of feeling. She's looking for something. Whiteness. She's looking for whiteness, purity, a natural thing—for the flow, the buzz of life."

"The buzz of life."

Loretta nodded. A look of great sympathy came over her face. "She's also trying desperately to get over Bernardo Bertolucci."

"Bernardo—"

"That's why she broke off her engagement."

Suddenly I remembered something about a coat that Bertolucci had given Allegra on location. It was a cashmere coat—long and red—to wear over her bikini when the wind was cold.

"But she became engaged to Tom Swimmer while she was making *L'Avventura,*" I said. The timing seemed off. "Although I guess it wouldn't be hard to fall in love with Bernardo Bertolucci."

Loretta laughed a little too gaily. "That's it exactly," she said, sweeping into a wing-backed chair and resting her hands on the polished wooden balls at the end of the armrests as if the chair were a throne.

"Do you know how attractive a director can be? *Do you know how appealing?* He's like a ship's captain, a president, a priest. He's running everything, every day. He makes the mountains move and the sets come and go. Of course, he's already a bit in love with you—because he picked you to be in his movie. So when you squeak just a bit, he rushes in. He coddles you, fathers you. He saves you from an unfortunate hairdo or an ill-fitting costume. All he cares about is you and how beautiful you are, how stunning and perfect. . . .

"I suppose," she continued, "that it's not too unlike the relationship between an editor and a writer."

"No." I shook my head. "Not the same."

"Oh, yes."

"Not really."

She looked at me intently with her implacable face.

"No."

"Like you and Ed Nostrum."

She shifted in the throne. Her smile was closed. She looked down and snuffed out her cigarette with a few tiny twists. Then she looked at me again.

"Only a couple of times," I said. "A few weak moments."

"Amsterdam, London. The Mark Hotel in New York. It was quite a lot more than that."

"It was stupid."

"You loved him."

"No, I didn't."

"You were lonely."

"Was I?"

She pulled another cigarette out of the pack. I watched her carefully. The way her hands moved. The way the cigarette looked between her elegant fingers. The way she held it in her lips. She lifted the lighter to her face and I felt another pang of desire—quite a huge pang, actually. It had been nearly a year since Ned and I had quit together. It had been nearly a year since other things too.

"I had the worst sort of crush on Orson Welles," she said, "when we were making *The Stranger*."

"Orson Welles?"

"Oh, yes. Oh, yes. Horrible crush. Embarrassing. I had trouble speaking sometimes, and other times I would babble on like a fool. Early in the morning, he'd come to see me in makeup, and I'd be smiling so, and laughing, that my foundation would start cracking around my eyes and around my mouth and it would all have to be redone. . . . His eyes were so dark. Just the biggest wet wonderful eyes. He seemed so terribly brilliant and—" She paused.

"And what?"

"Boyish, young. Alone. Somehow he needed me. He needed my love. He seemed so desperately hungry for something. Like he could eat the sky."

Ed was a bit Wellesian, I supposed—the young Welles, before he'd moved on to gluttony and wearing velvet Henry VIII hats on the Carson show. In my mind, Welles occupied a space—a dining room of the mind—with Marlon Brando and Shelley Winters. It was adjacent to the room where Judy Garland and Elizabeth Taylor were passed out. Was it talent or fame—or simply narcissism—that twisted people into cartoons?

"His eyes. That black hair. I remember swooning at the sight of it, staring at the back of his head. *The voice* . . . so deep. It was deeper than baritone. It went through my skin and into my bones."

"So you loved him," I said.

Loretta knit her brows faintly—not enough to cause a crease. "I don't think God wants us to love men besides our husbands," she said. "Marriage is a sacrament. Even having a soul mate is wrong if you aren't married to him."

"But it happens," I said. "Even if, as you suggest, God doesn't approve."

"I suppose so."

I thought about the love affairs she'd had—Tyrone

Power, Douglas Fairbanks, Ronald Colman, John Barrymore, Clark Gable, the list goes on and on—and wondered if she would have enjoyed them any more or less if she hadn't been so tortured about them.

"So you weren't in love with Orson Welles?"

"Infatuation," she said. "And years before he became so pitiful."

"I guess I'm not sure if I always understand the difference. Being in love versus loving."

"One is shallow and loud," Loretta said. "The other is quiet and deep."

I thought about Gloria falling in love with Henri, her glorious marquis and third husband. In *Swanson on Swanson,* she describes how "blissfully" happy they were. How perfect he was, elegant and refined and adoring! Fifty pages later, in Palm Beach, while Henri's off fishing one afternoon, she's making love to Joseph Kennedy—the beginning of a love affair. "I knew perfectly well," she writes, "that whatever adjustments or deceits must inevitably follow, the strange man beside me, more than my husband, owned me." Was that love or something else?

"Did I love Ed?" I asked aloud. "I don't think so."

"All you had was your work," Loretta answered. "You loved your work. It was all you cared about."

"I guess it was."

"And Ed was your work, so you loved him too."

"It's funny," I said, "but we were drinking one night after work, and the bar was dark. It was dark and smoky and full of people. We'd been working so hard. God—five, six years ago—before I started the profiles, the celebrities. Before he'd gone to *Flame*. He was still married, and somehow that made him seem more solid, dependable, not inflated or ridiculous. And he was fascinated by me. I'm not sure why."

Loretta shifted on the throne and crossed her legs again. "He was focused on you," she said. "He gave you his undivided attention."

"The way he looked at me. The way he stared. The way he'd swivel in his chair when I walked into his office."

"You were angry," Loretta said. "He liked that."

"I guess so. I had a kind of endless supply of rage and a sense of injustice. Our mothers were both dead, maybe that was it. They'd been dead a long time. We were angry and alone, and it felt like he and I were fighting a war together. Us against everybody else. Us against the whiners. Us against the hypocrites. Us against all those people who had been softened by money and success or their parents' love. We were orphans, both of us, and we were alone at our cocktail table in the Mark, and it was like a little boat taking us away. And the rain seemed to be coming down. It was raining on us, and we were under cover together, alone against the world. Huddling."

Loretta was resting her head in her hand. A hank of brown hair fell over one eye again, and for a second she seemed aloof and knowing, improbably like Veronica Lake—but not quite.

She took a drag from her cigarette. "I know that feeling," she said, and her voice was dreamy. The smoke streamed out of her mouth. "Two hearts under one umbrella."

"Something like that," I said. "Although not quite so corny."

"Cozy?"

"Corny."

She looked a bit wounded.

"Loretta, I've never told anybody that before," I said.

"Not Ned?"

I shook my head.

"He knows nothing?"

"No."

"Because you're smart," she said. "And very wise."

he maids woke me up with their knocking. The TV had been left on HBO, and there was a full ashtray in front of it. The room smelled faintly like lemons but mostly like a bar.

I showered, dressed, wandered down to the dining room and ate a plate of pancakes. Franklin reached me on the phone as I was walking to my car. "Sounds exotic," he said. "Bay of the Moors. Is it gorgeous there?"

"I haven't noticed," I said.

"Spectacular here. I can see the mountains, finally, and the Hollywood sign."

"People used to jump from the 'H,' did you know that? They'd stand on the horizontal bar between the goalposts."

"You're in a sick mood. England gets about three days a

year like this. Seems a sacrilege to actually work. Anyway, I have a huge package of mail for you, forwarded by *Flame*. Is it all right for me to go through it? Truthfully, I started picking through it last night. Your mail is getting very strange indeed."

I could hear papers rustling. "We haven't talked about *L'Avventura* yet," I said.

"What is there to say? No words. Do you want me to read all the mail and then answer it?"

"Just go through it. Throw out catalogs, magazines, brochures, flyers, and invitations. Send any bills back to Ed. And send him any intelligent reader mail—things that might be worth printing."

"Clem," he said, "these aren't letters to the editor. These are letters from genuine earnest Americans and other assorted crazy people. Volumes of it. Get-well cards, boxes of candy, books, some trinkets. Somebody sent you a satchel of polished stones with healing powers. Nothing looks valuable so far, alas. But you might autograph some eight-by-ten glossies so I can send them out."

"Oh, please."

"I'm serious. People will be flocking to your birthplace soon, chipping away at the bricks and leaving piles of crutches and tufts of hair. Or maybe it's tufts of your hair they'll want. As for *L'Avventura* . . . it still feels like sacred ground."

"Stays with you, doesn't it?"

"I was ruminating all night. So haunting. So sad."

"Is she better than Monica Vitti?"

"I never thought I'd hear myself saying this—"

"But what?"

"She's amazing. A magnificent hybrid. The reincarnation of Monica Vitti and Marilyn Monroe. There isn't much more to say."

"Did Monica Vitti die?"

"No, but you know what I mean. The *spiritual daughter* of Monica and Marilyn. She's yin and yang and everything in between. Allegra's even better than Gwyneth—or more powerful, anyway—although that might be due solely to the size of her breasts. And you know how I feel about Gwyneth."

"You think it's going to be a hit?"

"Blockbuster. But beyond now imaginable boundaries of that word. Not sure if that's good or bad for Bertolucci. Here's a postcard. Uhmm. From some kind of terribly gauche neopalatial spa. It looks like a Roman temple with a gigantic fountain. Marble statues—nude nymphs and other water creatures and demi-deities. The water's so blue, it looks like they've put those American toilet dyes in it. God, it might even be a swimming pool—" He paused. "It's blank."

"Blank?"

"On the other side, it's addressed to you, care of *Flame*. But otherwise blank. No message."

"From a spa?"

"Oh, I see what it is. Hearst Castle. San Simeon. 'The

three-hundred-forty-five-thousand-gallon Neptune Pool is dominated by an ancient Greco-Roman temple facade with modern colonnades to the north and south.' Blah blah blah. 'A hundred four feet long and graduated in depth from three and a half feet to nearly ten feet, the heated pool was filled with water from springs on Pine Mountain by gravity-fed pipeline.'"

I felt my heart speed up.

"The description is a tad archaeological," he said. "Who cares whether the pool is gravity-fed?"

"Hand-addressed?" I asked.

"Yes."

"Kind of cutesy, emotionally retarded, happy-person script?"

"What does that mean?"

"Does the *i* in Clementine have a circle over it instead of a dot?"

"No. But there's a super-adorable halo over the top of the *a* in James. Must be a reference to your well-known angelic qualities. The sweet, meek, compassionate Saint Clementine of Montclair. Or sometimes called Clementine of the Clear Mountain. Sainta Clementina di—"

"I get the joke, Franklin."

"Sent quite a while ago, actually. Huh. Weeks ago. February tenth. I can't make out the location. *Ben-Hur*?"

"Charlton Heston is never far from your mind, is he?"

"Can't help it."

"Try."

"Wait, I can read it now. It's postmarked Khartoum."

"I thought you were going to say *Planet of the Apes.* Never mind, I know where it's from."

"Where?"

"Big Sur."

"Oh, quite right! Amazing."

I could barely hear his voice, the blood was pounding so loudly in my ears.

"I'll be back at Shutters later this afternoon," I said. "We'll talk about the vigil then. And in the meantime, round up all the Loretta Young movies you can find—"

"Oh, retch. No. You can't be serious."

"And Myrna Loy movies."

"That's better."

"And call Marie-Claude and have her start forwarding all my mail overnight as soon as it comes in."

I put down the Luscus's windows as I pulled away from the quiet inn. I could hear the tires on the wet road. They rolled over eucalyptus pods and popped them open, little pops like bubble wrap, like the sound of faraway gunfire. A clean smell rose up from the ground.

She was alive. That was all I could think about. A girl who'd left me for dead, a girl I was jealous of, a girl I hated, a girl who was a moron, an airhead. A girl who had two eyes, unlike me, and perfect skin and not one wrinkle; a girl who was—just to return to square one for a second—*a girl.* But there it was.

My car climbed the road to the highway, and underneath

a canopy of dripping trees, I saw the morning sky ahead. It was deep blue and wide. The clouds were low—white and full and heavy, as if I could reach up and grab them. I could see spring in the sky, and summer ahead. I could taste corn and strawberries, and hear the sound of her laugh.

t was a loose affair, loose and spontaneous and, at the same time, elaborately concocted, like a wedding cake. Cosmos and *Flame* hadn't really come up with the idea of a vigil any more than they had created Allegra. But it was suddenly in the air like nerve gas, in the water like El Niño. It was happening, one of those naturally occurring events—an act of God, an involuntary reflex, a great manifestation of the collective unconscious. Something even bigger than the People's Choice Awards.

There was talk of a vigil, then a need for a vigil. Fan groups began organizing it, the websites promoting it, the media reporting it, and not long afterward, the studios and entertainment outlets were elbowing their way in, offering to donate goods and services, wanting to arrange for a suitable location, celebrity speakers, printed napkins, flowers, tents with tables of food.

Like advance buzz for *L'Avventura,* it was a public relations conundrum. Cosmos didn't want to be seen as profiting from a missing girl, a young star who could be dead, deranged, dismembered, ravaged, kidnapped—or simply insensitive enough to keep the world holding its breath and wringing its hands for eleven weeks.

A proper vigil required delicacy, balance. The purest of motives. And that was stressful for everybody.

I could hear the discomfort in Ed's voice when he left messages for me. He boomed confidence, made demands, and acted cocky. They wanted me at the vigil. They wanted me at the vigil in the worst way. Not just Ed but *Flame* and Cosmos—probably the Conglom lawyers too. (Who knew when Clementine James might become angry, a spoiler, and start suing for damages?) "It's important for you to be there," Ed intoned in one voice mail. "It's a gesture of goodwill," he said in another, "and good manners." *Her fans are our fans,* he wrote desperately in an e-mail, *and your fans too.*

"Do whatever you want," Ed said when I finally returned his calls. He sounded bored—another tactic. "I completely understand if you don't want to be there," he continued with a sigh. "It's going to be a zoo. All those L.A. people with their boobs and sunglasses."

Later on, Marie-Claude phoned to close the deal. She was Ed's longtime secretary, a dark-haired gamine with perfect diction. She also had a tireless need for resolution and clarity. "Clementine, I'm calling you about the vigil," she said. Her voice was cool and certain—the kind of voice that goes with bitten nails and bloody cuticles—and I imagined her sitting outside Ed's spacious white office, doodling tight circles on a pad.

"I'm sending an overnight packet," she said, "with event information, a ticket, and a VIP pass. Ed wanted to know if you need a dress. Lydia Forti at Gucci has offered you one and, I think, representatives from Tombella."

"Do you think I need fashion help, Marie-Claude?"

"Ed thought you might enjoy a new dress."

"I thought *Flame* had a policy against freebies."

"It was meant to be a loan, as I understand it."

"As for the VIP pass, I just want a seat in the audience. A seat for me and a seat for Franklin. Nothing else."

"But the fans . . ." Marie-Claude's horror leaked out.

"What about them?"

"Ed says it's going to be a bit crazy."

"Crazy" was a favorite Marie-Claude word, something that hadn't gone unnoticed at *Flame.* She said it like she was Brazilian or Cuban, *car-AA-zee,* suddenly becoming Desi Arnaz midsentence.

"And will you be speaking at the event?" she asked.

"No. Does Ed think I am?"

"You are just attending?"

"Yes. Just attending."

"Very well. As for transportation," she continued, "Bernardo Bertolucci will be picking you up at your hotel at five-thirty P.M."

"Who?"

"Bernardo Bertolucci. Ed made these arrangements. He would like you to arrive with Mr. Bertolucci. I'm not sure this can be changed."

———

He arrived in front of my hotel exactly on time, resting elegantly in the back of a vintage black Cadillac. I saw his silhouette in the smoked rear windows. The driver, a weight-lifter type with pale hair and nice teeth, opened the heavy door, and I climbed inside the dark cave, sank down into the soft black leather. The Italian director instantly exuded—as he had years ago, when I interviewed him for the *Journal*—dark elegance and boundless enthusiasm.

"Clementine!" He burst into a smile.

"Bernardo."

"Enchanting dress."

"Nice car."

His hair was longer than I remembered, dark and wavy, with threads of white. He wore all black, linen and cashmere, and no accessories like a collar or a tie, only a copper bracelet on one wrist and a heavy Rolex slipping around on the other. He leaned back, settled into the leather for a long ride through rush-hour traffic. After a pause, during which

I noticed the sound of air-conditioning and the smell of the driver's cologne, Bertolucci began a brief monologue on Erich von Stroheim.

"Your article in *Flame*," he started in. "Ed Nostrum faxed me this afternoon. So fascinating, so completely fascinating. Von Stroheim's perfectionism! The megalomania and genius!" He began chuckling. "Of course, I recognize myself too."

"But," I interrupted, "isn't the definition of a megalomaniac somebody who would never describe himself as a megalomaniac?"

"Self-awareness has nothing to do with it," he said with a laugh. "Von Stroheim knew he was a madman—and it didn't change anything. What a fabulist, what a liar! For all those years, telling people that he was Prussian nobility when his father was a Jewish hatmaker! Telling people that he'd served heroically in the cavalry when all he'd done was supervise the hatmaking factory! Of course, so many great artists are great fabulists. Aren't they? Truth is negotiable. Reality, a delusion."

I thought about Von Stroheim's monocle, his thin lips, the snug military uniform that fit him like a wet suit. His demeanor couldn't have been more unlike Bertolucci's infectious good humor and warmth. During World War I, when Von Stroheim was still an actor, the studios billed him as "The Man You Love to Hate." A poster for Bertolucci, if there ever were one, would say something quite different: "The Man You'd Love to Have."

"The impulse to create surely comes from the same place," he was saying. "The desire to reorder the world, to play omnipotent God. Thousands of extras. Millions of dollars in sets and costumes. The director is the center of this concocted world—the master of his or her own elaborate stories. How is that not egotism? Only a madman and a genius could have made *Greed.*"

"You've seen the full-length version?" I asked.

"Oh yes! Or whatever has been saved of the original. *Forty-two reels.* Can you imagine? Seven hours! Incredible! I screened it years ago, when my producers were making me cut *1900* in half. I needed courage and companionship, I guess. I wanted to see *Greed* as Von Stroheim had wanted it seen. *1900* was five and a half hours, and the producer was complaining. But why must movies be two or three hours? It's insanity, of course. Like saying a painting needs to be a certain size, or a book a certain length."

"People get used to something," I said, "like having three meals a day. A little meat, some vegetables, some starch. And they want their movies to be two or three hours long."

"Capitalism, not art," said Bertolucci with a laugh. "*Greed* cut down to two hours is ten reels of incoherent craziness. Very sad."

I looked out the window and thought about my Von Stroheim piece. I'd handed in twenty thousand words— four times the length that *Flame* wanted. I had been driven, kept reporting, kept writing and writing and rewriting. I wanted an open field, a big sky, the space to say everything. There seemed to be no containing Von Stroheim. In the end, Ed boiled it down to four pages of truncated banalities. It read like an entry in a film dictionary. Ned had gotten me through all that, of course. Ned had spent hours on the phone with me, listened to all my complaints and heartaches, all my anger. Looking back, it's hard to know why he did. Who cares anymore about Von Stroheim? The world has moved on, the movies have moved on, as well as the movie audience.

A river of red taillights flowed around and beyond us—old Subaru wagons, Chevy minivans, new Lincoln Towncars and Rolls-Royces and scores of shiny Mercedes-Benzes—all heading east on the Santa Monica Freeway. When I first came to L.A., I used to count the Bentleys I'd pass on the road. In Bel Air and Beverly Hills and the Palisades, they were always passing me—their glossy paint, their heavy bonnets and doors and chrome latches. The great sturdiness of those cars, the seriousness, the confidence. They seemed eternal somehow, while the people driving them seemed weightless—funny and sad, insecure, unreal, not people, exactly, but cartoons of people trapped in some kind of one-dimensionality. They needed to show the world how rich they were, to armor their fragile flesh with jewelry and expensive clothes and elegant cars. They stopped being people in the same way that a Christmas tree doesn't seem like a tree anymore, for all the lights and tinsel and dangling ornaments. I told myself that writing about movie stars was a temporary gig—something I did for sheer amusement. It wasn't me. It had nothing to do with me. Eventually I'd steal away from palm trees and brush fires and the flickering movie screens. My imagination would lodge itself in a sane place, a green place, a real home—not the dark depressing house in New Jersey where I grew up, not my cramped apartment in Brooklyn—but a home, a heaven, where youth itself wasn't the final resting place. Where I could age and wizen, wear old clothes and drive old cars and walk around for days without looking in the mirror and become the person I was meant to be before the movies were invented. But every year, the more I tried to stay away from movies, the closer I got.

"And *L'Avventura*?" I asked gingerly. "How are you feeling about it?"

"Very nervous," said Bertolucci. "Panicked but also very excited. We're having some problems with the sound. An homage to Antonioni has to have perfect sound, it goes without saying. You must get the wind just right, no hyped-up whistling or sense of enhancement. You want rustling, not whistling. And it must seem utterly real, like the wind itself and not movie wind. And until this, I never realized how difficult that could be."

His face changed then, as though pulled down by a great weight. "To be honest, I haven't slept since the whole thing started," he said. "A year without sleep. Eighteen months without sleep. I've tried everything. Acupuncture, yoga, tai chi." He paused. "Allegra is magnificent." He said the words as if resigned and disbelieving all at once.

I nodded. "She is."

We fell into silence. He pulled a white piece of paper from his jacket pocket and unfolded it—notes for his vigil speech.

The Cadillac drifted off 101 in the direction of the Hollywood Bowl. Along the curb of Highland Avenue, we passed people with sleeping bags and coolers, pillows and folding chairs—overnighters, folks who had camped out for seats. We passed a line for valet parking and slowed at a sign that said: VIP RECEPTION AREA. Clusters of limousines were letting off passengers and moving ahead.

The car came to a stop so subtle I thought we were still moving. Bertolucci turned to me quickly. "Are you ready?" But the driver had jumped out, and the door was soon open, and I was startled by the change in the air around me—its temperature and density. I heard crowd sounds, sensed movement. And then I saw bodies standing at the curb and along the walkways, ten deep. There was pushing, swaying. When I stepped out of the car, there were screams.

"The eye patch!" a voice called out.

"It's her!"

"Clementine!" ten voices seemed to holler at once, and then scores of heads, hundreds of heads, seemed to turn in my direction. A swarm was moving toward the car, pushing up against the velvet ropes and stanchions. Glistening faces, a desperate glistening. And so many smiles, desperate smiling and pushing and glistening. Bertolucci came around to my side and took my hand.

"Clementine!"

"Clementine, Clementine!"

"How are you tonight?"

"Who designed your dress?"

I saw flashes, heard metallic sounds, popping sounds. My heart raced, and I looked at the ground—at the cement pathway. I looked at the soft black perfection of Bertolucci's loafers as his feet walked forward. They seemed so quiet and complete. I lifted my chin, raised my head.

I felt Bertolucci's warm hand. Solid, sturdy Bertolucci. In the shifting sands of this strange world, he was consistent, true to something, even if it was just himself. Oh, maybe he'd made a few duds, maybe *Stealing Beauty* was missing something. Maybe *1900* really was too long . . . But then I thought of Dominique Sanda and Stefania Sandrelli dancing in *The Conformist,* Maria Schneider in the bathtub in *Last Tango,* Joan Chen in *The Last Emperor.* Twenty, thirty years of poetry, beauty, hard work.

And yet, here outside the Hollywood Bowl, nobody was yelling his name, nobody was saying, "Bernardo! Bernardo!" Did they know who he was? Did they care? Perhaps to them, he was just a fabulous-looking man who held my hand, a man walking in black linen and cashmere and perfect loafers, his genius and vision and integrity completely overshadowed by the intensity of the blinding new rage that was me.

People wanted me, needed me, reached out and repeated my name. A blur of hands and voices like a prayer, a chant, a song of the crowd. The way I imagined a mother would say it, Clementine. *Oh Clem.* I was wounded, a victim— a martyr. I was beloved. As the crowd roared its roars, I looked up again at the blur of hands and faces and glistening, and I felt something unexpected and strange: a joy, a jubilance. A sense of warmth and unyielding gratitude. I had strangers on my side. I had friends, teammates, a rooting squad. There were hordes—a living safety net—of unnamed and unknown human beings who liked me, who stood with me. They knew me—and my whole name. "Clementine James! Clementine James!" they called out. "Clementine, look this way!" And what I had always assumed was a downside of notoriety—the throngs, the sick and scary throngs reaching out to devour you—became at once a bath of lushness, fullness. A bath of love. The swarm wasn't a swarm but an embrace, and the calls were cheers. And this sweet blur of humanity in their Allegra T-shirts and Allegra ball caps and Allegra buttons and Allegra denim jackets was staring at me, centered on me, and wishing me well.

uards ushered us inside, to a white holding tent where it was air-conditioned and cold and nobody was calling my name. Everything was silvery and shadowy. There were linen tablecloths, white tulips, Mylar kites, and a huddle of people around a raw bar. I remember Bertolucci being embraced by Dyan Cannon and Liv Tyler and Ann-Margret in quick succession. I remember talking to Michael Tibbs—he smelled like oysters and wore a necktie with clown faces on it. He was saying something about bad chi, but then I realized he was talking about *Apache,* the movie Allegra was supposed to be making with him, and I excused myself when I saw Franklin across the way.

There were sounds beyond the tent—announcements being made. A stage crew was testing microphones.

"You're flushed," Franklin said. "Nice frock."

"It's wild," I said.

"The crowd?"

"Stay with me."

We stood at the periphery of the tent and looked out the clear plastic windows. Beyond, we could see the half-dome of the Hollywood Bowl. It was glowing pink like a seashell in the twilight, and hundreds of people were holding candles or lighting candles. They waited in lines with candles. They sat on the ground with candles. And they were setting down the candles on long curving tables that flanked the edges of the outdoor stadium. Big candles, votive candles, beeswax candles, all colors of candles. Next to us, on a table inside the tent, I saw matchbooks arranged neatly in stainless-steel baskets, matches that said FLAME in red-orange letters, and underneath was Allegra's face.

Outside, people were standing in line, hundreds, thousands, tens of thousands. People were lighting and people were singing, and by night's end, they were mostly weeping and swaying and laughing. And all the flames, thousands of twinkling, flickering flames, were swaying too. The Santa Ana winds came, hot and dry, lifting the wishes and prayers and songs up into the dark clear sky. Up, up, to wherever she was.

"Hey you," Margaux Clarke said. She had appeared out of the blue. "Nice hair. Zoro?"

"Francisco. He came to my hotel room," I said.

"Nice. Very nice," she said, coming too close. I could smell the wine. "Hey. Listen. I heard you heard from her."

"What are you talking about?"

Margaux looked at Franklin.

"That wasn't supposed to get out," I said.

"Oh," Margaux said quickly. "It won't."

Franklin's face had fallen. "Sorry," he said, "I didn't—"

"Was it Allegra?" Margaux interrupted. Her hair looked a bit wiry under the harsh tent lights, gray hair being covered up with a sunny yellow color. I remembered the old rumor that Margaux was a Scientologist.

"It was just a postcard," I said. "A blank postcard. I have no idea."

"San Simeon."

I nodded.

"It's her! You know it's her."

"You're talking too loud," I said.

Margaux moved into a tipsy stage whisper. "Michael Tibbs thinks you know where she is."

"I just saw him. Michael Tibbs?"

"Do you?"

"I have no idea where she is," I said. "I've only got a blank postcard sent from Big Sur."

"Have you been in touch with the police? The FBI have been calling some people."

"I haven't been in touch with anyone."

"But Franklin said—"

"Can we change the subject? I don't have anything more to add, Margaux. I just have a hunch she's alive, that's all. It's a gut feeling. It's nothing more."

I looked up and noticed that in another corner, people were watching us while we talked. They were staring without shame. They were gawking like we weren't real, like we were just flickering figures on a TV or movie screen. They were clumped in a huddle and looked dark and small under the creepy overhead lights. And then I realized that they were members of the media, the other media—the noncelebrity celebrity journalists—representatives from the distinguished pages of *We, Us, You, People, Speak, Gas,* and *E.* trapped behind red velvet ropes and brass stanchions.

Margaux wandered off, and a vast space seemed to open around me. The VIPs dropped by, made guest appearances in my vicinity. They sailed toward me like yachts in a Sunday-afternoon regatta. They smiled and touched me, fondly, familiarly, as though we were old friends. They moved their soft hands across the backs of my upper arms and puckered kisses in the air about my ears. They were sweet and lucky and spoiled and hardworking and lazy people. TV people, movie people, music people, artists, suits, showboaters, showoffs, dancing men and crooning women. They looked at me with kind eyes, with the softness of years of good meals and first-class seats and household help. They descended into me—bared souls, open mouths—ignoring Franklin completely, even after an introduction, and acting like I was standing alone in the spotlight of their own radiance.

"Dazzling," said Leslie Caron, staring at my dress. "Have you been working out?" asked Neil Diamond, holding my arm. "My sister lost her eye," said Snoop Dogg, "and once she got that new one, baby girl, you couldn't tell. I swear."

"Clementine, hi."

"Hi, Clementine."

I had a name now. It seemed to make everybody feel better just to say it.

"Did you hear about the spread in *Vogue*?" asked Michael Minor, the other producer of the ill-fated *Apache*. He was wearing a short leather jacket and blue-tinted glasses—and reminded me, as he always did, of the young assassin in *Ashes and Diamonds*. "The May issue—five or six pages, apparently. All the models have black eye patches."

Franklin and I left, walked down a long ramp to find our box seats in front. Beautiful girls in tight white T-shirts were passing out vigil programs. Allegra's face was on them, a shot from *L'Avventura*. She looked luminous and fresh, rubbery and alive. The wind was blowing her hair in her mouth.

In the distance, I saw Ed charging toward us.

"I might need to find the loo," Franklin said.

"Not now," I said.

Under the open sky and against the whiteness and grandeur of the Bowl, Ed looked shorter. He was dressed oddly too, in baggy jeans and a rumpled blazer.

"That dress worked out," he said to me. He leaned down, pressed his face next to mine, missed my cheek, and kissed me on the ear.

"Your blazer needs steaming."

"My luggage was lost."

He stared at me. He said nothing to Franklin. I assumed this meant they'd already talked.

"What are you doing after?" Ed asked.

"Nothing."

"Come with me. Johnny Mast is having a—"

"I'm doing nothing by choice."

"Lunch tomorrow, then."

I shook my head. "I'm not around."

Ed looked over at Franklin. "She's so impossible."

"I've got a date," I said.

"With whom?"

"Not sure yet."

Ed smiled. "You break my heart, Clem," he said. "You break it and break it and break it."

"Yes, I know." I reached up and patted him on the shoulder. I thought about the two King Charles spaniels I gave him when he left his wife. "And it feels good."

———

Things seen: Ed trying not to laugh while he lit his vigil candle. Franklin trying not to sit next to Ed. John Travolta air-kissing Margaux and holding her hand. Norman Lear with his smooth tan and smooth pate, casting his smooth gaze on Deepak Chopra.

"Tell me," Lear said to Chopra, "isn't being a movie star supposed to be a disaster, karmically—having to pay back for all that unrequited love? With horrible repercussions on the next incarnation?"

"It depends," said Chopra. "Have you been talking to Demi?"

Baggy "The Creeper" Billy sat down with Margaux in the box next to ours. I watched his long ponytail, his chiseled face, bony in a caveman sort of way. Margaux kept poking his chest with one of her frosted fingernails.

The Creeper twisted in his seat and faced us. "I don't understand why the FBI hasn't come up with something by now," he said in superserious tones, paranoid tones, as if he were a politician, a senator with a guitar and salon highlights. "The word I get is that they know everything and aren't saying. That Allegra's under some kind of surveillance, like a witness-protection program. Maybe she's spilling secrets, man."

Out of the corner of my remaining eye, I saw a very tall figure with sandy hair. He was scooting between chairs in Margaux's box. Heston. It was Charlton Heston. He was even taller than Ed—a towering giant with an enormous jack-o'-lantern grin.

"Hey, good to see you!" he said to everyone and no one.

"Hey!" Franklin answered. "Good to see you too!"

Heston nodded and then turned back around, began flipping through his vigil program. Within seconds, Franklin was whispering in my ear: "He's got a hairpiece. Look. Oh my God."

"Relax."

"It's almost a wig."

"You're so harsh."

"I'm very afraid," Franklin said, "'Soylent Green is . . . people.'"

I didn't recognize Tom Swimmer at first. He seemed too multilayered and tortured. It's funny how TV can make an interesting-looking guy seem bland. I thought he was coming to pay respects to the Creeper, but it turned out he wanted to see me.

"Thanks for calling me back," he said.

"I didn't."

"I know."

He smoldered in person, a wicked energy that didn't transmit all the way to the tiny TV screen. He was young—mid-twenties at the most—and quite tall, without the disproportionately large head of so many TV people. He was dressed entirely in gray. A pair of bug-eye Oakleys were hanging from the neck of his collarless shirt.

He smiled at Margaux and the Creeper and Heston. He pointed at me and walked away.

A childhood friend of Allegra's took the stage. She was beaming as though performing at a pep rally. She talked about Allegra's love of squirrels, her strong attachment to her Cabbage Patch dolls and Strawberry Shortcake comforter, her obsession with old Shirley Temple movies. Then the woman muffled a little sob.

"That was so fake," Franklin whispered.

"Bold of her to try."

"Hey, that reminds me," he said, "I watched *Come to the Stable* this morning."

"And?"

"I so wanted to hate her. That face. Those ghastly robes."

"I know. Loretta's so *kindly*. How did you like the ending?"

"Total meltdown. Hunched over and sobbing into my bedspread."

A Tibetan holy man blew a long horn, and there was a five-minute moment of silence. After Donovan and Donovan Leitch were done singing, after Radiohead had played "Kid A," and after David Byrne read a poem he'd written after meeting Kay Blyth at a retreat ten years before, Morgan Fairchild and Sally Field sat on two wooden stools and sang a song.

We were leaving—fighting crowds—when a group of women broke from a bathroom line to surround Franklin and me. They were heavyset, wearing neon-bright sweatshirts and enormous eyeglass frames set with rhinestones. One of the women had I ❤ RIVERSIDE across her considerable breasts.

"We've got something in common, Clementine," the woman said.

"We're friends of Allegra's too," said another.

Pushing toward me, anxious to talk, was a red-haired woman with a shopping bag for a purse who turned out to be one of the Mumy sisters and somehow related to Allegra's ex-husband. She introduced me to an enormous woman with sweat bleeding through her heavy makeup. Her purple sweatshirt said MOUNT RUBIDOUX DANCE.

She was Carmen O'Leary, Allegra's first tap and ballet instructor. She took gulping heavy breaths of air. She was out of breath just standing. Her son Angel had dated Allegra in junior high.

"She was very determined, a tough little girl," Carmen gasped. "That's why I know she's okay. When she was seven, I knew she was practicing, she *had* to be practicing. Nobody could have done the moves she did right, first time, otherwise. But she never let on. She never let you see the insides, the hard work, the pain."

"She's tough," the Mumy sister yelled out.

"She's a sweet girl," said Carmen.

"Just a little fucked up," said Mumy.

They struggled in a game of ownership, a land battle of who-knew-Allegra-best. It was interesting how even casual contact with a movie star—doing her nails, cleaning her house, walking her dog, having your cousin marry one—could start to distort the rest of your life, pale the moments of your day, your immediate family, your loved ones, even your pets. Next to the magnificence of fame, the ordinary sometimes held little value.

"Don't be fooled into thinking that her stardom was a fluke," Mumy said, poking my shoulder to get my attention again. "She wanted it all her life. And"—talking very loudly at this point—"I think she always *hated* her mother. *You know what I mean?*"

I nodded.

"The minute Kay started that goody-goody spiritual crap and renounced all worldly things, or whatever she did, Allegra became determined to get them."

I remembered what Allegra had told me about Kay Blyth—things I had promised at the time not to include in the profile. "I was my mother's mother, you know?" she had said in her white bathing suit by the Erawan pool. "By the time I was five. You know?" She told stories of finding Blyth passed out on the bathroom floor, cleaning up vomit around the sink, watching her swim naked one afternoon with the pool man, drunk and sinking and swallowing mouthfuls of pool water. Allegra watched her mother gulp pills and noon cocktails, glasses of wine, bottles of wine, then vodka straight, for months and months and then years.

We found Bertolucci to say goodbye. He was staying for an afterparty, then heading to Bancrofts; he mumbled something about "Johnny Mast's." Franklin was subdued, trying not to appear awestruck. And after Bertolucci had left for his parties, I found myself wondering if he was still a communist, if it was true about Allegra, and I wondered how many more movies he'd make before he died. Later I was sorry that I hadn't told him how great I thought his *L'Avventura* was.

"That's how it is," Franklin said as we stood in the shadows under a white scalloped awning, waiting for his rental car. "One can't say all the things one feels. It would be inappropriate, really, sort of artless. So you pretend that you're talking to anybody—otherwise you're groveling and embarrassing yourself and him and . . . Well, I was sort of flooded with feeling when I looked at him—weren't you? I was thinking about the end of *Last Tango in Paris* when Brando is standing out on the balcony and leaning in to the railing. He's been shot, and he's grimacing, and he's taking the chewing gum out of his mouth and rolling it between his fingers, then pressing it under the balcony railing with his thumb. Bertolucci, clearly a man like any other, but also the purveyor of memories that are now mine. It's so indescribably odd. He's a part of my life, part of who I've become, my soul in a way, and yet, of course, he has no earthly idea who I am."

There was a parade feeling—sad and happy, like the end of a football game when the home team loses. The wind was dry. The air was turning cool again. A blimp was flying overhead. A parking attendant was pulling up in Franklin's car.

"Hey." Tom Swimmer's voice was empty of all feeling. The L.A. voice. He appeared from the shadows in his cool gray clothes and brushed up close to me. He'd just chewed a mint.

"Where are you?" he said. His eyes were green. Sort of a shining hazel green. And magnificently shy.

"I'm right here."

"No, I mean, the Noguchi said you were at Shutters, and then the clerk at Shutters said you checked out."

"Oh, I did. Yes. I was getting sick of the roaring fire in the lobby—and all the baby boomers acting like the world is still theirs. And the seagulls were so loud in the morning. It was like *The Birds*. I just moved up the street, or down the street, to an undisclosed location."

"Casa del Mar?"

I said nothing.

"How will I find you?" He took a step closer.

"You won't."

He leaned over and kissed me on the lips. It was hard and then soft and warm. I didn't want to draw away, but I did when I wondered what Franklin was doing. He wasn't watching us, though; nor did he seem aware that his car had arrived. His eyes were on the curb, the sidewalk, where a TV camera was tracking us. Following Swimmer and me. It was a lumbering monster with black tentacles and black chains, cords, hoses, a giant hungry eye, and then its blinding blue lights flashed off.

om Swimmer's house was all corners and long walls, a midcentury showcase that he had paid a midcentury specialist to orchestrate. It was glass. It was bent wood. It was ostentatious only in its uninhabited feeling. Aside from a small cluster of California plein-air paintings in the foyer—dry gulches, eucalyptus groves, sand and sea—the house was utterly devoid of color, clutter, personality. The furniture, what little there was of it, consisted of exquisite museum pieces dating from the brief moment in time, a design sneeze, when the world wasn't deco anymore and yet not quite modern either.

"Roadie," Tom said, his voice bouncing off the walls of his spare living room. He dropped his motorcycle helmet on a sofa that was so sleek it looked like a bench with padding.

It was a dark night, a new moon perhaps, and his ceiling-high windows looked out onto blackness, except for a few scattered lights to the east, where houses were dug into the canyon like crabs in wet sand. Somewhere behind a dark hill was Van Nuys, I figured, and the rest of the Valley with its strip malls and delis and shrinks and two billion nail salons.

"Roadie?" I asked.

"Furniture designer," he said and began tapping his knuckles on the side of a sleek cabinet with big metal knobs. "American. It's spelled R-O-H-D-E. Gilbert Rohde. You pronounce it 'roadie.' Like a go-cup. Like a beer for the road. This piece actually came from Lucy and Ricky Ricardo's Hollywood apartment—I mean, from the set of their Hollywood apartment. From the show."

We had driven up through the canyon on his loud burring Harley, climbing through the darkness, leaning in to turns. He drove carefully, slowed for sharp curves, watched for patches of gravel on the narrow roads. The wind was dry, cool, almost cold, and I waited for wafts of heat to rise up from the exhaust pipe and warm my legs. My dress was hiked up, and I had no helmet—nothing between me and the air, the black sky. I heard whistling in my ears. I felt the glass egg vibrating against my right cheekbone.

Franklin had seemed confused at first. He was standing

beside his red Taurus rental with the driver's door swung open. His body looked tired—he slumped—and the sleeves of his jacket were pushed up above his elbows, a look that made him seem a little like a recording executive from the eighties. I put my hand on his back and whispered into his cheek: "Swimmer has a motorcycle. I'll talk to you in the morning."

I couldn't see all of Franklin's face, only the side. His eyes closed, squinting, as if he wasn't sure what I meant. Then he opened his mouth of beautifully crooked teeth and let out a laugh. "You're leaving with him?"

"On impulse," I said. "A very bad impulse."

A decision made before thinking, or made in a place I wasn't able to access. I was tired of trying to stop that from happening. Quite strongly, I had had an urge for something new, something different, to spend the night somewhere that wasn't a hotel, a place free of antiseptic smells and little wrapped soaps, no cavernous lobby with terrazzo floors and sun-washed silks and brown leather sofas. A place that didn't have so many blooming orchid plants—or hip/casual young faces behind the concierge desk, all dying to ask me about Allegra.

"What do you feel like?" Tom asked.

"Maybe this," I said, pointing to the deep end.

His pool was hanging over the hillside, suspended above blackness and a dry canyon. It was pale blue, almost white. A rectangle of light and shifting paleness. Dark specks were floating on the surface above the underwater light by the diving board: a gathering of dead moths.

I went in first, diving with my head down. An initiation, a beginning.

He followed. His body moved fast and made long shadows in front of the round light. Then he came up for air.

"Good idea," he said.

He was one of those people who looks completely different wet, almost unrecognizable. It was entirely about his hair. The water weighed it down, flattened it. Suddenly his face loomed too large, freakishly so. It was as though Tom Swimmer's hair were the largest part of him, his personality, his spirit; as though his very being were centered inside his heroic mane and the way it sprang pleasantly away from his face in dark hodgepodge undulations. At the valet stand, in the glow of the Hollywood Bowl, he had reminded me of a guy I'd known in middle school, a guy I'd liked, even yearned for, who left town one summer when his family moved to Chicago. He and Tom Swimmer had the same lean muscularity. They were both dark and too handsome, inarticulate jocks with a disjointed sad feeling beneath the unconscious exterior.

But those were my own private thoughts about Tom Swimmer, my own quiet sympathies, my unique reaction to him as a person, perhaps why I slept with him—feelings that were small and pointless because they had nothing to do with the public man, the poster man, the billboard man.

The actor who had appeared on the cover of *TV Guide* last year, dangling a blue rubber chicken. Whoever Tom Swimmer was, really, fame had simplified him and distorted him. He wasn't human-size anymore. He had only the illusion of humanity, the illusion of familiarity. We all knew Tom Swimmer—even I had a sense that I knew Tom Swimmer—from pictures in magazines, from the few times I'd caught him on late-night talk shows. (I'd never actually seen *Left on La Brea,* his hugely popular sitcom.) He seemed trustworthy and honest. And unlike the boy who moved to Chicago—from whom I never heard again—Tom Swimmer was traceable, accountable. He couldn't just go away.

But wet, he was a stranger. When his head emerged—his bulging face looking at me from the surface of the pool—I closed my eyes in a kind of shock. When I opened them again, his hair had dried and sprung out from his head. We were inside the house. We were in a dark room and taking up a small portion of a large bed with very good sheets. His body was warm and smooth, and there wasn't any part of it I didn't like.

"Do you need anything?" Tom asked.

"No, I'm great," I said.

We were quiet for a few minutes. His breathing became heavy and slow, a sleeper's pace. I stayed awake, curled on my side, my head sank into a thick down pillow. I watched most of the canyon lights go out, one by one, and studied a chest of drawers next to the bed. Another Gilbert Rohde, I had to assume.

I thought about what Allegra had said, wondered if my karma had changed. If my luck had changed. Who was that surfer from Newport Beach? She didn't seem to know his name. Where was he now? Allegra seemed to believe certain people were lucky, that sleeping with certain people gave you better karma. And if she believed that, then did she believe that sleeping with certain people could improve your health, perhaps cure disease and cancer? But you didn't have to sleep with them, apparently. Every time you met somebody, your karma changed "in subtle ways," she had said. Maybe just seeing somebody's picture changed your karma. Maybe watching certain people on TV was restorative, providing millions of subtle cures a day, little unnoticed miracles, cures and uplifts. Maybe watching *Cheers* was like that. Maybe *Gilligan's Island* and *I Love Lucy*.

Maybe watching *Thin Man* movies could do that. Maybe Myrna Loy could do that. Sitting in front of the television, avoiding the scene around my mother, that dumpy bedroom of hers, all her friends from the makeup counter at Altman's hovering around like cancer ghouls, I sat hypnotized by the annual *Thin Man* festival. Every day after school. Every day. For hours. I was transfixed, mesmerized—and received it like an infusion of some miraculous healing tonic. I noticed everything about Myrna Loy—the way she carried her head, lifted a champagne glass, arched her eyebrows when she uttered one of her wry put-downs. I watched all six—*The Thin Man, After the Thin Man, Another Thin Man, Shadow of the Thin Man, The Thin Man Goes Home, Song of the Thin Man.*

Myrna was a little like the Rohde chest across the room. She was deco, not quite modern. She was streamlined but not serious. She lingered between worlds, in midcentury, between phrases and feelings and moods.

Loretta wore ruffles, and her eyes were always misting over. She cared too much, like a hostess who meets you at the curb. Myrna held back. She never cried. She didn't meet you at the curb either. She had somebody else do that, and bring you a drink.

Just before sunrise, I left the bed and walked into the bathroom. My back felt good, stretched. My insides felt jostled. Above the toilet, there was a blue David Hockney swimming pool with a diving board. On another wall, a John Marin watercolor of boats. I opened the cabinets. There were shampoos and conditioners, toners, tonics, cleansers, scrubs, astringents, lotions, salves, and softeners. Under the sink was a plunger and a canister of Quaker Oats.

I found my dress and underwear in a puddle of black silk on the pool deck. I found my Manny Baba sling-backs and handbag by the front door. I drank a glass of tap water in the stainless-steel kitchen, and then I found the den.

It was like no other room in the house. Rather than spare and furnished with purchases from Christie's, it was quaintly comfortable and suburban. Two brown leather recliners were positioned in front of an enormous flat-screen TV. There were knickknacks and memorabilia cluttered on walls and shelves—an old Paris street sign, movie posters, driftwood, a collection of wooden giraffes. Bookshelves held stacks of magazines, biographies, memoirs, beach books and best-sellers and two copies of Stanislavski's *An Actor Prepares*. There were photos here and there—not studio head shots or oversized outtakes from Gary La Grange shoots but snapsnots in cheap plastic frames.

The other rooms of the house were easy to be in, free, sunlit, roomy, and half empty. But I imagined that the den was where Tom's decorator hadn't trod, where he was allowed to display and remember and collect, make cozy and be sentimental. But as I stepped farther inside the dark lair, I realized it wasn't Tom's life that was being celebrated and archived. The photos were all of Allegra.

She stood in baby fat and a black gingham dress for her second-grade class picture. Long-legged and thin, a bit older, she leaned against a lifeguard stand. In others, she was sweaty-faced and mugging inside a photo booth. She had her arms thrown around her mother and waifish half siblings in front of a pancake house. She was smiling beside her father at some kind of gallery opening. Max Coleman looked dignified in his ponytail and cape but also self-absorbed.

Up against the far wall, boxes were stacked, some of them open, some not. They held keepsakes, correspondence, a sticker and stamp collection, tattered Cabbage Patch dolls, a wobbly stuffed Jar Jar Binks, and an astrological chart for the birthday 1/11/79. There were Playbills from New York, ticket stubs from London movie houses, working scripts from *Vices* and *Sphinxa*.

I picked up a notebook. It seemed fairly new. When I looked inside, the pages were all blank but one.

November 7

Breakfast with Max. He seems better but still so thin. He was wearing the green kimono that I can't get him to throw out. The place is so messy too. Bird shit, stacks of newspapers, old rotting velvet curtains. I was ashamed to take Tom. So I lied and told him that Max wasn't up to meeting people even tho Max was dying to meet him. He loves Tom, watches *La Brea* faithfully. (That's more than me, I must say!) And sitting here right now, I keep thinking of Tom and how sweet he is and how he'd understand Max. How nice he would have been. And I'm ashamed that I was ashamed.

Baby flew into the parlor where Max and I were sitting, and Rita grabbed her by the tail and kept holding on. It was a riot. Rita was holding on to Baby's tail and Baby kept flying. Finally Rita got airlifted off the ground. At least two paws off the ground, I swear. I wish Tom had seen that. Baby made Rita fly.

November 14

I am a bug, I am a bug, I am a bug.

I heard a sound—or thought I heard a sound—and put the notebook back. I stood still for a few seconds.

I noticed a framed poster leaning against the wall behind the boxes next to me. After I'd waited a little while and heard no more sounds in the house, I lifted it up. It was a movie poster—old, very old—for a Brigitte Bardot picture that I hadn't seen, had never heard of: *Vie Privée*. Louis Malle was listed as the director. In the colored illustration, Bardot was walking on a roof. Her hooded eyes were looking down. Her hair was ridiculous—ratted to the sky and super-white like Dolly Parton's. Over her head, it said, PLUS CÉLÈBRE QUE MOI, TU MEURES! Fame. It seems to be killing her.

I put the poster back, left the room, and opened another door. It led to the garage.

It was a three-car garage with only two cars. Old cars and perfectly kept. I walked by a green Aston Martin sportscar. On the far wall, I could see some of Allegra's bottle caps hammered into the plaster—the ones she'd stood in front of, practicing her moves.

I opened the heavy door of a moss-green Woody station wagon and got inside. It smelled like gas and wax—clean and greasy at the same time. I opened the wooden glove box and found a remote control for the garage-door opener and pressed the button. Behind me, the door ascended without much sound.

The sunlight came in, and morning air. The key to the Woody was in the ignition. I took the car out of gear, twisted the key, pressed the gas. I put it in reverse and backed out.

The car dropped down into a canyon and rose out of another. It hugged turns, seemed to drive itself, passed manicured grounds and grand houses—colonials, Tudors, villas, haciendas, ranches—each seeming too large for its lot, too proud. I drifted onto Beverly Glen. The morning sun felt strong, and the fog was burning off.

I felt good, beyond the edge of a melancholy that I'd been fighting since the Hollywood Bowl, since stepping out of the limousine with Bertolucci. Since hearing the cheers of the crowd. Since the quiet alienating attentions of strangers, talented and well known. There had been a peak, then a valley. But now it was okay.

———

The footage of the Swimmer Kiss ran all night after the vigil—and then all day. I was on Sunset, weaving and wandering my way back to Santa Monica and Casa del Mar, when Franklin called my cell phone.

"Have you been watching TV?" he said.

"No. Why?"

"Your apotheosis is now pending."

"What are you talking about?"

"A very fine kiss. Nice timing, perfect angle. Awfully sweet, I must say. Your chin rises a bit to meet Mr. Swimmer's face. He's bending over you with that thick head of hair. Then freeze-frame. I've seen it nearly a dozen times already."

"On the news?"

"Well, the news of some kind or another. Gotten loads of calls too. Ed being one of them."

"Ed?"

"Yes, he rang at approximately two in the morning."

"How was he?"

"Amused. Curious. Possibly jealous. He used that old Valley Girl expression for kissing. It's so vulgar, I have trouble remembering it—"

"Sucking face."

"Yes, that's it."

"I hate that expression."

"My guess is that Ed does too. But isn't it nice to know that even your smallest gestures now have impact?"

The phone in my room at Casa del Mar rang like a fire alarm. By eight-thirty A.M. I had stopped answering my cell phone too. I began packing—lifting from the closet my black canvas T. Anthony bag that Ed had given me some years ago, with a monogram and no wheels. I also pulled my old camel coat out of the closet. It felt stiff with neglect and inordinately heavy, like something one would wear to the Arctic.

When I checked my laptop, I found that Franklin had forwarded the blurry blowups that would be spread across the *Post* and *Daily News* the following morning. Tom and I were identifiable only by our cartoonish attributes: his head of hair, the black elastic band of my eye patch making a dent in my hair. CLEM NABS ALLEGRA'S EX, one headline read. And under the photograph the caption read: IN THE LAND OF THE BLIND, THE ONE-EYED GIRL IS QUEEN.

I finished packing and listened to my messages. Franklin had called again, sounding a little too jolly while confirming my flight to JFK. Marie-Claude had called with a request that I contact Ed at the Marmont. Margaux had checked in, and so had Tom. His voice sounded both laidback and upbeat, the L.A. combo.

"Hey, Clementine," he said. "That was nice. But where's my car?"

CHAPTER 16

Maxwell A. P. Coleman was spray-painting his shoes gold the morning I met him. They were lined up along the dark walls of his Gothic brownstone, in the foyer and down the long hallways. Belgian slippers, moccasins, high-top sneakers. There were Pava sling-backs and chunky mega-mules too. Each pair—not much larger than my own—was set on top of unfolded newspaper and surrounded by a shaggy halo of gold paint.

"My dear, my dear," Max said as he opened the heavy wooden door. "Come in. Come in." His face was pale and powdery, and he looked thinner than he did in pictures—and a bit frail. His soft white hair was collected into a ponytail, and his eyebrows seemed to be either gone or vanishing, like the foggy trails of vapor his breath produced in the frozen air.

"Come in!" he said again. "Before the media hounds arrive or we die of exposure."

It was cold in New York, a dry cold that I found strangely exciting at first, after eleven weeks of Los Angeles tepidity. But in the early morning as I waited for the Carlyle doorman to hail me a cab, I was shivering on the sidewalk, and my hands were turning reddish blue. My camel coat seemed suddenly too thin. My legs too bare. In my rush to flee Los Angeles—two photographers from the tabloids had planted themselves across from Casa del Mar—I'd forgotten to bring a scarf or gloves. I'd forgotten an undershirt, or even tights, as though three months in Southern California had softened me, spoiled me, had made the reality of winter both vague and precarious as though it were a movie I'd seen long ago and couldn't quite remember.

My cab crept along Park Avenue in traffic, and I was still shaking as I passed women in fur coats and fur hats, women with thick cashmere scarves wrapped around their necks. And as I began to anticipate my morning with Max Coleman—the pancakes he'd offered to cook, the sound of his world-weary voice on the phone—my curiosity about him was replaced by more pressing desires: I just wanted to be warm and, perhaps later, to do a little shopping.

"Come in! Come in!" As far as I could tell, Max wore only a kimono printed with a fire-red chrysanthemum blossom. He held a very small brown dachshund under one arm and waved me inside with gold fingertips.

He'd been up early, spraying since dawn. "It's so practical," he explained. "Only sorry I didn't think of it years ago. All that sparkle without having to polish!" His teeth were white, and when he smiled, his mouth looked like the keyboard of a child's piano.

"Rita," he said, looking down at the trembling miniature dachshund in his arms. "This is Clementine." Rita squinted at me with nervous eyes. Her mouth opened, and I could see a slim pink tongue and pointy teeth.

"Green tea?" Max asked. "Sencha? Or perhaps a little ma huang?"

As I followed Max down a dark corridor, he turned periodically to check on me, as if to make sure I was still there. He put the dog down and she clicked off in the reverse direction, passing me, her furry bottom pushing its way toward a remote corner of the shadowy house. We kept walking, and the air grew warmer; the paint smell thickened and was joined by something else—cigarette smoke and patchouli, a moldy scent that clung closer to the ground.

Max stopped and let out a deep cough, a bowels-of-the-earth kind of sound that I'd heard before. He leaned against a wall. "Sorry," he said, waving a handkerchief that he'd pulled from his kimono pocket. He walked only a few more paces, then stopped again.

We were standing before an immense red room. It was filled with ornate furniture and thick velvet curtains that dropped and cascaded and then buckled at a golden Aubusson rug. There were dark heavy carved pieces from the nineteenth century. There was a crouching Aphrodite in marble. There were touches of Japan—bamboo; and China—red lacquer. There were touches of Louis XIV too, gold damask pillows and Sun King medallions. And in the midst of this eclectic opulence were several of Max Coleman's famous op-art paintings from the early sixties. On one wall was a canvas of yellow polka dots on a dreamy field of sky blue. On another wall, red-orange polka dots were set against a grassy field of chartreuse.

"That's *Dawn,*" Max said, pointing to the farthest wall, where a magnificent canvas dominated with hazy intensity: a solitary white-golden dot rising over a horizon line of white-violet and the palest indigo.

"And this," Max said with a sweep of his hand, "is the morning parlor. Except we spell that m-o-u-r-n-i-n-g to pay tribute to its rather somber decor. Ha ha. Our favorite room, really. A tad gloomy and *de trop* and too Addams Family, I suppose. But we love it anyway. Gra-gra and I like to sit here with the girls and confab by the hour . . . Anyway, let's have our tea here, and we'll chat before I get going on the pancakes. Why don't you sit there?" He pointed to a rigid little settee with a tufted back.

I felt a bit unsteady all of a sudden and took a few steps

toward the settee, then waited for Max to sit down first. But he remained on his feet.

"I hope you don't like them fat and cakey," he said distractedly. His arms were waving around again: another trait, besides the dire cough, that he shared with his daughter. "I hate thick pancakes that soak up all the syrup like a big sponge and make you feel really ill later. They're so fatal. And combined with fake syrup—that maple *flavoring* . . . Dreadful. Don't you agree? I do the thin cakes—the super-super thins or, as we call them, *delicate thins.* Almost a crêpe, really, served with whipped maple butter. We love them. And so does Baby."

He pointed up to a corner of the ceiling where an enormous fig tree was pressing against a sunny window—ten feet high, maybe twelve. The leaves of the fig were large, primordial-looking, and appeared diseased. They were dotted with mildew, a chalky kind of grit, and on the floor beneath the tree were old pink pages of *The New York Observer,* also spotted. There were drops of white grit all over the room, actually, the lamp shades, the rugs, the tabletops . . .

Max began to whistle and looked up to where a red wooden perch was wired to the trunk of the tree. "Flown off, apparently. Well, she can't be far . . ."

I began to feel queasy and disoriented. I felt too hot. I felt too cold. Dots were swirling before me, like dancers on a stage. Orange dots, golden dots, little white dots . . .

"My dear," Max said, coming closer. "Are you all right?"

——

The room was cold, and the ceiling was different. A window was wide open, and I could see a brick airshaft between town houses. Candles were burning somewhere—the smell of paraffin would come and then depart with each draft of cold air. I pulled a blanket up over my arms.

It was the paint fumes, perhaps, or the long airplane fight and the consciousness-lowering in-flight movie with Sandra Bullock. It was lack of sleep too—the way I had woken up several times thinking about Ned, wondering if he'd seen the kiss on TV, or if Bram had seen it—which seemed worse. It was the two lurkers also, the photographers who had positioned themselves outside Casa del Mar, and the way I had to elude stalkers in the lobby by taking the freight elevator to the garage. It was the vigil, Bertolucci, the crowd, the roar of the crowd . . . My feelings on the subject seemed in constant flux, warm then cool, excitement followed by bruising self-punishment. To gain some balance, I'd taken a Zopax at LAX. (Several of those small blue capsules remained in my arsenal after Cedars.) But I continued to find, as I returned home from Hollywoodland, that I felt either ashamed or triumphant depending on the hour. And at JFK, people looked lumpy and overly serious. They stared at me.

"Clementine James," I heard a preteen girl whisper to an older woman in baggage claim. The girl, her mouth agape, was stunned by the sight of me.

"Who?"

"Mother."

A cloud of paraffin came, went. I was dreaming. I must still be dreaming. A long slur of unrelated images drifted through my mind. I tried to construct a puzzle in which each piece had a proper place—the dots, the gold shoes, the kiss (now more important than the night of lovemaking that followed), the mirrored bathroom at the Carlyle, the minibar with Frujin shakes and salted cashews, the note Ed left at the hotel: *Tom Swimmer's car . . . where did you park it?*

When I woke up, I found myself reclining on an overstuffed sofa with a cashmere throw spread over me. A small needlepoint pillow was under my knees. Max was fanning my face with an issue of *Elle Decor.* He was talking softly. At first I thought he might be on the phone. He was recounting a long anecdote, something about Palm Springs.

". . . then, of course, Kay and I were married in Indian Wells. We liked it there—I'm not sure why. We were good friends with Johnny Weissmuller and his sixth wife, Beliza, and anyway, they had a house at Thunderbird right on the green, and they organized a small party for us. It was just ten or twenty people. Weissmuller was a funny guy and almost dead at that point. The desert is such a good place for the nearly dead. Kay had had a part in a *Tarzan* movie when she was a baby, and they'd stayed in touch . . ."

The fanning stopped. I heard the clink of a teacup.

"My dear, I'm so glad you've come around," he said. His elegant ghost face hovered over me. "I've been blabbing on, a fool—hoping to revive you with stories," he said. "Apparently it worked. I didn't want to call the doctor. I'm always calling the doctor, and I'm afraid I've become quite a nuisance to her."

"I'm okay," I said.

"I'm not sure you are."

An elaborate candle stand, like the kind you'd see in a church, stood behind him. Seven or eight of the white votives were lit. Something moved beside me, inside the blanket. Rita—curled against my waist.

I tried to sit up. Max motioned me to stay down. I felt my head, the side of my face . . .

"I put it over here," he said, pointing to the table between us. The eye patch was lying flat and looked for a second like one of Max's dots. He came closer and patted my hair. "You remind me of Kay a little. You know? Your forehead, the hairline. When she was young. Your brows. It's a bit haunting, actually. I suppose Gra-gra told you that."

I shook my head.

"No?"

"I didn't know you called her Gra-gra."

"Really? That's odd. But also very like her. She likes to keep things simple and mysterious. A big empty book. It's all quite deliberate, you know. Gra-gra believes too many details muddle the power of the overall picture. If the surface is distracting, there can't be depth—*that* sort of thing. But she goes too far sometimes, condenses too much. She's always smoothing things out. Honestly, when I read some of these articles about her, particularly interviews, it's as though she's trying to turn herself into a Zen koan or a sand garden—an event of great beauty and simplicity . . ."

His eyes drifted off to an open door at the end of the room. It seemed to lead to a closet or bathroom. And then he kept talking.

"Aside from my dot paintings, which are cartoons, really, and meant to be elemental and symbolic, I'm afraid simplicity is beyond my grasp. I'm all over the place. Quite sloppy and uncollected, in every possible way. Poor Gra-gra. I was never interested in presenting a cohesive self to the world. I'm a man, I'm a woman. I'm a father, then a mother. I'm a painter, then a performer. Actually, if you want to know, I never saw the difference between painting and performing. Everything is a performing art. Anyway, my tendency is to get as messy as possible. That's where life is for me—the mess of things, chaos, uncertainty. But Gra-gra is a bit of a spareness nut. She likes things very simple and specific. She walks away from complications."

He sighed, looked again toward the door. "Well, you know."

I nodded.

"And God knows, Kay was a mess. She was one grand prix mess, so disorganized. The pets were always dying. Gra-gra would ring up with this little weepy voice. Some puppy had run off—hungry. The iguana was dead in the bathtub. All the angelfish were floating at the top of the aquarium. She had this ancient cat, Hello Kitty, and it died giving birth—we marveled that it was able to conceive at all, after years of apparent barrenness. And then the coyotes came down the mountain and ate the kittens that Gra-gra had been so diligently trying to save, and it left their little bloody bodies in a water dish by the front door. She wailed and wailed. It was such drama, truly awful. It was. I'm sure. But she didn't want to come live with me. I was a freak. She hated that too."

He laughed, and his chest gurgled. Then the laugh became a cough, and by the time he had it under control, perspiration had broken out on his forehead. "Have you met the Riverside Halves and Steps?"

"Who?"

"The stepbrothers and half sibs. Gra-gra dumped them all about five years ago. Very bad boys. They were always stealing her CDs or trying to pull her clothes off. And their friends would show up and try to throw her in the pool, or to feel her up and grab her crotch. Kind of an awful scene. Kay couldn't handle it. Anyway, Gra-gra would have nothing to do with them—and I've been very very surprised that they haven't surfaced in this, wanting their fat greasy faces in *Speak* or *People* or *Flame*." He paused for a second. "Oh, sorry. You're *Flame,* aren't you."

"That's all right."

He was chuckling, and then his eyes landed soberly on my black eye patch on the table. He lifted it up by one finger. "I wouldn't bother with this anymore, if I were you.

Of course, it's your look and I respect that, but it's awfully harsh. Much too sinister and *True Grit,* even for me. You're a beautiful girl. *You are.* If you want to hide the glass eye, why not a pair of Jackie sunglasses—or even *Terminator* shades? I mean, my dear, when you first came to the door, I was trembling with fear."

"You did seem pale," I said.

His face came closer still. "Is that a clear glass eye?"

I nodded. "Like a little egg."

"Is it permanent?"

"I'm getting some kind of high-tech replacement," I said. "It'll be ready soon. Bionic or something. Being made for me in Switzerland."

"What color?"

"Matching."

Max took a deep breath, then let it out in a quiet but expressive sigh. "*Matching.* Are you sure that's what you want?"

Going across the room, he plugged in an electric kettle and began to make green tea. He carefully spooned out the green powder with a skinny bamboo spoon. "You know," he said, "Peter O'Toole is an old friend."

I sort of nodded—it was the kind of comment you had to nod at.

"And he once told me a very interesting piece of information. If you tie a piece of red string to a seagull's leg, he said, the other gulls will peck it to death. Apparently it's true. You tie some red string on a gull's leg, and the other birds will fly after it and attack it and kill it, if they can. They aren't happy until it's been destroyed . . ."

Out of the corner of my eye, I saw something move in the bathroom or closet. A cloud was drifting overhead, casting a shadow on a skylight, perhaps.

"The fear of being different, you see, is the fear of being destroyed." Max glanced over at the bathroom too. "Do you believe that?"

"It makes sense," I said, looking around. It was a large suite, mostly empty. The decor was vaguely Spanish. There was a large carved bed, a Moorish ceiling. The walls were painted the color of roasted pumpkin. There was only one object on the wall: a wooden Jesus with a throbbing *sacré cœur* in the middle of his chest.

"Where are we?" I asked.

"I brought you in this room," Max said. "It's Allegra's."

—

Max's delicate thins were presented on square plates that were lined with sliced kiwi and drowning in glorious liquid maple butter. In his small kitchen, I watched him create his magic pancakes. I sat at a table stuck off to the side, next to stacks of unopened mail and mail-order catalogs, programs from Wigstock and other drag extravaganzas, a collection of salt and pepper shakers ("I rescued them from the trash one day, after Gra-Gra went on a purge"). After we ate— and Rita had done dog tricks for bits of cooked bacon—

Max gave me a tour. Four floors and seven coughing fits. We saw his painting studio in the turret. We saw Allegra's yoga studio with bottle caps hammered into the walls and a poster of Steve McQueen on a motorcycle in *The Great Escape* ("Gra-gra's first love," he said). Max's bedroom was enormous and cluttered and decorated in a style best described as Pre-Raphaelite Liberace. An enormous grandfather clock stood just beside his door and tolled every fifteen minutes. In the far corner, inside a confessional that had been turned into a wardrobe with shelves, was Max's wig collection. There were twenty or so versions of his signature accessory—the chin-length blond pageboy that he wore as Ava Pillbox in the clubs and as the director emeritus of Night of a Thousand Gowns—sitting on Styrofoam heads. In a moment of giddiness, we stretched my eye patch over the face of one of the heads and left it there.

Toward the early afternoon, we made a foray to the outside world, looking for some "remedies" that Max had decided I needed for jet lag and fatigue and other maladies that he had diagnosed me as suffering from. To brave the cold, Max wore a gray fur-lined winter kimono with ratty sleeves over his indoor kimono, and Rita padded along behind him on a rolled leather Hermès leash. "Los Angeles always gives me a case of some unnameable malaise," he said. "It's the rotten air. I think you've got that too."

We wandered into a place called the Dharmacy, somewhere near the corner of Grove and Bleecker streets. The shelves were ceiling-high and crowded with glass cylinders of Chinese herbs. And in front of us, on the counters, were small containers of pollens and extracts. Max seemed to know the proprietor, Fred, quite well.

"My friend Clementine has the L.A. disease that Gra-gra and I always get," Max said.

"You gotten a ransom note yet?" Fred asked Max.

Max shook his head.

"She call you?"

"No," Max said, fondling a bag of dried mugwort. Beads of sweat again appeared on his brow. "Oh. I forgot to tell you," he said, quickly turning to me and away from Fred. "Your cell phone rang while you were napping, and I didn't answer it the first time. And then I did. Your assistant Franklin was looking for you. Awfully pleasant. We talked for quite a while."

"What about? I wasn't asleep that long, was I?"

"We talked about movies," he said.

"Kurosawa? Charlton Heston?"

"Fassbinder," he said. "And we talked about L.A. The Brits always fall for it, don't they? Just lap it up. Oh well, they think America is one big joke anyway. Maybe they're right."

"He didn't ask about Allegra?"

"He's not that gauche," Max said. "And neither, I gather, are you."

Later, walking home, after we'd gotten alfalfa, black co-hosh, dandelion, skullcap, and the mugwort, we made a plan to see each other the next day. Max was lonely, I thought. And he seemed to have more to tell me.

"She's in Big Sur—isn't she?" I said finally, after weighing whether to ask directly. Not asking had gotten me pretty far. "Or somebody wants me to think she's in Big Sur. I got something postmarked from there."

Max said nothing. We passed the park, and he still had said nothing. "I don't think she's allowed to make calls. That's what I think. And that's not the point. *Making calls.*"

He made it sound like she was in prison—or Promises rehab. "So you've heard from her?" I asked.

"Indirectly."

"What do you mean?" I asked.

As we turned the corner and his brownstone came into view, he leaned over and whispered, "Honestly, I don't know." He stopped walking and bent his head. When he looked up again, his eyes were pink.

"I miss her. Of course I miss her," he said. "And I'm worried and waiting, and I'd love her to come back. But whatever she chooses, regardless of whether she returns . . . I've lost her, don't you see?"

n winter's late afternoons, New York City becomes a strange netherworld. There's a sense of a breath being taken, a momentary pause. At four, the daytime cabs go off duty, and the rush-hour cabs have yet to scour the streets. As I left Max's brownstone, an expansive mood came over me, brought on, I suppose, by the herbal infusion, but even more than that, by Max himself—his gold shoes and gallantry, his outrageous kimono.

Downtown, I stepped into the hushed warmth of Paul Smith's and found myself lured into the cocoon of the accessories area. I needed some good sunglasses. I needed some other good things too. And it wasn't long before I had pulled out the green Conglom card that Marie-Claude had sent me—ostensibly to nurture the speedy production of an essay pondering the "vagaries of fame"—and bought a pair of suede gloves, a thick sea-blue cashmere shawl, a lizard wallet in Paul Smith's signature stripes, an overpriced but terribly attractive hair clip, and a pair of extremely dark P.S. shades. Even though they were not oval—the Jackie O shape had made me look like a gigantic fly—somehow I felt Max would have been proud of me. The sunglasses were brown and striped and rectangular and so enormous that my eyes were completely hidden.

Leaving the shop, I wandered uptown. The winter sun was sinking and an eerie gloam had descended on the streets. Sharp beams of light broke through in the oddest places. A street corner would suddenly become golden and a small pool of sunlight—the last gasp until tomorrow—would land on a woman's head.

I followed the bits of golden light and forgot about finding a cab. I continued like a homing pigeon toward the old Conglom neighborhood. I passed my Greek coffee guy, the pretzel vendor, the handbag man who sold Kate Spade and Bomba knockoffs from his kiosk, the homeless woman who wore newspaper hats and yelled at the shrubs. As I pushed closer to Thirty-third Street, I came upon the nail salon where I had sent Meg Tilly for an emergency pedicure, the vegetarian café where I had interviewed Andie MacDowell, and the little Japanese jewelry shop where, before the holidays—which now seemed like another lifetime ago—I had been eyeing a freshwater-pearl necklace but wondered, at the same time, what I'd do with it on a farm in Virginia.

The Gothic tower of the Conglom Building soon came into sight. The sun had dropped behind it and a burst of yellow flames seemed to engulf its crown. At the twenty-second floor was a row of four bright windows—whiter and more intense than the others. He was in there, I thought. Way up, protected from the gloomy sky and orange flames, he floated above me, dark and primitive and laughable, like one of the gargoyles on the tower. But in the ghostly light of dusk, I felt a pang for my tiny cubicle at *Flame,* for my cramped apartment in Brooklyn, my little hamster wheel of obligations and projects and complaints. Rising stars, cresting stars, fading stars, has-beens making comebacks . . . plugging a new movie, plugging a memoir, sporting a new hairdo or spouse. It was a pathetic life and deeply unimportant work, as Ned was always reminding me. But it had saved me, in a way, lifted me out of New Jersey and the tragic blandness of my past. The work had its pleasant routines too, its predictable pace, its little joys—joys that I had come to count on, rely on, and look forward to.

As I drew closer to the corner of Thirty-second Street, I worried that the revolving doors of Conglom might eject somebody I didn't want to face. I wrapped the blue shawl high on my neck to cover my chin and mouth, took comfort in the new glasses. (Why hadn't I bought a hat?) A few minutes later, once I was well beyond the zone of life around Conglom, I looked up from the sidewalk and noticed a figure ahead of me. It was hard not to. Her hair was yellow-white and wavy to her shoulders—the sort of old-fashioned gel wave that was everywhere in the twenties but seemed affected ever after.

She wore an unusual velvet cloak of the same yellow-white color as her hair. There was some kind of silver fur piece, a stole, around her shoulders. I realized that I had been trailing behind her for several blocks already—had vaguely noticed her in the periphery of my vision when a flash of sunlight had landed on her head and then on the small brown dachshund that walked next to her creamy evening slippers.

She was weaving, I noticed. Her shoes wandered from one edge of the sidewalk to the other. Her step was too dainty, her gait too light, to be Max's. When she stumbled, I saw a flutter of silk under the cloak. The dachshund wandered from side to side too, sometimes trying to lead, sometimes following, but always precariously positioned—possibly in harm's way, considering it was tethered to a person who appeared close to some kind of inelegant collapse.

I quickened my pace. I wanted to stare at her, I suppose. I wanted to see who she was, this figure who brought so much light—and lack of control—to the gray city streets. As I got closer, I saw she was rather tall and willowy, and so pale, so blond, that her head shimmered like a pale yellow moon. A drunken moon. Just as I reached her, she fell into me.

"Oh, I'm so-so-sorry," she said, clutching my arm with

a dire grip. Her nails were manicured into little points. One finger carried a diamond as big as a cocktail onion. She lifted her right foot and stared down at the satin shoe.

"I've ta-ta-twisted something, I think," she said in a voice that was more husky than helpless. "My ankle fe-feels like ru-rub-rubber."

She picked up the dog and surveyed the landscape, looking for a bench, perhaps. "Oh, but aren't we ne-near Keens?" She seemed to be speaking more to the dog than to me. Somehow her stammer didn't make me feel all that sorry for her. Besides, there were other, more pressing reasons to feel sorry for her.

"Woo-would you mind?" She gestured toward the other end of the block with her free hand and, after I nodded agreement, leaned on me with what seemed like all her weight. We walked slowly, as though neither of us truly had a destination, and I suppose we made quite a sight—an ambling, outlandish four-legged beast carrying an anxious dog.

At the edge of Sixth Avenue and Thirty-sixth Street, we arrived at the place she had talked about. It was an old joint—a long forgotten watering hole with leaded casement windows and other details that made it look like a fake Elizabethan tavern or castle. KEENS CHOPHOUSE, said the sign, SINCE 1871.

She turned to face me for the first time. I could see her eyes trying to find mine behind the sunglasses, and somehow they did. Her face was open and girlish. It was also a kind face. Her eyes were blue and sparkled almost as though glitter were drifting inside them. On the outlines of them, the mascara was so thick that the lashes clotted together.

"I'm Marion," she said, then bowed toward the dog. "And this is Helen. Woo-woo-would you join us for a dri-dri-drink?"

———

She found a booth in the darkness, in the way back but not far from the glistening bar. She ordered quickly, with apparent renewed sobriety, and a bottle of champagne and two glasses arrived, the grand marshal of a long parade of other bottles and glasses. Three bowls of smoked almonds were consumed as well, along with a dozen or so unfiltered cigarettes that she pulled from a jeweled case inscribed with *Marion* in chunky rubies and diamonds. When she switched from champagne to a gin "martini" (no vermouth), I switched with her—partly out of curiosity, partly due to either politeness or my new expansive mood—then drifted to Cosmopolitans after a while. Later, when I came to look back on the evening, I wondered whether I'd slowed down or hastened the tempo of her consumption by joining in—or if Marion operated at her own pace at all times, like some kind of liquid-seeking missile. She was a piece of work, as they say, and mostly there was no stopping her.

Keens was almost empty but still cozy, and reminded me

of "21." It had the same haunted, cavelike feeling, the same smell of fresh flowers and stale air. The leather on the banquettes and chairs seemed marinated by decades of smoke and booze. The walls were covered with old photographs—black-and-white and gray pictures of show people and movie people and ballplayers and politicians. A museum of the forgotten. Billy Rose. Jimmy Walker. Babus Feinman. Their bodies seemed stiff and their suits too tight. They posed in a wooden way that people no longer do, inhabitants of a more formal world, before strangers called one another by first names, before the invention of the Frisbee, before snowboarding and casual Fridays.

Marion used the bathroom a lot, and it seemed to require a great amount of time and energy to simply go there and return. I sat alone with Helen in the near darkness, eating the almonds and drinking slowly, looking at Marion's stole that she'd left on the table, a silver fox with its head intact and dead glass eyes looking out. I studied the walls and the lights of the great swooping bar with its polished mahogany and brass, its underlit bottles. It was a cluster of lights, a distant constellation in the black night sky. And around the bar, sitting on its rounded stools, I could make out the forms of a few figures, fellow drinkers, who looked, in the dark at least, confident and glamorous and potentially fascinating. I had to remove my sunglasses briefly, and squint, to examine the most surprising element of the decor. On the ceiling were hundreds, perhaps thousands, of small smoking pipes (clay or wood, I couldn't tell which). So many pipes were hanging from hooks that the space above looked almost alive, as though covered in scales or fur. Some of the pipes were labeled with names of the men who had put their lips to them and smoked: Teddy Roosevelt, Will Rogers, Florenz Ziegfeld . . .

Marion returned from the powder room. I put on my sunglasses again. The room grew as dark as the beginning of a Disneyland ride.

"Hey baby, look at that old ba-ba-badger over there," Marion said, shooting a glance at an unsuspecting fellow sitting alone in the corner.

"I can't see anything," I said, trying to control a laugh.

"That b-b-big sourpuss in the tw-tw-tweed jacket. He keeps scowling at me." She seemed to enjoy excursions into mockery, and doing impersonations.

"Maybe he doesn't like the way you're staring at him."

"What a gr-gru-grumpus! *Grumpasaurus maximus.*" She balled up a paper cocktail napkin in her right hand and pretended to aim. "Let's liven things up."

Marion had wicked schemes and plans—ideas about jokes she'd like to play on the other patrons (there were only three or four) and the few waiters who worked the shift between lunch and dinner. She seemed particularly focused on grave-looking older men and making them dance with her. People were being "no fun," she said, and her own fun seemed to consist of making fun of the no-fun people. She had ideas about the huge dinner she would order too—a three-pound steak, a two-pound lobster, baked potatoes and curly fries and creamed spinach. "Oh baby, I lo-lo-love creamed spinach. *It's so good here,*" she said several times during the evening, as though a bowl of creamed spinach were orbiting her mind, taking about half an hour to complete a revolution before entering consciousness again.

But she never ordered spinach or lobster—or interfered with the other guests. She remained planted on the banquette, chewing on almonds and drinking champagne and gin like somebody whose life was beginning to depend on it, except for the long absences when she wandered away.

"I need to pee," she'd say. "Wild call. I mean, call of the wi-wild."

How old was she? This question circled inside me like Marion's bowl of creamed spinach. In the darkness, her hair glowed and her teeth shone and I couldn't see any wrinkles. But the flesh was doughy under her chin, and her eyelids were puffy, like tiny pillows into which her eyes were embedded. When we'd removed our coats and stood at the Dutch door of the coat check, I noticed that her once-thin waist had mostly disappeared.

Just a few pictures left to make, perhaps . . . *Cain and Mabel* or *Ever Since Eve.* Not long ago in the span of things, really, she'd sung and danced on a stage about six blocks away. On Forty-second Street in the New Amsterdam Theatre, she'd been a Ziegfeld girl at just sixteen or seventeen—lying about her age and saying she was older—while William Randolph Hearst sat in the second-row orchestra staring up her short dress. Overcome by attraction or desire—or whatever it is that makes a fifty-two-year-old man do embarrassing things—Hearst came backstage looking for her, with flowers and a big toothy smile. His eyes were sad. His voice was very high. Later he sent watches from Cartier, rings from Tiffany. There were dinners at his hideaway apartment in the Bryant Park Studios building. There were love notes too. And by the time she was eighteen or so, he was allowed in her family's house. Hearst was a married man with children but a publisher of no small renown, and Marion's mother and father were pleased that their daughter was associating with a man who loomed so large and seemed so gentle.

Marion could sit very still for interminable periods of time, and the more she consumed, the more rigid she became. Her thin eyebrows rose higher on her forehead after she moved on to gin, and her face grew paler until the blood seemed to have evaporated completely. Aside from encore gestures to the waiter, it was hard to tell where her mind was—what city, what decade. Where was she? Asleep? Alive or dead?

An industry of academics and experts had tried to revive her reputation in recent years, declaring Marion Davies to be a genius—Hollywood's first screwball comedian—and an actress whose career was hurt as much as helped by her association with Hearst. Books had been written, documentaries had been made. She wasn't at all like the Susan Alexander character in *Citizen Kane,* they asserted. Yes, she did jigsaw puzzles at San Simeon. And yes, she tended to drink a bit, and her boyfriend produced all her pictures and then promoted them in all his newspapers, but she wasn't talentless or whiny or stupid. Orson Welles had even apologized for the cruelty of *Citizen Kane,* but the words of a bloated narcissist just looked self-serving by then. And by then nobody remembered Miss Davies, anyway. She occupied an ancient realm, a world of movies long gone—the silent era—while *Citizen Kane* lived on and on, at first a cult film for clever people and then, finally, a classic film for all people.

Around the time of her last martini, Marion's good cheer started to fail her.

"Are we still si-sitting here in Keens, for chrissakes? I'm getting ti-ti-tired of the view." She was looking at me. "Why don't you go bl-blond, baby? It'll bleach out your mo-mood."

Her head began to swing to one side, then jerk back. Her face flushed as if she had windburn. "They ca-ca-cared about appearances, you know. *Appearances.* They wanted me to make an ho-honest man of him, I suppose."

She tapped her index finger on the tabletop, and the rata-tat of her pointy nail on the hard wood started to echo her stammer. "But he-he was honest. *The most honest man.* So I wake up how ma-many hours later and . . . his body is gone. His things are gone. All his things. Cleared out. They make out like he ne-never lived with me at all. Like I wasn't that imp-po-portant. Do you think they invited me to the funeral? The creeps."

I wasn't able to watch her continuously while she rambled on. I steadied my eyes on the edge of my martini glass and studied the way it distorted the light. I focused on Marion's silver fox and diamond ring too. And the next time I remember looking up, an enormous fur coat was being thrown over a café chair next to me. And then a voice spoke:

"*Fuck* them, darling."

Hers wasn't simply a voice. It was a foghorn, a jolting baritone blast. The timbre of her southern drawl was so strong and deep that I could almost feel it in my blood.

Marion lifted her eyes but didn't move her head. "Hey, baby."

"Darling," Tallulah Bankhead continued, "that story is a bore and I hate it." She was wearing a gray wool crepe dress that was almost mousy. Her hair was not as pale as Marion's but was styled similarly, in waves that fell to her shoulders. Her eyebrows were also very thin, arching high over her large eyes and giving her a perpetually surprised expression.

She sat down and didn't look at me, only at Marion, while she picked a cigarette out of Marion's case, tapping it a few times on the rubies and putting it in her mouth.

"Broken record. I repeat: *broken record, darling.* Either abandon that story or devise a better version. Perhaps one where you don't come off like such a dope at the end." Tallulah then turned to me and paused. "She was stuck with Pops, old man river, darling, for thirty-five years. William Randolph Hearst was simply too kind and too generous to dump, you see? Not to mention a complete cipher. So he finally dies—a very old, very famous, very rich man who had refused to marry her, and all his boys come and take his body away and want to bury him. What the fuck is so bad about that? She was free, off the hook. Pops was gone, and she was sad, of course. Okay, so she doesn't get to go to the funeral. But"—she turned to Marion again—"get over it, darling. There are so many more interesting things to be depressed about."

Marion smiled a little foggily, unfazed, and tried to say something; but only two words, "Horace Brown," came out. Her head drooped again and swayed. Then it fell on the table with a soft thud.

We stared at her head for a few seconds, and then Tallulah started up. *"Whore Ass Brown,"* she said. "Old Whore Ass." Her knee was bouncing under the table, and a heavy bracelet—big diamonds set in interlocking squares—jangled on her wrist. "Now, *he* was a colossal creep. The creep of all creeps, perhaps. A blunder, darling. Excruciatingly bad judgment. We've all fucked creeps. We've all fallen in love with creeps. But we don't marry them—particularly when we're already rich and don't have to. But it's pointless to feel bad now. It was always going to end badly. Everything ends badly for us. There's no other way."

Tallulah was a monologuist, a talker, a blabber of blab infinitum and the greatest stage actress of her generation. It never got dull, only hard to break in. Mostly she seemed to talk to Marion's head, or the top of it. She was eloquent. She was raunchy. She was well read. She quoted Keats and Tennessee Williams, Edna St. Vincent Millay and Shakespeare ("Alas, poor Yorick! I knew him, Horatio," she blurted out at one point. "A fellow of infinite jest, of most excellent fancy"). She talked with a cigarette in her mouth like a hood in a Scorsese picture. She managed to make this look impossibly artful, at least until the ashes started dropping down her blouse. "Jesus Christ! There's an ember burning my tit!"

Marion's head moved a little, then stopped. Helen jumped into my lap.

"It's agony, darling," Tallulah continued, wiping at the ashes with a cocktail napkin. "Bitter agony—watching everything slip away. Your looks. Your dough. Your mind. Your ass. And having to contend with that sick shit Orson Welles . . ." She looked at me again. "Imagine how she feels. Just imagine . . .

"So you find compensations. The world is full of compensations if you look for them. Hotels, foreign places, new food. New everything. What's so wrong with that? You fall in love a million times—I'm bored to the point of suicide when I'm not in love—and your partners diminish in quality, but at least you keep meeting them and they want you, somebody wants you, and so you snort up lots of buzz and drink lots of drinks and fuck and fuck and fuck and hope for God's sake the lights in the room are dim. 'I cannot see what flowers are at my feet, nor what soft incense hangs upon the boughs, but, in embalmed darkness, guess each sweet.'"

Tallulah was drinking whiskey, and I watched her hold up the squatty glass, waiting for the last drops to descend into her mouth. "We're getting old, Marion. Jesus, it takes balls just to say the words. *Old lady.* It would be bad enough for any woman, anybody, but for us, for us . . ."

Another whiskey was set down in front of her, and the waiter promptly disappeared. "So you let your ass get fat to save your face. Then your arms go. Then your legs start to go about the time your face finally does—and all you've got is your name, darling, and *your voice* oozing with the sound of all the sex and booze and buzz you've ever had. All the kings you've met, the presidents you've kissed . . ."

Tallulah tapped Marion on the shoulder, then lifted her head by the hair and set it back down on top of the silver fox.

"Marion, I wish the fuck you were still conscious. We had *it,* you and I. Chemistry, devastating allure. A light, a youth, a brilliance that has been saved for eternity. 'What men or gods are these? What maidens loth? What mad pursuit? What struggles to escape?' We made people feel something. We gave them desire, dreams. All those beautiful people out there in the dark . . .

"Right, darling?" she said to me.

I shrugged, plucked a cigarette out of Marion's case, and looked at it. The paper seemed so white and clean and smooth.

"God, I was watching TV the other night," Tallulah continued, "and there he was, that fucking Paul Henreid propped up in a dinner jacket looking embalmed. He looked one hundred. Two hundred. And he was desperately trying to be Paul Henreid again, as though anybody cared. He was gassing on about *Casablanca* and how it was written into his contract that Victor Laszlo winds up with Ilsa at the end, but once filming began, he started to worry. And with good reason, darling. *Nobody wants Ilsa to wind up with him instead of Bogart.* That's the beauty of the picture. But Paul was babbling on, oblivious of this—such a hideous bore and pompous windbag. Did he have any fucking chemistry whatsoever? Honestly, the minute he comes on-screen, even in *Now, Voyager,* all one's sexual desire just plummets. He's in a league with Glenn Ford or Donald O'Connor. I mean, darling, who could be more unsexy than Donald O'Connor? The girls make the pictures, darling. And we've never quite realized that fact . . ."

She downed the rest of her whiskey like fruit juice. "But by the end, darling, all you have is your voice. You want to know how to sound like me?"

"Nobody could sound like you," I answered.

"Sure you can, darling. Scream in the desert. Scream and scream. Walk out to the empty middle of nowhere—away from the city lights and car lights, the whole world spinning away from you—and just scream your fucking bloody head off. It's such an appropriate response to life. And also happens to be how you get a voice like mine."

"Just scream."

"Scream and scream, darling," she said, "but at some point, after your legs and ass and face, your voice will go too. Or mine did. Wretched ending. Whatever you do, darling, don't get emphysema. I was on oxygen and cigarettes, bourbon and cocaine and codeine, and so fucked up one night, I lit one of my dogs on fire . . . With a cigarette. *An accident.* You know, darling, those sunglasses make you look vaguely crazy."

"Thanks," I said.

"I can't see your eyes, darling. My audience is veiled."

"I'm still here. I'm listening. Go on. Your voice. That's all you have . . ."

"And memories, darling. All the men, the women, all one's lovers. I may not have made many movies, darling, but I beat the rest of them in lovers. Only Louise Brooks and Grace Kelly might have come close . . ."

I put the cigarette in my mouth. Nearly a year without

one. I looked around for a book of matches, then settled on the votive candle in front of me.

"Garbo slept with nobody, of course," Tallulah continued. "She had her period every week, they said. That was the source of her agony, darling—the great pain that she communicated so well on the screen, the silent torment. Cramps. But she had a voice, didn't she?"

She took the candle from my hands and lit her own cigarette. She looked at Marion's head again, and her eyes were sort of sad, or angry, or something. I couldn't tell. Her voice was way out front, it seemed, and the rest of her was very far away.

"Late at night, I used to lie in bed and listen to the radio shows," she said. "And sometimes I'd call in and talk to the hosts and guests and send people money. A bighearted drunk, just like her"—she pointed at Marion. "She gave money to everybody—orphans, widows, hospitals, animal shelters. She sent everybody through college—her cooks, her maids, her gardener's kids. And at the end she had a whole army of leeches living off her—sisters, stepsisters, brothers-in-law, aunts, cousins, nephews. The Good Ship Marion. She was a sweet person—generous, kindhearted."

Tallulah laughed demonically. "That counts for a lot, as it turns out," she said. "Something Orson discovered a little too late." She was still laughing when I motioned to the waiter for the bill.

"Of course, darling, I'm no picnic. Whoever said 'A day away from Tallulah is like a month in the country'?"

She exhaled a long plume of smoke, and her mind seemed to drift after it. "I've had lots of time for reflection. Eons and eons. You know what brought me almost as much joy as acting?"

"What?"

"Taking drugs and watching soap operas on TV in the afternoon." She paused. "Come on, darling. Have some buzz. I've got pills and powders. All kinds. And I won't take no for an answer."

———

It was getting late when I realized my cell-phone battery had died. The room was starting to spin a little too. I don't remember leaving the table. There was a blurry exchange with the waiter, a fumbling for the *Flame* credit card. I remember yanking Marion to her feet, calling for her cloak. I remember carrying Helen to the door.

Afterward, I found an old public telephone in a dark hallway. It had an old-fashioned dial—no buttons—and the mouthpiece smelled sour. But that could have been my nose.

"Who's this?" Franklin asked formally.

"It's me."

"Oh. You sound weird. Bad connection or something," he said. "I returned the car."

"What car?"

"The wood-paneled station wagon. Are you all right? You sound strange."

"Been drinking," I said. "Wasted, actually."

He was quiet for a few seconds. "Your voice has a very nice boozy sweetness, come to think of it. Maybe you should drink more often. In any case, Tom Swimmer says hello. He was there at the house when I brought the car back."

"How was he?"

"The same. He had that cheerful disoriented look, like he'd just heard a very loud sound and was waiting for his head to clear. By the way, as long as you're drunk, I might as well tell you that Ed is a maniac. I was going to wait until you'd left New York, but as long as you're sounding so sweet and pliant . . ."

"What now?"

"I think it was the kiss—which is still news out here. There's even some fresh footage, I'm afraid, new angles with spittle. Actually, there's a shot of you straddling the motorbike and I'm afraid your frock is hiked up and your knickers are showing, and *like that*. At any rate, the outlets were calling Ed's office. And Swimmer began calling, trying to find his car. After that, Ed sort of deepened into a more profound rage. He said he'd left several messages at the Carlyle and you weren't calling back. When he was talking about it, I think I heard him throw something across the room."

"Oh my."

"Oh yes. I must say, it's been loads of fun."

e picked up right away. I didn't hear anything unusual in his voice, only the end-of-the-world sound of Radiohead in the background of his long pauses. He was working late, closing the May issue.

"Where are you?" he asked.

"Three blocks away."

"Asia de Cuba?"

"Keens Steakhouse."

There was a pause. "The place with all the pipes on the ceiling?"

"That's right," I said, trying to sound as sober as possible, but at the same time, a string of bizarre thoughts had started to bombard my mind, beginning with the sudden perception that fame had made me irresistible. "There's Teddy Roosevelt's pipe and Will Rogers's pipe . . . Pipes everywhere I look, but no Ed Nostrum pipe. It's so lonely here."

He laughed uncomfortably. "What's that sound?"

"I'm smoking."

———

The Morgan was spare and open in the way that Keens was not, and it didn't feel haunted by anything except maybe Ian Schrager's sensitive taste. I don't remember getting there, really. I could have walked and didn't. The mist had turned heavy, almost rain.

Ed was in the lobby when I arrived. He looked sort of bored, or serious, or maybe just sober. His raincoat was soggy, and his hair was wet—his forelock hanging down, sort of limp and not knowing what to do with itself. When he saw me enter, he ran a beefy hand against his head and smoothed things back in a nice way that he never could have planned.

"Those sunglasses are too much," he said.

"So is your hair."

He leaned down and gave me a kiss on the cheek. There was something reserved about it, withdrawn. If I hadn't been so numb (yet strangely alive), I might have been bothered by his excruciatingly polite expression. With Ed, formality—a type of accentuated good manners—tended to precede difficulties. It meant that sharp barbs were coming, a frozen silence. He liked to manufacture tension—seemed to need a struggle—maybe because it helped him dominate the conversation. I knew all that and didn't care.

I gently pawed his coat. "You're all wet," I said. And then I must have giggled.

"You're in an unusually cheery mood," Ed said. "You're actually smiling, aren't you? A smile. Wow. I don't think I've seen one of those in over a year. Am I coming in on the second half of a drinking orgy?"

"Oh, a few Cosmopolitans. A few cigarettes."

"And your drinking companion? Am I allowed to know with whom you reached this giddy state of enlightenment?"

"An old actress," I said. "A couple of old actresses— movie stars, actually. You wouldn't know them."

"No?"

"'Vagaries of Fame.' It was a liquid lunch, I mean a working drunk."

"Not Max Coleman?" Ed asked, leaning in my direction while he took off his dripping coat. "Clem, you smell like an old fireplace. On Drudge, there's a picture of you and Max walking down Fifth Avenue together this afternoon. Have you seen it?"

I shook my head.

"Should we go around to Asia de Cuba—dinner?"

"So loud in there."

"It's loud everywhere."

"So what's the picture like?"

"You're not the most attractive pair. It's a little scary, actually. Coleman has a blond fright wig on. You're propping each other up."

"Really? I don't think we were on Fifth Avenue."

"It's you and Max Coleman and his dog. Trust me," Ed said. "My God, Clementine. Next time you decide to get that trashed, at least use a car service."

———

How to make sense of the day, the night, the in-between—how to describe it in a way that's believable and true but also doesn't make me terribly unsympathetic? To attempt this, I must return for a moment to Tallulah and Marion.

I was carrying Helen, that quivering little sausage, in my arms. I was walking to the front door—and just as I should have been pausing at the coat check to retrieve my old camel coat, I followed Tallulah and Marion outside just as they were about to disappear into the brume. I asked an obvious question, I suppose.

"Any regrets?"

Tallulah sucked on a cigarette and then took Helen from me. "Marion," she said, "answer that."

"What?" Marion smiled.

"Any regrets, darling? The reporter wants to know. For her book. You know."

"Regrets? Not really, baby." Marion giggled. "We had fun."

———

The noise inside Asia de Cuba was blinding, and the food didn't seem meant to eat. Nobody really eats at such places, anyway. They go to be there and fight the noise and look at each other. They go to become the people they want to be, actors on a dimly lit restaurant stage.

Ed held a tiny red plastic sword that he'd pulled from the olives in his drink, while I described the interior of Max Coleman's brownstone. When I got to Allegra's poster of Steve McQueen, he interrupted.

"McQueen. That's not bad," he said. "Who was yours?"

"Who was my what?"

"Your first movie star?'

"My first . . . ?"

"The first one you fell in love with," he said.

"That's so personal."

"I know."

"It's like a Barbara Walters question."

"Love. Not a crush."

I didn't say anything.

"It's Lee Marvin, isn't it? I remember the poster from *The Wild Bunch* in your apartment. You like guys in jeans who shoot guns and tequila. And they have to walk a certain way."

"No, I don't. And Lee Marvin isn't in *The Wild Bunch.*"

"*Dirty Harry.* Clint Eastwood."

"No."

"John Wayne."

I just looked at him. I noticed a colleague from *Flame* walking into the bar. It was a researcher, a young girl, a friend of Franklin's. She looked at me, and then Ed, and then began staring at the floor.

"Arnold Schwarzenegger. Sly Stallone."

"Now you're being cruel."

"You're right. They aren't macho enough."

"I'm not into this game."

"I have it," he said. "Rhett Butler." And then he leaned across the small café table and put his hands on either side of my face. " 'Scarlett, I want to take your head between my hands . . .' "

"You're close," I said.

"Gable."

I didn't say anything.

"I knew it was Gable. That explains why you like me so much."

———

Fritz was waiting for us outside in his black Lincoln Towncar. He had been Ed's driver for a long time, since the *Journal.* He was a Jamaican with a shaved head and an accent that Ed and I used to imitate when he wasn't around.

"Hey, Miss James," Fritz said with a big smile. "You doing so great! You so famous now. Saw you on TV last night with dat new boyfriend."

Ed was folding his raincoat and laying it flat on the seat, pretending that he wasn't listening.

"Tom Swimmer," Fritz continued. "I like dat show. *Left on La Brea*. Berry funny."

"He's not my boyfriend, Fritz," I said.

"No?"

"Oh no," I said. "Just a one-night stand."

Fritz started shrieking. "Oh, you so funny. Always so funny. I miss you, Miss James."

I stepped into the car. Ed was looking at me, watching me get in.

"Allegra—she been missin' a long time," Fritz continued. "She dead? She gettin' dat Oscar? Dey say she get it for *Sphinxa*. I saw dat movie. Why anybody make a movie like dat?"

"I don't know," I said. "I liked it."

Ed was quiet.

"Can dey give an Oscar to somebody who dead?"

"Why not?" I said.

Ed clicked off his reading light. He moved closer to me and whispered, "Quit talking to Fritz."

"You think she alive?" Fritz asked. He was pulling away from the curb.

"Sure," I said. "She's too big to die."

Fritz changed lanes and drove the dark car up Madison.

It was beautifully quiet, finally—until Ed started talking. He went on about the All-Allegra issue, which he seemed inordinately proud of. ("What will I do after that?" he said. "It's so upsetting to watch yourself peak.") Then he talked about the vigil and the afterparties—which seemed like ages ago, not two nights.

"Bancrofts was kind of fun," he said. "Brad and Jenny were there. George and Julia. I got to meet Frank Sinatra, Jr. But the deal at Johnny Mast's was a little too *Hollywood Babylon* for me. Johnny had a gaggle of girls that I think he paid to be there—or they paid him. God, don't these girls have parents? I'd be horrified if Letitia dressed like that."

Letitia was Ed's daughter—fifteen or sixteen. She did well at Andover and had small thoughtful eyes.

"It's so depressing out there, isn't it? People seem so disconnected from everything—from the past, the news, the world, even the *weather.* And when they try to say something intelligent, it's usually about the interconnectedness of all things." He paused and waited for me to say something, but I didn't. "The small-screen types are the worst," he said.

Swimmer. It was all about him.

"I hate that L.A.-cool act too. Nobody wants to look like they give a shit," he went on. "They're convinced that they're living at the center of cool and the center of everything else."

I cleared my throat. "But you're at the center, Ed. Not them."

"That's right. *I am* the center." He laughed a little, seeming loosened up by the joke. "But really, Clem, I don't see how you've endured all these months. Two months, three months—how long has it been? How can you bear it out there? I'm always so anxious to escape."

"It's been okay," I said. "Not too bad."

"It always amazes me," he said, "how the movies can be so profound and the people who make them seem so cheesy."

I thought about that line for a long time afterward. Maybe it was the only thing Ed said that ever made complete sense.

"My Bio-eye is almost ready," I said. "Might as well stay out there for that."

"And then?" Ed leaned toward me. I felt his thigh against my thigh. I could feel his breath. "Don't tell me you're still planning to move to Virginia and train dogs."

"It's a horse farm," I said.

He fiddled with his tie. "Franklin says things aren't great between you and Nick."

"No, they aren't. His name is Ned."

"The Swimmer thing must have pissed—"

"It wasn't about that."

"No?"

"No," I said. "I don't think he even knows about that."

"He doesn't know? Is he alive? My brother called from Tangier to ask about it."

I'm not sure when we arrived at the Carlyle, partly because I was on his lap and we were already kissing. Our mouths had been open a long time, for many blocks of the ride, which had finally, thankfully, become quiet. I remember thinking that his lap felt warm. His eyes looked black and kind of lost, and I could smell the gin and the Altoids, and I remembered all over again what it was like, kissing Ed—the way it always comes back to you after it's been a long time. It wasn't so bad, but it wasn't so incredible either. Kind of empty, a little automatic. And suddenly the car became very still, and I looked out the window and saw that we had stopped, and that Fritz was talking to the Carlyle doorman under the awning. The lights of the hotel seemed very bright.

"Clem, where's your coat?" Ed said when he handed me my sunglasses. "Is it in front?"

"No, it's gone."

"I'll send Fritz back."

"It's not there either," I said. "It's somewhere else." I thought about the coat check at Keens, and my old camel coat stuck between the coats of other revelers, interred forever under the soft dim light, being marinated by all that smoke next to the little Dutch door with its shelf and wicker baskets of bills. And it made me glad.

———

I watched Ed's face while he tried to put the hotel robe around me and tie it. I was sitting on the edge of the bed. His black eyes, the high wide expanse of forehead. The hair—and all the vanity and tragedy and humor that seemed embedded in the atoms of it.

The door opened. A crack of light came in. The door clicked closed. I was in the dark again. Alone.

I found a note in the morning, after a long night of strange dreams, which were full of secrets that I kept from myself. The note was crumpled and under my head on the pillow. I must have rolled over it several times in the night.

C—

You never told me who your first movie star was.

E.

CHAPTER 19

The room was dark in the way that only hotel rooms can be—the sort of sunless void you can never fully achieve at home. In the night, I could feel the darkness pressing on my face, surrounding me, lifting me upward. There were no faint sounds in the corridor, no swoosh of an elevator on its cable, no wheels of a maid's cart. I floated beyond my bed, somewhere amid sleep and numbness and death. My dreams were drunken and borrowed and strung together like beads.

I was walking in Monument Valley against a spare landscape of a John Ford Western. It was a black-and-white dream—with strong shadows and blinding sunlight, a wide and open sky. I was on a horse and riding alongside Wyatt

Earp, except he was also Henry Fonda. His hair was black. He needed a shave. He sang the song that people always sing to me, but the later stanzas that almost nobody knew:

> *Ruby lips above the water,*
> *Blowing bubbles soft and fine,*
> *But alas, I was no swimmer,*
> *So I lost my Clementine.*
>
> *In my dreams she still doth haunt me,*
> *Robed in garments soaked in brine;*
> *Though in life I used to hug her,*
> *Now she's dead, I draw the line.*

Then I was in the audience of a small theater. It was the talent show in *Viva Las Vegas,* and Ann-Margret was shimmying before me onstage in a one-piece bathing suit and heels. I stayed in my seat, but the theater changed, and I was in the front row at the Follies, and there were Busby Berkeley dancing girls, all white feathers and loose sequins, moving in a circle, twirling and being spun, a birthday cake alive with women and white light. Joan Crawford was a girl, twirling. Louise Brooks and Marion Davies and Mae Murray, twirling. Hedy Lamarr, Billie Dove . . .

Sometimes the actresses called out to me as they twirled. They stretched their arms toward me, as if beckoning me to the stage. Joan Crawford was excruciatingly young and fresh. Her eyes were wet and still looking outward—open, hungry, like the world held something she wanted to eat. Her arms were so thin they looked like they might break. Her mascara was thick, her eyelashes looked like spikes. She knelt down at the footlights. "All I ever cared about," she whispered, "was dancing."

Then I was at Keens again—but it was crowded, jammed with people. I saw Lee Marvin and Burt Lancaster at a table near the bar. They'd taken off their holsters and pistols and draped them on the back of their chairs, like they were in between takes of *The Professionals*. Raoul Walsh came up to my table. The director was older, wearing his eye patch. He pointed at me, nodded, then walked on. Kay Francis came around too. Her hair was bobbed and slicked back, the way she wore it in movies like *Girls About Town* and *Man Wanted*. Her dark eyes were languid and knowing. A little sullen. She leaned forward and, with the faintest lisp, said: "Yes, it's true. I can't wait to be forgotten."

I was walking down a street. It was dark, foggy. It was Ed's street, in the Eighties on the East Side, and in my dream I stepped inside the shining lobby of his apartment building and found Mary Astor standing at the door to the elevator looking at me with that meek, intense stare of hers. It was that *Maltese Falcon* gaze; she seemed guilty of something. She was wearing a felt hat. She smiled thinly. She handed me a copy of her book.

"Oh, thanks," I said.

214 ★ MARTHA SHERRILL

"I've signed it to you."

"Thank you," I said in my dream. "Very kind." But I didn't want her book. I'd already read it, was already sick of her. At seventeen, she falls in love with John Barrymore—her first big mistake but followed by so many more. She has trouble with drinking, is increasingly dependent upon psychiatry. She converts to Catholicism. Her book was unusual and smart and thoughtful, the product of a good mind or a good education or a good ghostwriter.

"I'm tired," I said. "So very tired. Can't you go?"

The next time I looked down, my clothes were different. I was dressed in very fine white chiffon—a robe or nightgown with enormously baggy sleeves, like deflated silk balloons. I sat down at a vanity and looked in the mirror. I was an actress in my dream, and I was playing Greta Garbo—her long face, her lanky, liquid movements, and tired, oh so very sad and tired—and the movie was *Grand Hotel,* because John Barrymore was in the dream too. He had a small dog with him, a King Charles spaniel or a dachshund, I couldn't tell which. Barrymore was hiding behind the curtain in my hotel room. He was a hotel thief. And he was stealing my pearls.

—

The curtains of my room were pulled open with a screech. It was a metallic sound, aggressive and awful, and the sunlight exploded inside the room as though I were suddenly under interrogation and being tortured with strong light. I had been slumbering or dead—and now forced alive. My coffin lid creaked open.

I heard the crackling of paper under my head. It was loud, violent crackling. I was shocked to see Ed's handwriting. Ed? Was he in my room? Then I remembered and grew instantly fretful. It was the way of all hangovers—frantic thoughts, regrets circulating. And where was my coat?

I needed to call Franklin. I needed a reservation and an airplane ticket, an avenue of escape. I needed to call Max. I wanted to see if Max could meet for lunch instead of dinner. Where should I go once I got to L.A.? I was finished with Casa del Mar.

Sounds came from the hallway of my $1,100-a-night "junior" suite. Sounds near the minibar. The stirring of an ice bucket. The mixing of liquids. I was thirsty, so thirsty. But then I smelled something warm and spicy. Not hotel soap but perfume. Shalimar. It was a smell I hadn't smelled in a long time, years, twenty years, since my mother. It was this smell, I think, mixed with the memory of cigarettes, that made me suddenly sick.

The floor of the bathroom had black and white interlocking marble tiles. The tiles were warm, almost hot, from the pipes running underneath. That's where I wound up—sort of crouching on my knees with my elbows shaking on the edge of the toilet seat. My head was bent over the bowl. I watched a long string of spit leading from my mouth to the water.

I heard ice again.

Ice in a glass.

A woman was holding a tray and standing over me. Her red hair scared me. It was so red that it looked colorized. It was so red that I barely knew who she was.

"That's awfully cute," the woman said. I wasn't dreaming anymore. Myrna Loy was real, so very real. "Is that a new yoga posture," she said, "or are you trying to flush yourself down the toilet headfirst?"

She was wearing evening sandals with ankle straps and, above them, a long blue satin sheath. Atop her fabulous head was a black peaked felt cap with a feather.

In a quick gesture, she handed me a towel. I wiped my face.

"Come on now," she said. "You're better already. I can see that. Time to stand up. I brought you a glass of my very own hangover cure. Nectar of the gods. Ingredients to remain secret."

I pulled myself up slowly and looked at the tray. "I hate tomato juice."

"For one thing, it isn't tomato juice"—she pronounced it "toe-MAH-toe." "For another thing, don't be a brat. There's pineapple in it, some ginger too. It's good for you. A great tonic for those in spiritual decline. If you'll get back in bed, I'll give you an ice bag for your pounding headache. I'm taking a wild guess that you have one."

—

The others' visits had been intrusions. They disturbed a natural flow of some kind, a flow of life, of energy. And they demanded inordinate attention, as though every atom of my being were needed to fill the seats of a large stadium inside their minds. Their eyes fixed on me with great need. They watched for boredom, signs of disaffection. They bent themselves like a 360-degree flashing billboard, surrounding me on all sides. They were misshapen—curiosities, freaks, loonies visiting from the fringe of a John Waters movie. But in just a few minutes, I could tell Myrna was different.

"I won't bother you," she said as soon as she'd gotten me back in bed. "I'll just sit in my little corner and read." She walked to the next room, where the sun was coming in the windows and a blue velvet love seat and chair were awash in golden light. She picked up a book. She was reading Ibsen.

The minutes passed quickly. The ice pack grew slushy and began slipping off my head. I finished the nectar and set it down on the nightstand, streaks of pineapple and tomato pulp running down the sides of the glass.

As I waited for breakfast to arrive, I began to devise ways to get Myrna back in the room. So we could talk, so she could talk—so I could listen to her voice again and watch her up close. Whatever she was made of, it was solid. The part of her that was Myrna Loy was Myrna Loy throughout—not a veneer or an act or a triviality conjured for the screen. She wasn't a still-photographs kind of beauty like Lamour.

She didn't communicate with her shoulders and chin, like Swanson. She was stationary, stable—except for her eyebrows and her voice. And with these she could do anything.

But people called and people knocked and the outside world intervened—and once it had, there was no stopping it. Breakfast arrived, along with the newspapers. The *Daily News* ran a picture of me walking alongside Max Coleman, both of us hunched, making our way through the cold. Max's face looked frail and he was wearing his shabby kimono. My face was entirely covered by my hair, except for the eye patch. Underneath, in very large typeface, it said: EVERY DAY IS HALLOWEEN.

"Would you look at that," Myrna said.

A few seconds later, an enormous vase of white lilies was delivered to the room—the smell made me immediately sick—along with an impressively large and elegant box from designer Gaston La Fille. Inside, I found a long red cashmere coat with epaulets and gold buttons. "Don't lose this one," Ed's note said. He had also enclosed a preview copy of *Flame*'s All-Allegra issue.

Myrna fiddled with the lilies, sort of rearranged the arrangement. I kept the coat on and flipped through the new issue of *Flame*.

The images were dazzling. The array was dizzying. The colors were rich, deep, redolent of winter and summer and life being lived marvelously, in fullness and extremes.

The layout was stupendous—mesmerizing, haunting, compelling, fulfilling. Each page seemed more miraculous than the next, and I could tell, even as I first held the issue in my hands, that it was Ed's masterpiece, the culmination of all his talent and imagination, probably a bit of his heart too.

He'd assembled a remarkable cluster of never-before-seen pictures of her. Allegra at various ages and stages of self-awareness. There were stills from her movies, on-location "candids," and a lengthy black-and-white series of Stieglitz-like soft-focus photographs taken in Riverside, inside rooms at the Mission Inn. Allegra was naked in most of them. We saw her hands clasped. Her long legs akimbo. Her elbows. The bend of her knee. The back of her neck. We saw her breasts triumphant and rubbing up against a rug.

At the front of the magazine and again toward the back were photographs of her family and friends—and the supporting cast of the unfolding Allegra drama, like planets orbiting her sun.

The Michaels were photographed inside Musso & Frank's on Sunset. Margaux was wearing white leotards at the Vivekananda yoga studio. Max Coleman was in his Ava Pillbox outfit, performing in a club. There were pictures of Kay Blyth as the child star of *Tarzan in Hollywood*.

And the group photos: Manny and Moe and the rest of the Kern County sheriff's office. Allegra's boyfriends of the past three years, seven of them, lined up along Hollywood Boulevard's Walk of Fame, including Joaquin Phoenix, Storm Rockefeller, Tom Swimmer, and Charles Bronson—a boyfriend I hadn't known about or figured on. Where had they met?

Then I found myself. I was spread across two pages—sequential pictures from the day with La Grange. I was sideways in the orange chair, my face in profile. In the next photo, I was turned toward the camera. My hair looked very large, very *Valley of the Dolls*. My eye patch was slightly crooked. It was a startling image in which my injury, my freakishness, and my somewhat chilly persona were fully exposed and exploited.

Franklin was fully awake when I reached him, and seemed energized by my latest descent.

"Fabulous headline—don't you think? 'Halloween Every Day.' I must admit I laughed aloud."

"I'm not talking about that picture. I'm talking about the April issue."

"Allegra? You saw it?"

"Just now."

"You don't like it?"

I said nothing.

"What?" he said defensively. "I love the hair. I love the chair. The whole thing is wild. Very *Barbarella*."

"Have you talked to Ed?"

"Just a while ago, actually. He woke me. He seems to enjoy doing that. Anyway, he said he saw you last night and that you looked fabulous. I think that's how he said it. Might have been *absolutely* fabulous. But he was reeking of enthusiasm. He was positively discreet otherwise—neglecting to mention that you were pawing each other in the darkness of Asia de Cuba like young lovers."

"Oh God." Then I remembered the researcher from *Flame* who'd been at the restaurant. "Don't start in. I can't bear it."

"You sound so desperate."

"We weren't pawing each other," I said. "Everybody at *Flame* must have heard by now."

"From what I gather, your sunglasses were so dark, it's entirely possible that you didn't fully realize what you were doing." He let out a wicked laugh.

"We weren't *pawing.* That's ridiculous. Besides, what we do—or did—isn't anybody's business."

"Of course not," Franklin said. "I never said we were making it our business. It's our amusement."

I looked up and saw Myrna in the next room. After perfecting the lilies and approving the coat, she had drifted back to the sitting room, by the sunny window. Against the blue love seat, her hair looked fiery. She was completely engrossed in the All-Allegra issue.

"Hey," I said to Franklin in a quiet voice, "we never talked about Myrna Loy."

"Why are you whispering?"

"Did you ever find her book?"

"Wait," he said. I heard his hands on a computer key-board. "Oh."

"What?"

"It's Max Coleman."

"What?"

"He was admitted to St. Vincent's last night."

CHAPTER 20

We circled the hospital in a cab, looking for a discreet way inside. Camera crews were waiting in bored clumps, dotting the exterior of the drab brown-brick building like large shrubs. They wore black jeans and polar fleece, carried bags of camera equipment, folding chairs, stepladders. At first I assumed a horrible accident had taken place downtown, an explosion, another bombing. What else could it be?

But as our cab approached St. Vincent's, easing up slowly to the white curb for unloading, I caught sight of a reporter gaping at me—gaping as though I weren't a person, really, but a billboard. He studied me the way a museum curator studies a fake or a bargain hunter scans the shelves for markdowns. A call rang out through the crowd—a kind of shriek, an animal yell—followed by hollering and a dramatic turning of heads, like a wave sweeping through the audience at a football stadium. I told the driver to press on, continue past the hospital, and circle around.

"Sticky little mess," said Myrna as our cab rounded the corner. She said it in the droll way she said everything. There was something comforting about her consistent lack of excitement.

"Just wondering how to get inside," I said.

"Scale the walls?" she said.

I leaned forward to talk to the driver through the foggy Plexiglas divider. "Is there another entrance—on the back or side of the hospital?"

"Where's triage?" asked Myrna.

"There's an emergency entrance." His eyes looked at me in the rearview mirror. They were light brown or green. "It's on Seventh."

"Let's do that."

"Fans are so loyal. They're always there, wherever you go, wherever you turn," Myrna said. She chuckled, then uncrossed her jodhpurs and paddock boots, the aviator's costume she wore in *Too Hot to Handle.* "But you get used to it. And you even start to miss them—when they go away."

"Not me," I said.

It started to drizzle. Backslashes of rain appeared on the windshield. We made it to Greenwich Avenue and got stuck in traffic. Myrna continued, "Drunks drooling over you in bars. Corporate titans sending bottles of champagne in restaurants, looking at you across the room with their tight smiles. Notes written on business cards or napkins. And let's not forget the autograph collectors . . . People lined up at your lunch table with scraps of paper, pages torn from books. I signed a Bible once."

At first she had insisted on driving—she had "access" to a car nearby, she claimed. When I refused, she decided to ride along as far as the hospital. She had a way of being pushy and getting her way without being annoying. As we had left the Carlyle together, nobody seemed to notice us or care. When we stepped outside on the curb, a cab was waiting with its back door already open.

"After 1936, when Ed Sullivan proclaimed me Queen of the Movies, I had to stop shopping at Macy's," she said, carefully watching the pedestrians on the street as though they were visiting from Mars. "I'd walk in the store and be mobbed by the time I got to the handbags. The store manager called and asked that I not return. The police were tired of doing crowd control. I was instructed to place my orders over the phone. And if I ever needed to shop in person, special arrangements would be made so I could come after hours." She grimaced, wrinkling her upturned nose.

"That's not so bad," I said.

"Oh, but not the same. Have you ever shopped in an empty store with two store managers following you around like prison guards? It's lonely. Creepy too. I remember being sick with a horrible head cold once and watching an episode of *The Twilight Zone* where Anne Francis gets trapped inside a department store overnight. In the morning, she's been turned into a plastic mannequin."

Myrna did her grimace again and looked like she was chewing on her tongue. "But you're not really famous until you have to bag your own trash. That's always the watershed."

I could still see the eyes of the driver in the rearview mirror. He was listening. And then he started nodding.

"Bag your trash?" I asked. "I don't get it."

"If you leave your dirty dental floss around," she said, "or napkins and nail clippings in the hotel trash can, the maids will paw through everything and sell the relics. So you bag your own. Only at hotels, of course. And if I were traveling with my own maid, I'd ask her to do it. Tennessee Williams told me Vivien Leigh's technique when she was making *Streetcar.* She used those dry-cleaning bags—and shoe bags—in the hotel closet."

I shook my head kind of slowly, in disbelief.

"Otherwise, you're just asking for problems," she continued. "I blew my nose into a handkerchief at Nickodell's once, then forgot it on my seat. I heard later that the kitchen staff fought over it."

I caught the driver's eyes again. He seemed to be studying my response. It wasn't until he'd pulled in at the entrance on Seventh and I was getting out of the cab that I noticed he'd turned off the meter.

"How much do we owe?" I asked him.

He waved his hand. "Don't bother, sweetheart."

———

The emergency room seemed crowded at first, but only with the truly sick. The waiting room was full of people—holding their heads, holding their abdomens, rocking back and forth. A few of them were waiting on stretchers, in neck braces and back braces and with their clothes ripped open in places. I suppose if I hadn't just spent six weeks in a hospital, I might have been unsettled by the scene. Instead, it felt like a homecoming—another hotel, a maze I knew—and I navigated its corridors as though I'd been living in St. Vincent's all my life. I walked beyond the boundaries of the ER and through a hallway leading to an elevator that took us to the main information desk. Behind it was a young guy with a goatee and creamy brown skin and a blue hospital jacket. The name on his badge was Felix.

"I'm here to see a patient who checked in yesterday," I said. "Max Coleman."

Felix looked skeptical. "Visiting hours are over soon," he said while looking down at a computer screen. "I'll need to see some ID."

As I dug for my wallet, Felix's eyes fell on Myrna. He squinted at her.

"You have ID?" he asked.

"No," she said.

He stared at her for another moment. "You look familiar."

"I am familiar." She gave him a hypnotizing look—amused and mocking at once—that I guessed was supposed to put him off. But it didn't.

"I'm serious," he said.

"So am I." Myrna smiled mysteriously.

Felix looked at my driver's license and handed it back. "Mr. Coleman left word that only his daughter was allowed entrance to his room. I'll have to call his floor for approval."

He tapped a pencil on its eraser, looked at Myrna again. "I got it," he said. "You're married to Warren Beatty, aren't you?"

———

Max's eyes were closed when I stepped into his room. I was alone—Myrna had disappeared—and Max looked very thin under the white bedsheets, delicate and small. It was jarring to see him stripped of his surroundings—his baroque furniture, his paintings, his Aphrodite, the piles of magazines and cheerful sunlight of his brownstone. Because of all the hubbub outside, the milling reporters on simultaneous deathwatch and Allegra watch, I had expected to see more signs of life and interest in Max. But no flowers had come, no cards or other tokens of affection from well-wishers, friends, or family. Max was stretched out, his legs and bony knees covered with a dingy cotton blanket the color of pea soup. He was breathing steadily, slowly.

And under the fluorescent lights, his skin looked rubbery and unreal and vaguely yellow. There were bruises and some swelling on the top of his left wrist where somebody, a nurse I suppose, had botched the placement of an IV tube.

His eyes weren't completely shut but at half-mast. And then they fluttered open. "Clem. You're here. Clem! I hoped to see you today. I love the sunglasses, darling. I'm just out the door. I'm going home," he said. "Care to join?"

Max was determined to die at home, it seemed. Or he seemed determined to die, period. There was no talking positive, no upbeat proclamation of imminent recovery, no discussion of a possible untried cure in a faraway country. Just good humor, a kind of bemused acknowledgment, a resignation, I suppose, about some inevitable journey he didn't seem remotely afraid of. And I remember thinking, as I watched Max gather strength and wobble to the bathroom, then dress in his winter kimono and tights, how much easier it was to be around a sick person who wasn't trying so desperately to be well again, a person who wasn't exhausting everybody around him with lies and fairy tales and endless great pretending.

It took several hours door to door, from the beginning of the journey at St. Vincent's back to Grove Street. It was only seven blocks away but miles of paperwork. There was also a delay as we waited for Max's hospice worker, a nurse and caregiver, to arrive. Dudus was his name. A middle-aged African American guy with the body of a pro wrestler.

"Did I hear that right?" Max asked. "*Dudus?* How interesting . . . sort of a gladiator name, isn't it?"

Dudus picked Max up like a bag of cotton candy, gently dropped him into a wheelchair, then pushed him out the door and down the corridor so quickly that I had to run to keep up. Waiting for the elevator, Max reached out for my hand. "Sorry I messed up our lunch," he said. His fingers felt lean and long and warm. He looked at my face for what seemed like a long time.

"Oh, Clem, you so remind me of Paulette Goddard, minus the sunglasses, of course. What was that ridiculous movie of hers that I loved? *Babes in Bagdad.* So gorgeously campy."

"I thought I looked like Kay."

"Oh, sure. Her too. And if she'd been half as sane as you are, my dear, I never would have left."

"And today," I said, "you're reminding me of Melvyn Douglas in *Being There.*"

"That good? Not bad for a dying queen." He patted my hand. "You'll stay for dinner, won't you? Please stay. You're such a sturdy girl, Clem. Such a fine old-fashioned stoic."

"You don't think I'm too tough?"

"You?"

CHAPTER 21

Max wanted to be near his terrace—and his garden. He wanted sunshine, he said, although it only poured rain. When the hospital bed arrived— a rollaway on wheels—Dudus and I moved away stacks of old magazines and newspapers in the mourning room, a cluster of gold shoes still lined up against the wall, a Louis XIV side table and its surface debris, along with several peeling gilt chairs. We made a clearing for Max by the tall windows, where he could see the fig tree with its empty perch.

Once in bed, Max drifted off to sleep. The afternoon had been tiring—the preparations for departure, the papers to sign, the crowds of fans and cameras and curious pedestrians at the curb outside the hospital, not to mention the policeman who seemed a bit too eager for overtime pay. As we wheeled Max into an Odyssey minivan, he turned to me. "The longer she's gone, the more famous we become. Have you thought of that?"

Max snored while the rain poured down. Swinging above him, next to the bed, was a bag of clear liquid and a tube leading to his left arm. Rita was curled near the wheels of the rollaway. Dudus retreated to the kitchen, where he did dishes quietly. He could part a sea of reporters with one swoop of his ham-hock arm—and it was sweet, almost comic, watching him do small things like dishes, or handling the amber bottles of tiny pills and studying their tiny labels, then making marks on his chart with a pencil dwarfed by his beefy hand.

I sat at the kitchen table nearby, eating a sandwich, and soon afterward felt drowsy. I was still hungover and stretched out on a long Empire sofa that was more comfortable than it looked.

I thought about calling Ned. I wanted to call, but it was hard to know what to say. Or maybe I was afraid. While I pondered this, kind of randomly, I looked across the cluttered room at *Dawn*—so dreamy, haunting, achingly so—until I fell asleep.

Max woke me up calling for Dudus. "Doodus. Doooodus . . ." A toilet flushed down the hallway. A door opened.

"Oh, there you are, Dudus," Max said. "How about some TV? Can we bring one in here?"

A large television was hauled into the mourning room.

It took Dudus a few minutes to arrange the wires in back, and while he did, I moved a chair beside Max and brought him some green tea. He didn't drink it, though. He just looked at the foaming green water like it was a pond he wanted to dive into.

Dudus pressed the power button on the TV, and quite miraculously, we were looking at Ed's face spread across the television screen, large and monstrous. He was being interviewed on an entertainment channel, on a dimly lit, quasi-intellectual talk show about actors and acting and movies.

"Instead of an Oscar issue, we thought this was more exciting," he said with an almost sleepy nonchalance, like an aristocrat in a Van Dyck painting, "and closer to where people's heads are these days."

The interviewer had a beard and glasses and seemed professorial except for the paisley cravat around his neck. He gushed about the All-Allegra issue but in slightly esoteric ways. It was "hype" and "unhype" at the same time. It was a "psychic link to an unforgettable land of enchantment, if you will." He talked about Ed and used words like "genius" and "mastermind" and even "auteur."

Ed deflected the slavering, but another part of him, hidden from the camera but apparent to me, was enjoying every syllable of praise and locking it up inside him like buried treasure. With his mouth, he exalted the work of Gary La Grange, he praised his staff at *Flame*—the photo editor, the art director, the researchers, the staff writers—

referring to "our amazing exclusive access." He praised Allegra too, with depth and apparent sincerity.

"She's not just made more fascinating by her absence," Ed said, "or by all the mystery produced by her absence. She's fascinating because we're seeing a great, great talent rise before our eyes. We're seeing a woman on the threshold of enormous stardom—on the verge of immortality, in a way."

Max and I looked at each other. He opened his mouth and curled his tongue downward, as though about to be sick.

"Fascinating," the interviewer said, stroking his beard.

"And immortality is endlessly seductive," Ed continued in his casual tone. "I can't remember another actor who has risen so quickly—and who also seemed so deeply talented and so immediately mythical. There's a James Dean analogy, I suppose. He's an actor who died very young, of course— at twenty-four—but managed to leave behind three stunning pictures."

"I assume," the interviewer interjected, "you mean *Rebel Without a Cause, East of Eden,* and *Giant.*"

Ed nodded. "Not that I think Allegra Coleman is dead. Actually, I feel very strongly that she's alive. But what I want to say—and I seem to be fumbling around so awkwardly in trying to say it—is that whether this very fine actress ever makes another movie, I believe an important legacy has already been left. *Vices* is being reconsidered as a classic. *Sphinxa* is an unusual and daring picture and obviously a front runner for best picture at the Academy Awards on Sunday. I just saw a screening of *L'Avventura* two days ago in Los Angeles. I doubt there'll be much debate about its greatness. So she's close to something of a James Dean–like trilogy."

James Dean trilogy. Ed liked movies, but I'm not sure he liked them enough to have sat all the way through *Giant.*

I looked over at Max. He was dozing. By the time he woke up again, Ed's face had become a postage stamp at the bottom of the television screen, which was dominated by a clip from *L'Avventura.* Ed was still talking, but it was hard to pay attention to anything he said. The *L'Avventura* sound-track was playing, and the wind was blowing hair into Allegra's face, and she was looking out to sea.

A commercial for a Barbra Streisand film festival came on, scenes from *The Way We Were* and *Yentl.* Max held up the remote and turned it off.

"There are so many brilliant people in the world," he sighed. "So many smart, talented people. The world is teeming with them—the way it's teeming and teeming with rich people. There must be millions and millions of rich people—where do they all come from? You drive around a place like East Hampton or Edgartown, Dallas or Houston or Palm Springs or Bel Air. Go to Miami or Honolulu. Even Minneapolis, for God's sake. Chicago. Everywhere you go, there are all these unimaginative rich people with their cashmere robes living in their cozy slipper worlds. Fancy cars, plasma TVs, the swimming pools and golf courses and tribal rituals involving inebriates. It's all so funny. And rather depressing too."

Dudus was in the kitchen chopping garlic. I could smell it and the olive oil. And a minute later I could hear something sizzling in a pan.

"It goes so quickly," Max said, "the life of the mind, the life of an artist. Life. So many distractions, complications. You think you'll always have your art. I thought I would. *My art.* How could I ever lose that? But then success comes and gets in the way. It gives you more freedom, but it takes away everything else."

Dudus arrived with a dinner plate—two lamb chops sitting in a puddle of balsamic-mint sauce—and set it down on a tray next to Max.

"Very nice," Max said, looking at the plate as though it were a creation that he didn't want to disturb. "Beautiful, Dudus. Thank you."

Dudus nodded once, then set down four red capsules next to Max's napkin and left. Max looked at the capsules and put them in his mouth one at a time.

"The verge of immortality," Max said. "Oh Lordy. It's more like a slow death. Poor Gra-gra's life has seemed like a slow death for a while now. It's been like watching one of those self-sacrifice scenes in a B movie with a bad soundtrack, you know, where the maiden tosses herself into the volcano accompanied by the thumping of drums and blaring of horns? . . .

"She finally saw that, of course. Let's face it, that's what this mystical disappearance is all about. I warned and warned her. Maybe I was a nag. I never wanted to be a stage mother. I just wanted to pass along some wisdom."

"Max, aren't you going to eat something?"

"We all saw what happened to Kay. She wasn't able to handle any of it, you know—the ascent, the descent, or practically anything in between. That much should be obvious to you. She became a joke, really. A laughing-stock. And I assure you, being married to a has-been is only slightly less awful than being married to a full-fledged star. But Gra-gra wanted it. She thought she could handle it, I suppose. Or she thought she could do it a different way, or perhaps she wanted to best her mother at something, which would be the predictable Freudian explanation. But at some point all explanations are limited, like saying that a human being is the result of an egg and sperm coming to-gether. So true—yet so lacking.

"Anyway, you can't ask for anything more than aware-ness and thoughtfulness in a person—in a daughter. Can you? Gra-gra knows what she's doing. She really does."

Max sighed and pushed away the tray. Abruptly there was an eerie sound—scratching, a loud rustling of feathers. A bird flew overhead, an enormous green and red blur that swooped over Max and me and then ascended quickly to the top of the fig tree.

"That's Baby," Max said. "The macaw . . . On loan from Allegra." He rolled his eyes. "She bought her, and I wound up with her . . . but that's okay."

Rita jumped to her feet and began yapping at the foot of the tree.

I looked at *Dawn* again. The colors called to me, sang to me. The bleached golds, the pale blues . . . the thin long stroke of deep indigo. I felt a coolness washing over me, splashing inside me, a rinse of freshness and calm, and when it was over, I wanted it to happen again.

"I like your paintings, Max."

"Why, thank you."

"No, I mean I love them, Max. I really love them. And it seems like I always have."

———

I cried for a long time, alone in my room, thinking about Max and the clear tubes going into his arm, his cheerful tone, the way he insisted that I stay. The way he seemed more himself, not less, while he died. By the time I came out again, he was sleeping and breathing hard. Dudus was asleep in the chair next to him. I turned off a few lights. And then I picked up Rita and carried her into my room, Allegra's room. We sat on the sofa in the dark. Beyond the windows, the moon was full and rising up in the wet cloudy sky like a flashlight under a thin blanket.

Rita jumped off my lap and padded into the closet. A minute later, Myrna emerged. She was wearing a long quilted dressing gown. Her feet were bare. She stared at me for what seemed a long time.

"I used to live here, you know," she said. "After I gave

up movies, after my fourth divorce. I moved to New York City. My theater years. That's how I came to think of them." She sat down on the bed. The moonlight touched the edges of her red hair. "Lots of us were living in New York then. I was great friends with Roddy McDowall and Montgomery Clift. Actually, with Monty, it was a bit more than friends—although I couldn't say exactly what it was. He was confused and sad in the way that Judy was sad and confused—and you'd spend all kinds of time on the phone with them, at all hours of the night, and never get anywhere. It took me a while to realize that. They were just treading water."

Myrna was sitting on a satin comforter, and as she talked, I remember looking down at the satin underneath her. The moonlight spread away from her body in rays of reflected light.

"Joan Crawford used to call. Quite a bit, particularly after her last husband died. She wasn't what you think, you know. She wasn't the way everybody remembers her now. She made herself, scratched her way up the hard way—different from me. I had a refined mother who doted on me, sent me to good schools, exposed me to art. Joan had none of that. She was a shopgirl. She'd been a laundress, a waitress. And she'd won a Charleston dance contest and was discovered by a Hollywood talent scout who got her a pretty nice contract with MGM. In the twenties, when I first saw her in *Our Dancing Daughters,* I remember feeling aware that she didn't belong. She was a success—

the best possible example of the flapper, as F. Scott Fitzgerald said—but she didn't look like the other silent stars. Her face was long and lean. She had a hardness, a muscularity, an angular strength. And yet she was so natural, so totally unaffected.

"I think of her in *Rain*. I think of her in *The Unknown* with Lon Chaney. Oh, these are movies nobody sees anymore. They just roll out the clips when you die. Roddy and I used to watch old pictures together. He had a really fine collection, a lovely screening room . . . *Grand Hotel.* Now, that's Joan Crawford to me. That's the actress I remember—her white silk blouse, the tight dark skirt. Her sweet face and those scared, soulful eyes. I'll always remember the way she looks at the baron when he's on the floor, John Barrymore, the hotel thief, after he's been killed.

"We were the same age, you know. Just a year apart. She was a huge star at twenty-four, and I was still playing exotics. I was the vampire, the Oriental, the gypsy, the Mexican, the South Sea Islander, the murderer, the villain. They actually called it 'The Exotic Type.' I was stuck there for years and years. A producer had changed my name from Williams to Loy, so people probably thought I was half Chinese."

Myrna lifted her right hand to the corner of her eye and pulled it, made the lid slant. "I wore a lot of headbands. But then, when I was thirty, I made *The Thin Man* and everything changed. . . .

"Anyway, when you've grown up with somebody, you

don't have to rely on books written by their children, or on over-the-top screen performances, for your last memories. You have your own. I don't think about *Mommie Dearest* or *Mildred Pierce* or *What Ever Happened to Baby Jane?* I think of Joan the way she was when we had our last lunch. She came by in her beautiful car. She was wearing a beautiful suit—her clothes always fit her so well. And she looked so happy to see me, she smiled so warmly. 'I've been grounded,' she said. 'The doctors won't let me fly anymore.' She had cancer, of course. *I've been grounded.* That's all she needed to say.

"We went to '21'—and she was so gay, so funny. She was full of stories and laughs, and we talked about work—and wanting to work—the way we always did. We were both old. My God, close to seventy. And at one point, I complained about the age spots on my arms. Joan immediately piped up, 'Oh, my doctor gave me some wonderful lotion for that! Come back to the apartment with me and I'll give you some.' She was always like that, you know. Very up. Very caring. And the lotion . . . you know, it worked pretty well for a while."

She paused. "Max isn't going to make it, Clem."

"I know."

"But you can't stay. It's time to go back. You need to leave him alone with her. Allegra. She'll be coming soon."

CHAPTER 22

t was dark in the morning and sunny by night. The day
began cold and gray, a heavy rain coming down in sheets
against Allegra's bedroom windows, against the windows
of the mourning room where Max waved goodbye from
his white bed under the fig tree, and beating down against
the windshield of the gypsy cab I took to JFK.

Hours later, a handful of short hours, I woke to the same
day. The sunlight was bright and golden, and the clouds
were white and low. The sky was brilliant and deep blue
over L.A., the wide sky of the West, the open sky. Time had
gone backward. All over again, it was twelve noon.

—

There had been delays at the airport due to weather, and due to other things more predictable than weather. I was mobbed at the Delta ticket counter—everybody had a smile, vacuum eyes, hands extended. JFK authorities ushered me to a private lounge, a secret waiting area for famous people. It was black and shiny like a disco.

I read a book that I'd found at Max's but was interrupted at regular intervals by my cell phone. I checked the screen to see who was calling. *Flame.* It was always *Flame.* "Clementine," Marie-Claude said in her crisp hostile way, "where would you like me to FedEx your Oscar tickets and party directions? I called the Casa del Mar, and the things you left in your room have been moved to storage. Please don't forget to check out when you are leaving these places. They continue to bill us otherwise. Also Shutters . . ."

Ed called and left messages from his apartment, his office, his car, and the greenrooms of various television studios. He sounded harried and nervous. I could almost hear the makeup on his face. "I'm on my way to do *Charlie Rose,*" he'd say, or "Doing a quick segment for *ET.*" In his third message, he sounded exasperated—an emotion it was gratifying to arouse. "Listen," he said, "don't pay any attention to the Page Six thing. Lulu ran into Richard Johnson at an event last night, and he cornered her. And don't be mad about the pictures we ran of you in the Allegra issue." He took a great big breath and sighed. "The eye patch is great, darling. After I found out about the *Vogue* spread, I sort of had to. Don't you see? It's part of the story. It really is. Your trademark."

Across the lounge, on a round gray vinyl chair that looked like a giant marshmallow cut in half, I saw a copy of the *New York Post,* grabbed it, and quickly flipped it open.

FANNING THE FLAMES

Star scribe turned siren **Clementine James** seen canoodling with *Flame*'s dashing philosopher king **Ed Nostrum** at Asia de Cuba the other night. The two have been linked before but never quite like this. The next morning, a *Flame* rep confirmed that the editor sent five dozen roses to Clem's suite at the Carlyle and a new cashmere **Gaston La Fille** coat. It's red, of course. The color of love. Stay tuned . . .

Franklin called a few minutes later. I answered.

"Does the coat fit?" he asked. "I hear it's very luxe."

"Between us, the epaulets are a little extreme," I said. "And there are so many gold buttons. I feel like I've enlisted in somebody's army. But I don't know whose."

"His. Ed's army," Franklin said. "The Battalion of the Flame. Where are you?"

"The VIP lounge at JFK. I was mobbed by fans while I was standing at the counter. Security brought me here."

"People are so taken with the eye patch, aren't they?"

"I had sunglasses on. But apparently I'm just fabulous and famous no matter what I'm wearing."

"Does Ed know?"

"That I'm fabulous?"

"That you're at the airport."

"Oh, please. I just saw the Page Six item he planted—a new low. I can't wait to get out of New York and drop off his radar screen. He's a menace."

"Yes," Franklin said, "but he's *your* menace."

I paused for a second, sort of calculating the downsides of total honesty. "I didn't sleep with him the other night, if that's what you're driving at."

"No?" He perked up.

"No. Drinking got me into trouble but ultimately rescued me from lots more. I passed out cold and slept for twelve hours."

"Sort of a *Philadelphia Story* scenario? It looks like you did but you didn't?"

"A little more like *Snow White,* except kissing Ed turns out to be the opposite of Prince Charming. It makes you fall into a sleeping death."

I looked down to my lap, at the book Max had insisted I take. He had shelves and shelves of movie star as-told-tos and a separate, sort of enshrined off-limits section devoted entirely to Judy Garland. I found Myrna's book between Zsa Zsa Gabor's *How to Catch a Man* and Charles Higham's *Princess Merle: The Romantic Life of Merle Oberon.*

The cover of Myrna's book was odd. It bore a color-tinted image of her—bright red hair, green blouse—but her eyes were closed, almost rolled back into her head. "Hey,"

I said to Franklin. "I found a copy of Myrna's book. The cover's weird."

"The subtitle's even worse: *Being and Becoming.* So pretentious," he said. "I couldn't finish. She marries a couple of lounge lizards with good taste who spend her money, then she compensates by hooking up with a Hertz rental-car heir who beats her. In her dotage, she becomes a dreadful political bore. Sanctimonious and preachy. When I got to the part about Harry Truman, I gave up. She even moves to Washington and marries a bureaucrat. Didn't Liz Taylor do that?"

"Don't tell me," I said. "Don't tell me anything else."

"She lies too. There's some skirting around the issue of William Powell and whether she ever slept with him. And she spends an entire paragraph discussing why she never cries in any of her movies. I just saw *Test Pilot* again. And she cries twice."

"*Test Pilot?*"

"Big studio release. With Spencer Tracy and Clark Gable. Actually, I think both of them were in love with her in real life. Isn't there something in her book about shoving Gable into the bushes when he tries to kiss her one night? Anyway, Victor Fleming directed *Test Pilot* when he was on a roll—immediately after *Captains Courageous* and before *The Wizard of Oz* and *Gone with the Wind.*"

"Gable is a test pilot? How did I miss that one?"

"It's dark—and much less mythic and hokey than *The Right Stuff.* Gable is a tortured guy who needs to chase death and drink. On a coast-to-coast flight, his plane crashes into a Kansas cornfield. It's Myrna's cornfield—psychologically symbolic, I suppose. Anyway, she's terribly regal and full of delightful put-downs, considering she's a farm girl."

"What did you expect?"

"Then she and Gable fall in love. Lots of superb verbal banter. He loves her. He hates her. He loves her again— and that's only the first twenty minutes. Once he gets his plane fixed, there's a terrific scene where he flies off into the sky and leaves her behind to marry some young Kansas dweeb—is that the word? Gable's plane is in the air just a few minutes before he turns around and comes back for her. She's wearing a sweater set and nice skirt when she climbs into his airplane and they fly off together."

"Sounds like a Harlequin romance. Oh, wait, my flight's boarding. I have to—"

"It gets very grown-up after that. Gable goes on binges and disappears for days on end. His test-pilot buddies are being roasted alive in their exploding planes. Spencer Tracy is a sidekick, and he's in love with Myrna too. Anyway, the movie becomes a tortured triangle, and obviously some-body has to die."

"Who?"

"Tracy. He's the sidekick, so he has to. Myrna cries once for Gable, when his plane crashes and she's afraid he's dead. And again when Tracy goes down. Not a flood of tears, but there's liquid, actual fluid—a bit more than brim-ming. Doesn't that constitute crying in a movie? Or does one have to wipe one's face?"

"Franklin, I have to get going."

"Wait. She has the best line when she meets Gable for the first time. Unforgettably delivered, perfectly timed, and on the edge between earnestness and incredible irony—which is hard to pull off. She watches his plane crash, and she sees him getting out alive. He's wearing a leather flight jacket and a long white scarf. His face is so amazing—his mouth is always loaded with emotion. And she looks at him, completely unimpressed or trying to be completely unimpressed, and she says, 'Oh. I know you. You're the prince. A nice charming prince right out of the sky. A young girl's dream. And I've been waiting for you all my life.'"

———

A guy in a wilted jacket met me at the gate at LAX. He had sad blue eyes, strong lines in his forehead. He carried a handwritten sign, MISS JAMES scrawled on the lid of a shoe box. And I followed him, just as Myrna had instructed me, through the airport, with its old linoleum tunnels and new smoked glass, until we finally reached the outside and the cool dry California air.

She was waiting at the curb, behind the wheel of an incredibly long lemon-yellow Duesenberg convertible with whitewall tires. The interior was green—the same color as Tom Swimmer's Woody—and Myrna was wearing a powder-blue suit with a plunging neckline. A gardenia was pinned at the plunge.

"Where'd this come from?" I asked, crouching down to look at her.

"Borrowed it from Gary Cooper," she yelled against the traffic noise. "Come on, get in."

She pulled away quickly but otherwise drove slowly, almost too slowly, like somebody who had spent years in the back of a limousine. The top of the car stayed up too. I don't think she liked being blown around. She avoided the freeways, stayed on surface streets. She took Lincoln Boulevard, passing miles of seedy shops and gas stations and more nail salons, and turned east onto Venice Boulevard.

"I used to live down this street, you know," she said, pointing to the left. "A couple blocks down, on the edge of Culver City."

"Want to take a look?" I asked.

"Oh, it's gone now," she said. "A little house, a courtyard bungalow not far from Venice High. We moved there from Montana after my father died—my bereaved little family. I used to dance between the palm trees out front and stage dance recitals with Jean Vandyke, my best friend. Sometimes we climbed over the back fence and walked around the Goldwyn back lot and took pictures of each other."

She moved into the passing lane. Cars kept speeding up or slowing down to drive alongside us and wave.

Myrna concentrated on the road and reminisced about the old days, about dancing school, Grauman's Egyptian Theatre, and again, how long it took her to make it in movies. In the strong, almost blinding sunlight of L.A., her face seemed different. The plains and valleys of it had been flattened, and surface wrinkles were more pronounced. The old car turned north on Fairfax and began climbing toward Sunset. In the distance, the Hollywood Hills were brown and dotted with scrub brush and patches of green grass. I reached my hand out the window to feel the air.

"So, were you in love with Spencer Tracy?" I asked.

"Terrific actor," she replied.

I laughed. "That's it? That's all you have to say?"

Myrna kept her eyes on the road.

"Go on, Minnie," a voice in the backseat said. "What's the big deal?"

Dorothy was wearing another sarong—a blue-and-pink Hawaiian print. The wind from the open window was blowing her long hair up behind her head like a giant brown nimbus.

"I was always in love," Myrna said, looking at me. "There's really nothing more to add. I had crushes on people. I was always in love. That's just how it was. My first substantial role was in something called *Across the Pacific,* with Monte Blue. Remember him?"

I shook my head.

"Big Warner Brothers star. Part Cherokee. A former stuntman. Nice guy. I developed a huge crush on him until he cured it by taking me home for dinner to meet his wife. But let's just say that most of the other movie actors I encountered were somewhat less honorable. John Barrymore was incorrigible and ran with a changing gang of girls that I didn't feel like being a part of. Leslie Howard wanted to fly off to the South Seas with me. Gable was like wrestling an octopus. But they were married, all of them. And I didn't go in for that."

"And Tracy?"

"Keeping ahead of him wasn't easy. Chased me for years and then sulked adorably when I married someone else. I think he was still heartbroken when we met—his big affair with Loretta had just ended."

"Loretta Young?"

"It wasn't much of a secret. And I gather she insisted that he do the right thing and return to his wife."

"They didn't even hide it," said Dorothy.

"No?"

"Spencer drank," said Myrna. "He drank a lot. It seemed romantic then. He used to disappear for days. After a while, I got pretty good at figuring out when he was about to slip away. His eyes got dark and miserable. When we were making *Test Pilot,* he disappeared in the middle of filming. I drove all around Riverside, where we were shooting, and went into every bar and flophouse I could find, looking for him." She rubbed the side of her face. "People don't seem to understand," she said, "how you can be terribly in love with somebody and not sleep with them. But I do."

"I guess he had a thing for redheads," I said. "Or strong women."

Myrna didn't say anything, just drove for a while, but I could tell from her face that she was about to say something and trying to figure out how to say it.

"He hit her, you know," she said finally. "He'd hit Kate and yell at her and make cracks and insult her in public. It was very ugly sometimes. She'd just smile and nod. She stuck by him when nobody else wanted to. Strong woman. I guess she was strong, all right. She took it."

Dorothy giggled in the back. When I turned around, Loretta was next to her, whispering in her ear and wearing buckskin and braids, her costume from *Ramona.* "You're such a wonderful *talker,* Minnie," Loretta said with a hint of sharpness.

"Clem has a way of drawing us out, doesn't she?"

"Oh yeah," said Dorothy.

"That's her gift," I heard another voice say. Gloria was wearing head-to-toe leopard skin, and there were bracelets jangling from her wrist to her elbow. "She's absolutely divine. So hypnotic! When we were together, I did a soliloquy that went on for hours. I was surprised she didn't take notes." She jabbed a fingernail into my shoulder. "Just don't get Myrna started on the subject of politics."

"Or you, darling," Myrna said to Gloria, "on yoga."

Gloria pulled a pair of large round sunglasses from a beaded bag and put them on. Dorothy giggled.

"And I guess," Loretta said, "nobody wants to ask me about God."

The car climbed up a steep hill and turned onto Hollywood Boulevard. Then it swerved abruptly between rows of cypress trees. At first I thought we were headed to an old mansion or a cemetery—there was a pervasive embalmed feeling to the driveway—but soon enough we were pulling up to an enormous wooden Japanese temple. YAMASHIRO, the sign said. It was a restaurant, one of those old Hollywood joints that had been around forever.

At the top of the hill, we circled around and stopped at a small kiosk with a red gate. An older man came out, dressed in a uniform. He nodded and handed Myrna a key. Then he waved the car inside.

At the end of another steep drive, hanging over the hillside, was an apartment complex, the Hollywood Hills Hotel Apartments. It was a beige modern building with two long, low-slung floors. Seven or eight metal doors ran along a railed balcony.

As I walked away with my things—my laptop and coat, a duffel of clothes—they were all waving their perfect waves and smiling their perfect smiles. Somebody turned on the radio, and Dizzy Gillespie was playing the horn, and then Cab Calloway was singing. Myrna turned up the volume, and the girls all began to jump in their seats, shake their heads, and croon.

> *Oh Lady Luck*
> *Is the meanest chick in town*
> *I know it, because she brought me down*
> *Hard times got me topsy-turvy.*

Another head appeared in the passenger seat. Her face was turned away from me, toward Myrna. They were looking at each other, talking or singing. I couldn't tell. And as the car drove off, the new girl raised her right hand and pressed a lock of soft brown hair behind a small ear. She turned slowly in my direction. Hello Natalie. Hello Natalie Wood.

t was five or six P.M. by the time I settled in. The sun was sinking behind the copper roof of Yamashiro, and I could hear cars coming up the drive, people arriving for cocktails or dinner. In the pauses between cars, I heard crickets.

We hadn't talked in a week, actually ten days. It was funny how you could forget about a person—or fool yourself into thinking you'd forgotten—and then realize a part of your mind had been dwelling on him all along. It took me an hour to wrestle up the courage, and then I called.

"Clem." Ned's voice sounded shaky, or maybe just surprised. "What's happening?"

"Too much." I paused. "How about you?"

"I'm okay," he said. "I know about Swimmer. I mean, I

saw you guys. Bram made me watch the vigil with him on *Entertainment Tomorrow.*"

I heard a wooden kitchen match striking a rough surface and then a sucking sound.

"You're smoking."

Ned exhaled. "He looks computer-generated."

"I'm not sure what to say about it—about him," I said. "It happened. And it was stupid, I guess. Although it doesn't even feel important enough to be sorry about. I hate to sound callous."

"Yeah, that's the kind of thing a guy would think but never say. I thought women were supposed to be kinder and more romantically inclined."

"He's okay. He's a nice guy," I said. "But there isn't much else *to* say. I went temporarily insane, or maybe it was meant to happen. Anyway, I've called about something else. Something else I need to tell you."

"What?"

"It's about Ed."

"Jesus Christ." There was another long exhalation and I could almost feel the smoke in my face. "Don't tell me that you're in love with him again. I'd be embarrassed for you."

"No. It's not that," I said, feeling flustered. "We got together a couple nights ago. I drank too much. We kissed. But we didn't— What do you mean 'again'?"

"You and he had a thing already—right before we got together. I've always assumed that I came along and ended it.

Anyway, by the time I finally met him, he was already with Eva, the Danish girl. Or maybe she was Finnish."

"You assumed?"

"Jesus, Clementine. I think everybody knew."

All the hiding and secrecy, the games to meet in dark hotel rooms, climbing up stairwells instead of taking the elevator. All the e-mails instead of calls. Everybody knew. Of course they did.

"Ned?"

"Yeah?"

"I wasn't sure if we'd broken up or not. Last week."

"I don't know," he said. "Did we?"

We moved on to easier things—to Bram, who was better, to the dogs, the snow. I talked about Max and the hospital and the rain, about Baby and Rita. It felt vaguely like an experiment, like we were testing what it was like, how it felt, to have a regular conversation.

Later on, when I got to thinking about Ned again, and how things had gone, I realized he never asked where I was—or where I was staying. And I felt suddenly like a helium balloon on a string that he'd let go of. I was bobbing and flying and drifting into the darkening blue sky, rising upward, higher and higher, until I was gone.

☆
☆

CHAPTER 24
☆

The Hollywood Hills Hotel Apartments was a quiet place, so quiet that I wasn't sure whether the other eight units were occupied. It didn't seem connected to an actual hotel, or affiliated with the Yamashiro restaurant. There was no room-service menu that I could find. The bathroom had no basket of soaps and shampoos. There was a small galley kitchen with wooden stools around a red Formica bar, but no midget coffeemaker, and the refrigerator was empty.

Two red corduroy sectional sofas were pushed up against a corner of the sitting room, with a coffee table made from a polished tree stump in front. The floor was cork, soft on the feet, but a puddle had dried near the back door and left a large dark stain.

A sunny courtyard made up for the otherwise dispiriting aspects of the ground-floor apartment. Camellia trees and climbing bougainvillea had been planted around a redbrick patio. A thicket of white jasmine brought a sweet fragrance to the bedroom while I slept. In the morning, after the jasmine blossoms had closed in the hot sun, the scent of honeysuckle took their place.

As I was dressing and wondering where I might find breakfast, I heard splashing sounds in the courtyard, the gentle lapping of water, as though a large fountain had been turned on. Soft voices echoed off a wall, and music was playing. Yamashiro, I surmised, was opening for brunch.

Beyond the courtyard, I found a gravel pathway at the top of a flight of steps. I guessed that it must lead to the restaurant, but after a few minutes, I found myself on a rise that overlooked a secluded swimming pool. The pool wasn't large—not the size of a hotel pool—but was nicely proportioned, kidney-shaped, and surrounded by cypress, live oaks, and red bottlebrush, the red needles of which floated on the surface of the pale turquoise water.

Two empty chaises sat on the pool deck, near a few round tables still wet with dew. Nestled into the hillside, off in its own corner, a small Japanese shrine was hidden between shrubs and live oaks. The shrine looked old and vaguely important. It had a pagoda roof and a red spire; a rock garden had been carefully designed around its base, with moss and low holly and some arthritic-looking bonsai.

Beyond, the city of Hollywood rose up. It looked pale,

the color of bleached bones. On the side of a tall building, a man was standing on a small platform held by ropes. He was washing the windows of the Renaissance Hollywood Hotel. In an alleyway behind the hotel and the Kodak Theatre, where the Oscars would be staged in just a few days, a bunch of delivery trucks were angling for space while rolls and rolls of carpet were unloaded.

I heard the soft voices again, the faint music. I leaned over the railing to look closer, to verify again that the pool was empty, and was startled to hear the *thrung* of a vibrating diving board, followed by the splash of a dive.

I continued down the gravel pathway, and by the time I reached the pool, the landscape had been transformed.

Girls were everywhere, in clusters and crowds, gangs and swarms. They sat at the pool's edge, dangling their legs in the clear water. Along the deck, they were stretched out on golden-yellow towels, rows and rows of them in chaises angled to face the sun. Some stood waist-deep in the shallow end. Others wore quilted rubber bathing caps with colored flowers and were swimming on their sides, holding their heads above the water's surface.

Yellow cabanas lined one side of the pool area. They had peaked roofs like small Moroccan tents. One cabana seemed to be set up for beauty services, for manicures and hairstyling. The other cabanas were closed, the front flaps down. Every so often, girls—women—came and went, mingling by the pool as though at a cocktail party, a reunion, a sorority get-together. They gabbed and laughed.

They nibbled on fruit from small plates. They drank from old-style champagne saucers. Some were smoking, a few with cigarette holders. They were all about the same age or, rather, approaching the same acme of freshness and appeal. Their skin was taut. Their bodies were lithe and young. Their faces showed no signs of wear or boredom or much anxiety—only hope, expectancy, entitlement perhaps, and the sort of unconscious charisma that made them seem numb to defeat.

A girl in black bra and black underwear was approaching the diving board. She was a dark blonde with a round face and red lips. At the edge of the board, she began jumping up and down, bouncing until she had gotten the attention of those reclining in the front row of chaises. A group of small dogs stood at the edge of the pool—a few poodles and terriers, a Chihuahua, a longhaired dachshund—watching with great interest.

"Beat this!" the girl on the diving board yelled out. Her voice—a husky southern drawl—seemed familiar, but before I could place it, she sprang from the diving board, twisted gracefully in the air, and vanished underwater.

Ava Gardner looked up briefly from her chaise, smiling a little vacantly, and then went back to scratching something on her upper arm. I think it was Dolores del Rio who looked over at Grace Kelly in the next chaise and made a playful scowl.

Myrna emerged from one of the closed cabanas. She was wearing a white bathing suit with a long tank top pulled down over short knit shorts. Her skin was very white and freckled. Her arms were skinny, her chest flat, her legs quite muscular—a dancer's legs. She was younger than yesterday by nearly a decade.

She put her hand over her brow, shielding her eyes from the sun. She looked across the pool and waved.

Attention shifted toward me. Girls lifted their eyes from copies of *Photoplay* and *Confidential* and *Pic*. A few standing in the pool began waving. One of them, a girl with waist-length dark hair, the tips of which were underwater, put two fingers in her mouth and dog-whistled. And then a casual sort of parade began.

Ann Sothern sauntered by with a big dreamy face and half-closed eyes. She looked a little like Ann Sheridan, who came next, and a little like Rita Hayworth, except Rita had reddish hair. Betty Hutton had a beauty mark on her cheek—I couldn't tell if it was real—and a bathing suit with padded cups and marabou feathers. The Talmadge sisters, Norma and Constance, walked by together smiling, laughing, in thick black and white tank suits with wide straps. Other silent-movie stars appeared. They seemed to travel in clumps. Some I recognized, most I didn't, but I looked up their faces and names later on, in books and on websites. Vamps and flappers, innocents . . . and lots of bee-stung lips. Vilma Banky and Nita Naldi and Olga Baclanova wore headdresses. Lina Basquette had an enormous brindle Great Dane on a leash. Billie Dove's eyes were so blue it looked like she was wearing colored contacts. Barbara

La Marr had a baby-pink suit and seemed disoriented, or sleepy, or tipsy, but so did Marie Prevost and Olive Thomas. A very silly conga line of girls danced by, laughing: Thelma Todd, Zasu Pitts, Corinne Griffith, Lili Damita, and Fay Wray.

Mae Murray had golden hair, curls pinned up at the back of her head. Her ivory bathing costume was loose on her body and sewn with small pearls. She wore a diadem of rhinestones—or perhaps they were real diamonds, who knows. Her lips were small and so dark red they were almost blue.

"I was the Original Girl with the Bee-stung Lips," she said to me, "and the Gardenia of the Screen."

"I was the Hungarian Rhapsody," said Vilma Banky.

"I was the Whoop-dee-doo Girl," said a woman with sharp bangs, a flapper. Her lips were bee-stung too.

"I was the Oomph Girl," said Ann Sheridan.

"I was the Sweater Girl," said Lana Turner. Her hair wasn't quite as platinum, or stiff, as it would be later on in life.

"I was Norma Shearer," said Norma Shearer.

Clara Bow arrived, accompanied by two red chow dogs that were the same color as her short flyaway hair. Her face was small and taken up mostly by her eyebrows, two large slashes drawn with a black pencil across her forehead. "I was the first Jazz Baby," she said conspiratorially, in a Brooklyn accent, "and Hollywood's very first 'It' girl." She was short, a bit plump, wearing a black suit with carved cinnabar buttons and other Chinese details. She stood close to me. "I got the most flowers. I lived in the biggest digs," she whispered. "I made the most dough, had the best time. I screwed the entire USC football team in one night—when John Wayne was quarterback. I was big," she said, "bigger than anything." Her eyes were wild, dangerous. Once you started looking at them, it was hard to look away. But I had to.

"Darling, take a dive!" hollered the girl in the black bra. Her face was fresh and uncomplicated. I barely knew she was Tallulah. She was wet and sitting on the edge of the diving board with her arm around Lizabeth Scott. "Clementine," she yelled out, "come on in! The water's goddamn beautiful."

Just as I'd gotten down to my underwear, another girl arrived from an overgrown passageway in the wall. She studied me with an imperious look, though she couldn't have been more than sixteen. Her hair looked like Shirley Temple's, but the curls were longer and bounced below her armpits. Her bathing costume was baggy and blue—like a child's romper—with three rows of inelegant ruffles.

"Oh Christ," said Ida Lupino.

"Party's over," I heard somebody whisper. "Mary's here."

Lizabeth Scott let out a low husky chuckle that seemed to egg on Tallulah, who yelled, "Hey, look, everybody! If it ain't America's fucking Sweetheart."

Mary Pickford kept walking as though she were alone

and perhaps listening to some very sweet, inspiring music. When she got to the last cabana, she disappeared inside.

I stood on the end of the board. The water looked very blue, as blue as Billie Dove's eyes, deep and flecked with shadows—a great liquid world, another world. I heard the *thrung* of the vibrating board beneath my feet. I heard a chant rise up. "Go, Clem, go!" I sprang up into the air, then quickly sank under the surface, where I was alone and it was quiet and the water was warm and cool at the same time, exactly the temperature of the air.

———

Afterward, I drifted to a table for some food. It was a surprisingly bland array. Celery and carrot sticks, grapefruit sections, cherries. There was a bowl of sunflower seeds, a salad without dressing, an omelette without yolks. There were fresh pressed juices and four kinds of bottled water. A few dogs were nearby and begging for scraps, although I hardly knew why.

I took a silver serving spoon and shoveled some omelette and cut pineapple onto a plate. And then I walked down the rows, looking for an empty chaise.

Jane Russell was reclining on a chaise longue next to Jayne Mansfield, four enormous breasts in sequence. Betty Grable was putting sunscreen on her legs. Constance Bennett and Joan Bennett were giggling about something— their hair was cut short and dyed very white—and playing a game of bridge with Barbara Stanwyck, who looked ex-

actly as she did in *The Lady Eve.* Veronica Lake had found
an umbrella and sat in the shade with Theda Bara.

Off alone was a pale thin blonde with a wistful expression who turned out to be Helen Twelvetrees, a star of
thirties melodramas, weepers, *King for a Day, Love Starved,
Times Square Lady.* She came over to where I was standing.
Her mouth was very small, and something about her, a lost
look, reminded me of Lillian Gish.

"My name isn't really Helen Twelvetrees," she said.

"What is it?" I asked.

"Helen Jurgens. They said I was a suicide, but that's not
true either."

"No?" I asked. There were a lot of suicides, and it was
hard to keep them straight.

"Suicide makes it sound so dramatic," she said, shrug-
ging. "I just died the way everybody else does."

"They said I was beheaded," said Jayne Mansfield, lifting herself up from the chaise.

"I thought you were," said Betty Grable.

"Decapitated," said Jane Russell.

"Isn't that the same thing?"

"Really?"

"That's a laugh."

"No way."

"Where are you buried?" I heard one of the bee-stung
girls say to Helen Twelvetrees.

"I died in Harrisburg."

Jean Arthur motioned me to share a chaise with her. She

was bubbly but not all that pretty without makeup. "Remember the year—was it during the war?" she said to everyone and no one, "when they covered the deck of the Beverly Hills Hotel pool with sand, and it was like a beach?"

"I wish we were at the beach now," said one of the bee-stung girls. She closed her eyes slowly, like a snake.

"What a scene."

"I like scenes."

"Pickfair has the best pool," said Claudette Colbert, carrying a tray back to her chair. She was so short I thought she might be a child actress. Her head was enormous. "Everything Mary does is the best."

"There are so many nice pools," said Jean Arthur. "Preston Sturges has a good pool, Harold Lloyd and—"

"Yeah, yeah," said one of the vamps.

"I've got an idea," said Dorothy Dandridge from the shade. "Let's do tomorrow's party at Pickfair again. And I'll dance on the stage."

Peggy Lee came out of a cabana. She was tall and thin, and her hair was long and white-blond. Music picked up, and she began singing:

> *Is that all there is?*
> *Is that all there is?*
> *If that's all there is, my friends*
> *Then let's keep dancing*
> *Let's break out the booze and have a ball.*

On the other side of the yellow beauty cabana was a bamboo bar crowded with girls. I went there looking for something to drink, but the champagne turned out to be ginger ale, and the vodka was water.

Loretta appeared out of nowhere. She was wearing a pair of shorts and a striped halter top. Her face was full of freckles, and her hair was down and brown and not too fussy. "We've been trying to discourage alcohol," she said in low and serious tones. "Such an occupational hazard. It's so hard to cope, and so many of us had terrible drinkers for parents. Although most of us, according to an informal poll, grew up without fathers. Except Tallulah, of course, who was raised by hers. He was Speaker of the House— did you know that? But Dorothy didn't have much of a father, really. Veronica's died, and Gloria's. Lana Turner's was murdered. Myrna's died in the flu epidemic. Marilyn Monroe certainly never had one. I'm not sure what happened to Mary Pickford's or Ingrid Bergman's, but they weren't around. Mine skipped out when I was four—or my mother kicked him out—we've never been completely sure which story is true.

"Our mothers got us here," said Loretta. "They sacrificed, didn't they? Our dear *darling mothers.* Isn't that right?"

A cheer rose up from inside the beauty cabana. Glasses of juice were raised at the bamboo bar, and toasts were made.

"My mother was everything to me," Dorothy Lamour said, and you knew she wasn't kidding.

"My mother wasn't everything," said Gypsy Rose Lee, "but close."

Over a loudspeaker, a voice said: "This is Mary Pickford, and my mother was all I had until I married Doug."

"A psychiatrist once told me that I kept marrying my mother," said Myrna, peeking out from another tent. "After that revelation, I stayed single."

"I didn't have to marry Mama," Loretta said, "she never moved out. And when I died, I had my ashes put inside her grave."

"Where are you buried?" the same bee-stung girl asked Myrna. The girl had glossy black hair, and a Louise Brooks haircut, except she wasn't Louise Brooks.

"Montana."

At the end of the diving board, Tallulah was peeling off her wet underwear and tossing it at the girls sitting poolside. "To our fucking mothers!" she yelled before she jumped. "May they all be dead!"

———

The closed cabanas were somewhat mysterious. I gathered that Mary and Myrna each had her own. "Do you know where Gloria Swanson is?" I asked a clump of women by the Japanese shrine. "I was hoping to see her."

"Up on the roof," one of them answered in a tiny pulsating voice. After a few moments, I realized it was Billie Burke, almost unidentifiable out of her Glinda the Good

Witch costume. "Gloria believes in the healing power of the sun. She likes to bathe naked—and alone."

"She never comes," said the bee-stung girl who asked where people were buried. She had the kind of face that got prettier the longer you looked at it, but gloomier too.

"That's not true. Gloria does the food," said another vamp, a blonde.

"Orders it."

"She's never here. Neither is Garbo."

"Garbo doesn't come?" I asked.

They shook their heads. "She can't bear groups," Billie Burke said. She was wearing a floppy straw hat pinned with a huge jeweled brooch. Her face was white as an aspirin. "She's much too sensitive. I think she worries that Marlene might show up."

"Marilyn Monroe?" I asked, mishearing.

"Dietrich," said Billie. "Marilyn always oversleeps."

"Neither of them come," said Ginger Rogers as she approached our group. "Hoity-toity." Her hair was loose and wavy around her face. Her bathing suit had sequins. She reminded me of Betty Hutton, except her beauty mark was on her chin.

"Snooty-snobby," said Colleen Moore. She pushed up the tip of her nose with her index finger and rolled her eyes. I wondered where the other comediennes were.

"Wouldn't be buried near any of us either," said the gloomy bee-stung girl.

Clara Bow wandered in and immediately began talking

too loudly. "They said that Greta was a lesbian. I say she's nuts."

"Shut up, Clara."

"Let's not—" said Billie Burke, her hands gently motioning the girls to be quiet. Then she turned to me, her voice infused with extra sweetness. "Garbo is really quite pathetic. Socially inept."

"She's cold," said the blond vamp.

"Never says hi to nobody," said Ginger.

"I heard she has awful cramps."

"Always on the rag, didn't you know?"

"None of that is true," said Billie, turning to me again. "Don't listen."

"Where are you buried?" the bee-stung girl asked me.

"I'm not dead," I said.

"Oh, that's right," she said. "You're a drop-in. Like Betty Hutton and Fay Wray. They're not dead yet either. We get visitors all the time, you know. We had Liz Taylor here last week, and—"

Clara interrupted. "Clementine, do you know Mae Busch?"

I smiled at the bee-stung girl. "Hello."

"She's fixated on burial," Clara said.

"I noticed."

"Why not?" said Mae, putting a stick of Fan Tan gum in her mouth.

"Personally," said Clara, "I'm more interested in how a person spends their washed-up afterlife."

"Ferncliff Cemetery is awfully nice," interjected Billie, who hadn't been following the conversation too carefully.

"Where's that?" asked Mae.

"New York," I said.

"All that rain and snow," said Colleen Moore. "And who wants to wind up next to Joan Crawford?"

I shrugged.

"I'm in Glendale," Clara was saying to Mae. "If it's good enough for Bette Davis, it's good enough for me. Gable's there. He's got a semiprivate area with Carole Lombard. And Bogart has full private."

"Full private?" I had to ask.

"At Forest Lawn, semiprivate pretty much means you get a corridor that's roped off," Mae explained. "The fans can still come see you, but they gotta step over a rope. It works if you want to make out like you're aloof—like you're the private type—but you really aren't. With full private, you get the iron gate, the private garden, the works. Nobody can come."

"Family members can," said Billie. "Film historians and biographers. Mary Pickford has full private."

"Tacky sculpture," said Clara. "The worst."

"I like it," said Billie.

"Mother Earth with zillions of fat little cherubs. You'd think she was Marie Antoinette."

"Wasn't she beheaded?" asked Mae.

Myrna was approaching with a smirk. "I can't imagine anybody would want to be buried among a bunch of movie stars," she said. "Even when we're alive, we make the worst friends."

"You don't get classier than Norma Shearer," Clara said, a little agitated. "Errol Flynn's in Glendale, and Alan Ladd and W. C. Fields. Carole Lombard—" She yelled toward the pool, "Carole, aren't you in Glendale?"

A blonde on a raft turned her head. "What?"

"I thought W. C. Fields's grave says 'I'd rather be in Philadelphia,'" said Mae Busch.

"It does," said Myrna.

"Where are you, Mae?" I asked.

Myrna gave me a look that said I shouldn't be asking.

"It's a long story," Mae sighed. "But I spent many years in a cardboard box on a shelf in the back of a storage closet at the Motion Picture Country Home in Woodland Hills. That's a rest home for movie people."

"I've heard of it," I said.

"Anyhows," said Mae, with no sense of disappointment in her face, "after I was cremated, nobody came to get me."

———

Bad luck, or bad timing, or both got me stuck in the beauty tent next to Clara while she got a French manicure. She kept nudging me with her little elbow and honking at me in a loud voice. "I was crazy," she said. "Crazier than Frances Farmer and Mary Astor and Marilyn put together."

I nodded.

"I wound up in a straitjacket. Sanitarium. Asylum. Oh, I

married a cowboy star, Rex Bell, and after he became a politician he'd drag me out for holidays and fund-raisers. But it wasn't so bad. I'd take the nuthouse over an eternity of these parties. I'm tired of being twenty-two. And I'm sick of this bathing suit."

Several hours later, mostly spent avoiding Clara and dozing—turning myself over and over again like a rotisserie chicken on a chaise between Ava Gardner and Susan Hayward—Myrna walked me back to the apartment. She was wearing a cover-up over her bathing suit, a sheer chiffon dress with ropes across the breasts, kind of a Grecian look. She seemed a little sleepy and was walking slowly. Her hair had gotten a little frizzy in the wind, and her nose was red, a bit burnt. She was carrying a yellow flower, and when we reached the end of the path, she handed it to me. "The prophet Mohammed said, 'If you have two loaves of bread, sell one and buy hyacinths.' We're just purveyors of hyacinths, my dear. That's all."

I looked down at the flower. A sweet fragrance floated up to my nose.

"This is goodbye," Myrna said, kissing me on the cheek. "Hope you enjoyed your time in the sun."

———

The evening brought news of her. She'd come back, reappeared, just as Myrna had predicted. I wondered if our planes had passed in the sky. I flew to the West. She flew to the East—except it was as though she were still hovering over the world, like Glinda floating over the Munchkins. It's hard to remember now what I saw on TV or my laptop, or what I heard later from Dudus.

It was raining in New York, and Allegra walked up to the door of Max's brownstone holding an enormous golf umbrella over her head. She had no coat. She wore a lavender dress that was wet and stuck to her thighs, and brown boots. Her hair was longer, wispy at the ends. And she seemed thinner, worn out, with a slight trace of gray under her eyes. Eventually, I realized it was her new look—the extra layering of eyeliner that raccooned her eyes. She kept her mouth closed, her head down.

In the morning, I woke up to more news of her, streaming across my laptop. Her face bounced at the top of my home page, where a list of links to Allegra stories grew by the minute.

MISSING STAR APPEARS

NUNS TOOK HER IN

"I NEEDED SOME TIME TO THINK"

ALLEGRA HERE, CLEMENTINE GONE

My disappearance didn't last long, of course. Allegra had been gone an interminable ninety days. I could barely manage one. But when I emerged from seclusion, I was brown as a nut. My hair was golden, like strands of pale honey. And there were three dozen unanswered calls on my phone.

"How'd you find this spot?" Franklin asked when he came to pick me up. "A bit dodgy, isn't it?" We loaded my things into the silver Luscus, drove up to the small kiosk—now uninhabited—and down the narrow driveway that encircled Yamashiro. We retraced the route Myrna had taken the night before, along Sycamore, across Franklin Avenue, and left on La Brea.

We ate lunch on the patio of the Ivy, where it was sunny

and birds were singing and lots of other people were wearing sunglasses. Franklin didn't ask too many questions; he just seemed relieved to have me back in L.A. He kept saying how good I looked. "Your hair's brilliant, by the way. Haunting. Very *Persona* slash *Mulholland Drive*. The most amazing color."

We talked about the Allegra docudrama, airing later that night; about Ed and Margaux and how they'd both grown so preoccupied with the impending Oscars and *Flame*'s afterparty that they seemed to have dropped off the face of the earth. We placed a bet on how many awards *Sphinxa* would win—I said three, he said eight. Over mango sorbet that I ordered for dessert but which we both ended up eating, we listed our top ten favorite movie heroes and heroines in order of appeal and discovered our only overlap was Takashi Shimura in *The Seven Samurai,* and Shrek.

Then, in his ever cheerful way, Franklin walked me the four blocks to Cedars-Sinai.

The Bio-eye had arrived.

———

Surgery would take longer this time, installation being more difficult than extraction, but not nearly so complicated as figuring out what to do with the flowers. There were daisies and wildflower arrangements, peonies and lilies and tall sheaths of lavender. "You're almost at the Helen Hunt level," said Wim, the delivery guy from Nightingale's. "Everybody loves Helen." There were tulips and more tulips—white and purple and tiger-striped—standing in silver bowls, in copper urns, and arranged by the dozens in folksy crates with sphagnum moss.

"What's all this?" Franklin exclaimed when he returned later that night with a take-out dinner from Lucques.

"Flowering cherry branches," I said, pointing to one vase, "from Steven Soderbergh."

They came from people I knew but mostly from people I didn't. They came from New York—from Ed, the staff of *Flame,* the staff of the *Journal,* old editors and old friends and people who, frankly, I'd briefly forgotten. They came from Gaston La Fille, Calvin Klein, Matt and Katie, Diane and Barbara, and the producers of every television show that I'd turned down. They came from Cosmos, the crew working on *Apache,* Tom Swimmer ("Hey, give me a call sometime"), the Michaels, the assistants to the Michaels, the assistants to the assistants of the Michaels. They came from Margaux and her clients, as well as anybody I'd ever interviewed who was still alive, except Allegra.

As Franklin and I drank chilled sherry in my room, then ate pork tenderloin and garlic mashed potatoes, we watched television. We took in a few minutes of the news. We flipped to E! and caught bits of the New York premiere of *L'Avventura.* Bertolucci was walking into the Ziegfeld Theatre with his wife, Clare Peploe, and fending off the shouts and cries of inquiring simpletons who descended upon him, wanting to know about Allegra. He said nothing, only

raised his arms in the air, over his head, in a show of sur-
render, and continued inside.

Franklin and I settled in for the HBO biopic. It was
a reenactment of Allegra's life that dwelled, for dramatic
purposes, on her troubled childhood and her mother's
drinking and ended with the crash. Max Coleman was
played by David Carradine. I was played by an actress who
looked something like Jane Withers, the thirties child star
who went on to become the lady plumber in the Comet
commercials. The girl who played Allegra was very pretty
but a made-for-TV type—a tamer, plainer, smaller, weaker
version of the real thing. She had the face of a Romanian
gymnast, small eyes, a marked-for-death look. She didn't
seem comfortable smiling, and her laugh was hollow.

"Pretty pathetic," Franklin said. "She's nothing like Allegra." He was lying across the foot of my bed.

"You're on my leg."

"Sorry. Oh dear. Look at her pointy teeth."

"She's got something," I said. "But not a lot of whatever
that is. She'd be really good in the Olga Korbut story."

"She's jewelry-advertisement pretty," Franklin said.
"Miss America–contestant pretty. Sort of tarty."

"She's not tarty. You sound like a casting agent. She's just
too small."

"Well, she's vulgar. Or she's not vulgar enough. A chain-
store Allegra."

"The expression is *dime-store,* not chain-store."

"She's generic. An Allegra with fuzzy slippers and a bath-robe. And there's something so very depressing about that."

During a commercial, we switched back to E!, where a quickie news report about my return to Cedars was just beginning. There was a before-accident picture, the one where my hand is curled up under my chin like a claw. There were clips of me walking down the street with Max, followed by seven seconds of the deranged-looking crooked-eye-patch photo from *Flame*. Alan Dershowitz was being asked whether I had a legal case against Allegra and Cosmos Studios for assault and battery, attempted manslaughter, and leaving the scene of an accident. He seemed to be shaking his head, and Franklin and I were both howling but also listening intently.

"Can I use your loo?" Franklin asked, and while he was in there, I hit the mute button on the TV and watched the screen in silence.

I could hear the traffic outside on La Cienega, a jet in the sky, the wheels of a cart in the hallway. I could hear the tolling of the elevator bell. I could hear Franklin flushing the toilet and running the water in the sink. All the people, all the scenes and stories, all the lives. I thought about the frenzy of the world, the frenzy of the climb toward success—the going, the getting, the grabbing—the miles traveled, energy spent, years spent, summers gone, the dreams, the sighs, the sadness, the misery, and the endless attempts to end the misery.

"What if," Franklin said when he reappeared, "I run out and rent a movie? Something with Peter Sellers, maybe *Hoffman*. Wouldn't that be more fun?"

Early the next morning, I was draped in green and blue sheets. My hair was covered in a clear plastic shower cap, the circumference of which was taped to my skin. There were needles, injections of Novocain inside and around my eye socket. An oxygen mask was put over my face briefly. And there was a lovely dripping of clear liquid into the crook of my arm.

The glass egg was removed with a suction-tipped instrument. It came loose without a sound, without a pop, without fanfare or cheering. And the real work began. Bio-eye arrived to meet my face. It greeted me. I welcomed it in. And I have always imagined its installation—the hooking up of wires and fasteners and rudder—as something like the attachment of a television set to the wall. The only difference is, my eye never received or broadcast anything again.

———

My memories of Oscar night are foggy and indistinct. Franklin stayed at the hospital until I was asleep and a doctor told him that the surgery had gone okay. I woke up groggily and watched him changing into his dinner clothes—a Dolce & Gabbana velvet jacket with Nehru collar. "Was that a freebie?" I asked. When I woke up again, he was gone.

Ed came by for a few minutes, on his way to the Garden of Allah for the *Flame* party. And I remember thinking, when I heard his big booming voice in my room, that it was time to stop torturing him and being tortured by him. He was just a person, after all, another human being. No bigger or smaller than that, probably not much better or worse.

I remember Margaux too. She was wearing a long white dress with a neckline that ended somewhere in the middle of her stomach. She saw my face and started to cry. She held my hand, blubbered, "You poor thing," and splashed warm tears on my arm. After she left, I imagined what I had looked like to her. I tried to see myself in a detached way, as though from the lens of a camera on the wall. But it was impossible, too depressing. The bandages were so white and so high and so voluminous that it was like a snowy Mount Fuji had grown on the right side of my head. I turned away from all that whiteness and thoughts about self and cast my eye instead on the corner of the ceiling where the TV was suspended.

A pre-Oscar show was starting. It was sunny and perfect out there in the world, in Picture Land. The sky was blue. The unrolled carpet was so red, so long. And the windows of the Renaissance were clean. The stars sparkled in their ceremonial garb, long comet trails of sparks against a sea of black clothing. I was happy to be far away, in my little white bed, on my own. Happy that I was away from the glare and the glamour that, up close, just looked like a lot of people trying too hard. I didn't have much respect for fame, I guess. It seemed kind of cheap, and went away too easily, and required a crowd.

And beauty—it was like a one-dimensional kind of genius. The kind of thing that got you lots of compliments for a while, and guy problems, and maybe a nice life by a swimming pool. Sometimes it got you fame too.

The stars came down the carpet in twos, like animals heading into the ark. Their eyes hunted for TV cameras, looked around for familiar faces to help them. Their eyes found our eyes. The stars looked out to us through the cameras, out to me in my lonely bed, and they held up their beautiful magical shining charming heads and somehow hid their desperation. That was the greatest show of all.

And then, at the very last, when it seemed that all the magic had disappeared inside the Kodak Theatre, two more figures appeared at the end of the long glowing flying red carpet. "Allegra Coleman is here!" the reporter from E! started yelling into her microphone. "Allegra Coleman! She's here! And she's crying, everybody. Allegra Coleman's crying!"

She walked on the arm of Bernardo Bertolucci. Her hair was curled and fell loosely to her shoulders. Her face was rested and tanned and smooth. She wasn't the biopic Allegra, the docudrama Allegra—small and hollow. Nor did she appear to be crying. She was fresh and dewy. And she looked as breathtaking as a girl could without also looking artificial. She wore a golden-yellow halter dress. In her hands she carried a daisy.

———

She'd hit her head, maybe she'd had a concussion—that's what she'd say, anyway, when she finally gave interviews. She experienced a temporary loss of proper reasoning ability, perhaps a kind of temporary insanity. She was disoriented from the crash, she said—not to mention from stardom or life or newness or having all her dreams come true. She got out of the totaled car and went looking for help on the road. She walked for a while in her shorts and mules. It was hot. The sun was strong. And then she forgot why she was walking or where she was. She hitched a ride to San Luis Obispo—although it would always be a mystery why the driver of that car never came forward to verify this—and then she'd paid cash for a bus ticket to San Francisco. On the bus, she met a nun. "My mom was a nun," Allegra said, "for a while, anyway."

At St. Euphemia's of Big Sur, on a cliff overhanging the wild surf of the Pacific, she mowed the grass on a loud tractor during the day and studied historical martyrology at night. She planted a lettuce garden and introduced the nuns to arugula. St. Euphemia's was run by a cloistered order of shoeless renunciates who lived in silence. Allegra agreed to remain barefoot and silent too, as part of her meditation and practice. After a month, when it was discovered that she was making phone calls from the tractor while mowing, she was asked to leave. She took out a pencil and wrote on a piece of paper: "I never spoke into the cell phone. I only placed a few calls. Please, sisters. I beg you, let me stay."

The whole thing added up and didn't, of course. But that night in the hospital, watching the pre-Oscar broadcast, I felt very far away from Hollywood and Allegra and whatever explanation she might cough up. I wasn't really interested anymore—in Allegra, or what happened to Allegra. She had ceased to fascinate me. But that's the sort of thing you think—or feel—when you have just increased the flow of synthetic morphine going into your arm and you are feeling sorry for yourself for being half blinded but you're not much interested in suing anybody either.

———

Standing by the sink in the bathroom, I pulled off the snowy buildup around my right eye. I pulled off as much tape and gauze as I could, and looked at my face in the mirror. Way inside the pinkish-purple swollen flesh was Bio-eye, or what I could see of it. A tiny dot of hazel. I saw it. But it couldn't see me.

I smelled something sweet. Maybe it was the hand soap, I thought, or the flowers in my room. I heard sounds—footsteps or a soft knocking on wood.

I turned around.

"Is that you?" I asked.

But nobody was there.

———

I dozed off before the Oscars started and missed the entire broadcast. It was a first—and I survived. What I know about the show itself, I heard from Franklin. He returned in the middle of the night, stumbling from Cosmopolitans and champagne and smelling like an ashtray and second-hand perfume. He slipped past the night nurses. He talked for a while, rather excitedly, and then passed out in a recliner near a box of candy and an antique trunk filled with tulips.

Newspapers never quite give you the sense of the broadcast—the immediacy, the ridiculous banter of the comedian, the soapboxing of politics, the montage of clips of all the stars who died in the last year, the way the envelopes sound like they are made of the softest calfskin when they are being torn open. But talking to Franklin was almost as good as being there, perhaps better, until he fell asleep with a chocolate in his mouth.

Highlights: Allegra (backstage) refusing to name the designer of her dress. The alpine skier turned actor Bode Miller taking off his shirt, and then Clint Eastwood copying him, and Tony Curtis after that. Marisa Tomei presenting the award for best adapted screenplay and wearing a black eye patch. "I suppose it was an homage," Franklin said. "But it's so last week."

The best of all, though not exactly an Oscar highlight, took place at *Flame*'s Garden of Allah party, when Ed asked Franklin to profile Charlton Heston for the July issue, but Franklin took a job with Bertolucci instead.

It wasn't until the morning that word came in about Max. The newspapers were so overwhelmed by Oscar coverage, it was squeezed in on the bottom of the front page, one line: "MAXWELL A. P. COLEMAN, OP-ART LEGEND AND DOWNTOWN FIXTURE, FATHER OF . . ."

Outside his brownstone, people lined the road, stood at the curb for blocks—socialites, artists, drag queens, club performers, Allegra fans—an impromptu wake of thousands of mourners, well-wishers, and strangers. The media arrived in vans, by the droves. There were dozens of cameras on tripods, dozens of reporters doing stand-ups on Max's front steps.

He died publicly. He died crazily and with great personality. He died with the cameras rolling. Telephoto lenses were trained on the windows of the mourning room and recorded its contents. The lenses saw Max's paintings, his eclectic furniture collection, his fig tree. They saw Max too, in his roll-away bed. He died with his clothes on—his satin evening kimono—and he was watching Sissy Spacek smile and hand Allegra her golden statuette, and Dudus is pretty sure that Max was still conscious when she began what would be known later as the Broken Clock Speech:

"I've been gone, as you know," Allegra said from the podium. Her voice was calm, almost unnatural—not quavering, not one word out of place, not one moment when you felt, as you watched her, that she was just a person, a young woman, a girl really, who might be scared or nervous or overwhelmed. "And while I was gone, I thought a great deal about certain things. And one of the things I wondered about was what I might be doing tonight, and whether I would still be an actress, and still working, and indeed whether I would still be Allegra Coleman. And I find that I am."

The applause was deafening. "Almost immediately," Franklin said. There was a feeling of sympathy in the room, of affection. "That theater felt very small suddenly," he said, "like a small-town rally, as though she were our girl and we were all rooting for her."

She smiled a grateful smile with her mouth closed. "At first I wanted to dedicate this award to all the other actresses who didn't win tonight. For the ones who never won this award, or any award. For the ones who didn't get the chance to make a movie as good as *Sphinxa.* Or for those who did but were overlooked or not acknowledged. I wanted to accept it on behalf of them, and also the ones who have inspired me—women like Anna Magnani and Monica Vitti, Pola Negri and Faye Dunaway. There are so very many of them: the great Greta Garbo, the magnificent Joan Crawford, Gloria Swanson and Marilyn Monroe. The extraordinary Mae Murray. The unbelievable Clara Bow. Women who brought something to the screen—magic, enchantment, intelligence, sensitivity. Women who watched audiences spring to their feet before them, women who were bestowed with fame and riches and popularity, but who also lived long enough to endure the change in tides, the recession of love, the moment when nobody returned their calls. Women whose youth and vibrancy and beauty has been captured on the broken clock of film—but whose time came and left, whose beauty faded before their eyes and ours."

People were mesmerized—where was she going with this? Where was Allegra going?

"But why generalize when I could be more personal," she said, "and reveal something more intimate and human. Why not accept this award on behalf of my mother instead—"

The audience began roaring . . .

"—my beautiful mother, a woman who faded so slowly, so painfully . . . As Pablo Neruda wrote, 'That Tree of our being with its nondescript autumns. A thousand leaves dying.'

"The world turns on and on and on, and new days come and new girls and new sensations—they always feel new— and we lose ourselves in their newness, revel in the sunshine. So fresh, so fair. But not too long from now, I will be fading, and we will be gone, all of us here in our fine clothes in this fine theater. You will go, and you and you and you. All our nondescript autumns, a thousand leaves dying . . .

"We come and go, we bloom and fade, but the movies seem to endure."

———

Franklin's reaction was mixed. He gave a short soliloquy before passing out into the greenery and flowers. "She was breaking all the rules, of course. Too serious and morbid. Almost sickening. You could tell by her face that she thought she was being utterly profound and having epiphanies that had never entered the mind of any other person on earth. And, of course, it might well be true that they'd never entered the mind of a starlet. But what I found most stunning was the reaction. There was the most bizarre mob behavior. People rose to their feet. People seemed delirious—weeping, hugging each other—and there was a frightening surge of black dinner jackets and glittering gowns toward the stage as though everybody had forgotten where they were or who they were. It was a mosh pit, frankly—and it took another ten minutes to get the theater under control."

The frenzy continued for days, months, years. Academics debated the origins of the speech. Psychologists debated Allegra's sanity. Film critics discussed whether she was talking about her father when she talked about her mother, or whether it was about both of them, or whether it was meant to transcend references to actual people. The speech was loved. It was hated. It was mocked and revered, attacked and defended, but mostly immortalized, remembered, referred to, played back, repeated, quoted—parts of it cross-stitched and framed like "Home Sweet Home" on the den walls of ordinary folks across the land—and ultimately responsible for launching interest in two new pictures about Pablo Neruda and a remake of *Il Postino*.

It endured not just as a part of Oscar history or movie history—or Hollywood history—but as almost a pop philosophy, a way of living, a religion. Snippets were played on television for the rest of my life, and beyond that, for years to come, during the lives of my children and my children's children.

—

The morning after the Oscars, the sunlight came into my hospital room, and so did Ned. He looked very fine and sturdy. He looked tall. He bent over me with a kind of rough masculine grace, a feeling of pain being endured but not mentioned, and he kissed me on the mouth. I reached out for his hand. I could see the farm under his nails and smell the smoke.

"I decided," he said, "not to leave you alone anymore."

e are laughing. She is laughing, and in my head she is smiling and driving, and she's thinking, holding a notion, the whole thought of her life and her stardom, in her laugh. Allegra is sitting in a pointy old Jaguar, a racing bullet of a car older than she is, even older than I am. We are speeding. The road is winding. The top is down. Her thin brown shoulders are shaking. Her hands on the steering wheel are vibrating. The enormous blue sky is overhead, and palm trees are lined against the roadway as far as we can see. "Do you ever wonder what's buried underneath the sand?" I ask Allegra. It's the kind of thing she loves to talk about. "All the rusted car parts, the cigarette lighters, the old signs? Do you ever think about all the layers of things we're driving over right now?"

"Bones," she says. "The sand is made of granulated bones, isn't it?"

She laughs with her mouth open. She bends her head down, squeezes her eyes closed for a few seconds, as if she's trying to suppress more laughter. The car begins drifting into the center of the road. But just as I'm starting to worry about when Allegra might look up again, she does. And she's singing: "'Dem bones, dem bones, dem crazy bones . . .'"

Her hair is dark and glossy and perfectly straight because of *Apache.* The new color has changed the shadows of her face, the depth of lines. It has brought out the small hollows under her eyes and made her cheekbones look even wider, if that's possible. But something else has changed about her, something that has nothing at all to do with her hair. Allegra is more subdued. She's more poised, as if steadied by some kind of elegant gravity. She's more Audrey Hepburn and less Calamity Jane Valley Girl. I could hear it over the phone in her voice—a tone shift, a deepening—but now, in the strong sunlight, I see the difference in her face, in the way she holds her body. Perhaps it's the weight of fame, the touchiness of it.

It's hard to fathom how famous she is now—her popularity, her ability to hold the world's attention, is profound and unaccountable and almost frightening, as if she's moved into a territory of fame previously undiscovered and unimagined. It seems to have happened so naturally, at first through her compliance—her willingness—and then her refusal—her running, her disappearance—and then her compliance again—her teary apology, her confession of mental breakdown. In three acts, she became worthy of our love. She has a gift, a genius, along with fearlessness and bravado. And she is alone, all alone—parentless—an icon of great beauty and tenderness and mystery. She inspires suspense whatever she does, wherever she goes, as we await another boyfriend, another disappearance, another bout of madness, or another performance as breathtaking and unforgettable as her Claudia in *L'Avventura*.

For the last six weeks she's been in Needles, a small desert city on the California-Arizona border where the exteriors of *Apache* are being shot. She spends her nights in a Best Western motel room that she's decorated with Target beanbag chairs and pictures ripped from magazines, mostly *W.* She spends her days in a refrigerated trailer on location, her body slathered with sunless tanning creams and makeup to make her skin darker, closer to the "hazelnut hue" of her character, Swala, the troubled half-breed princess of the best-selling novel. The production of *Apache* hasn't been easy—there've been a lot of headaches, setbacks, bad weather, and waiting. In frustration, Allegra sent for her acupuncturist in New York. She hired a speech coach, Ben LoudSky, to help her with proper pronunciation of the Athabascan dialect, although LoudSky abandoned the project after three weeks. Allegra then hired a macrobiotic chef from L.A. and, in addition to Rita, her father's miniature dachshund, adopted a mongrel puppy from the Palm Springs pound. "I'm trying not to have an entourage," she said on the phone a week before my visit. "I'm trying, but it's so hard."

We'd been talking on the phone since late March, early April—since Ned brought me back to Virginia. She called pretty regularly. She called to ask how my eye was. She talked to Bram sometimes, or Ned. She asked questions about her new puppy. She asked if we were having a big wedding and offered to sing. We all decided she was lonely—had to be. But she never complained specifically about that. She never complained much, period. She was bubbly, upbeat. She was full of jokes and wisecracks, always making fun of somebody, usually herself.

———

She's in almost every scene of *Apache,* but she gets a day off here and there. The director, Michael Minor, has gone farther out into the Mojave, near the southern tip of Death Valley, to shoot some scenes with Allegra's costars, Peter Coyote and Ben Affleck. Her boyfriend, Yo-Yo Ma, is also gone for a few days, driven to Vegas, where he and his cello have been performing to packed houses at the Bellagio. When she hears I'm in L.A.—via Margaux, via Franklin— she calls my room at the Beverly Hills L'Ermitage and asks if I want to come see her. "It'll be so great to spend a day away from the trailer," she says, "away from the sun, and without all that body makeup. How's L'Ermitage? I've never stayed there."

"It's nice. Low-key," I say. "Kind of modern, in a forties way that I like." I could have said it's hidden and womblike and discreet, or that I like the staff. I could have added that it's convenient—near Cedars-Sinai, where I've needed to be twice since the end of March for minor adjustments to my Bio-eye. The orb sometimes moves clumsily, with jerking motions. "Well, it won't ever be absolutely perfect," the doctor said when I complained that the eye hadn't lived up to its hype. Nothing lives up to its hype. Nothing in my lifetime has lived up to its hype, except her.

I fly into a small airport outside of Bullhead City, and she is already there on the tarmac, waiting inside a fabulously restored 1961 silver-blue XKE Roadster with the top down. Her hand is over her brow, and she is squinting and smiling and looking up into the sky as if willing the tiny airplane to drop down beside her. Through my scratchy window, she looks like a kid—her shorts and long legs, her hand over her brow, her other hand waving with unrestrained enthusiasm—but when I get down on the ground, I see something else. A wistfulness, a sobriety, the elegant gravity that I'd heard on the phone. A spark is gone. But Allegra has so many sparks left, it hardly seems to matter.

"That dress is groove city," she says, after giving me a rib-cracking hug. "Moda Matta?"

"Von Furstenberg."

"So cool."

In Needles (population 5,989), we find a bakery that serves burned coffee that's also too weak. We find some sticky buns and glazed doughnuts and a couple other stale pastries—maybe things get stale faster in the desert. While digging in to a sticky bun, she talks about why she "went macrobiotic" and asks if I've ever "gone macrobiotic" too. When I say "Are you kidding?" she scowls at me, then laughs.

"It works, you know," she says.

"Works for what?"

Afterward we drive to the Best Western where she's been living. The room is cluttered, almost impossibly so, with tacky purchases from nearby strip malls, from weekends in Las Vegas with Yo-Yo. Taking up one corner is an incredibly large humidifier. "It gets so cold at night," Allegra says, "like, it's freezing. And this motel's got the driest heat. It makes my hair cling to my neck. The first week, my lips were so chapped I couldn't smile." There are two queen beds. Allegra sleeps in one of them. The other is for all her clothes that haven't been put away in the closet yet. There are several piles of them. The garments look new, still unworn. The wholesale tags are still dangling from the sleeves. On the floor are more bags and boxes shipped overnight from New York.

Allegra takes off her shorts and changes into a pair of tight riding breeches. Except for a flesh-toned stretchy bra that squishes her nipples flat, the size of poker chips, she isn't wearing underwear. She picks up a thin sweater off the floor. "I was getting free clothes sent to me before, but not that much," she says, "and it was from kind of bad designers. Now the stuff comes by the truckload—bags and bags. I mean, I can't stop the flow. Do you know how many hours of thank-you notes this translates into? I churn out stacks of these little handwritten notes every week, or postcards. I mean, what am I going to do with ten Gaston La Fille cashmere sweater sets—one in every color—in the middle of May in the Mojave Desert?"

"Ten La Fille sweater sets?"

"Oh God," she says. "They're yours."

We drive on, toward Barstow. It's almost noon, but it feels later, and we're starving again. The sun is baking us, and the air-conditioning in the car doesn't seem to be working—if there is air-conditioning—and Allegra can't figure out how to make the fan go. Lots of billboards start up for something called CALICO EARLY MAN ARCHAEOLOGI-CAL SITE. There's a museum, rest area, and excavation pits started by Louis Leakey. I wonder if the museum is air-conditioned. Allegra seems more intrigued by another bill-board, for CALICO GHOST TOWN. She takes the exit for both, parks the Jaguar in an empty lot, and we enter a visitor's center that feeds into a museum where we find glass cases of arrowheads and spears and bones that have been carved into tools, some of which date back two hundred thousand years. The museum is air-conditioned but smells like mold, the way hotels in Las Vegas smell. Allegra crinkles her nose. "Hey, where are the dinosaurs?" she asks.

There aren't dinosaur bones at Calico, apparently, but we find lunch, or a snack—it's hard to tell which when you're macrobiotic. At a cluster of vending machines, Allegra gets a Dole pineapple juice and an apple juice. I get a Dasani.

"Come on, earthling," she says. "Let's blast off."

Her next movie is a science-fiction space feature. She plays an alien. The part is "my first broad comedy," she says.

Back on the highway, I see a sign ahead for Apple Valley, and the turn-off for Big Bear Lake. Allegra takes both hands off the steering wheel in order to fasten her hair with a clip. She puts the clip between her teeth while she gathers her hair in both hands. When she's done, she puts the radio on, a country station playing Johnny Cash.

"Have you ever been to Big Bear?" she asks.

"No," I say.

"Lake Arrowhead?"

I shake my head.

"How could you grow up in California and not ever go there?"

"I grew up in New Jersey."

"Really? Oh, that's so weird. Are you sure? Don't look at me like that. I'm sorry. I thought you were from here. Haven't we ever talked about this?"

"Forget it," I say.

"Anyway, there's something so depressing about Big Bear. Don't ever go there."

"Lake Arrowhead?"

"Equally depressing. Sort of scary. Lakes are scary anyway—like, murky and moldy, and you don't know what's all the way down at the bottom? And so cold and still. It's not like the briny sea, the healthy moving exuberant briny sea. Anyway, I can't believe we scattered Kay's ashes there," she says. "That was such a stupid move."

She's been thinking about her mother lately, she says. This has puzzled her. She assumed that she'd be overcome with grief about Max, but she's found herself "thinking all the time about Kay and what a disaster her life was." About a week after she won the Oscar, she was in New York and eating dinner at the Fungi Palace in the Village and she had a vision. The restaurant was dark, and the tables were lit up with small votive candles. "Margaux was with me—she'd flown out to look after me for a while," Allegra says, "and we were drinking some wine, maybe a couple glasses, I'm not sure, and all of a sudden the white napkins on the table started flying around the room like doves. Then it was tons of doves flying over me, flying over my dinner plate, over the organic vegetables and organic mushrooms, and all this flapping noise."

Allegra holds her head cocked in a poise of fear as she tells this story, the way Tippi Hedren holds her head in *The Birds,* as though the doves were still flying above her. "And the doves kept coming, and I thought they were really beautiful at first—and they really were, the way they looked in the candlelight, really exquisite—but then there were so many of them, such a crowd of birds. And they started flying into each other, hitting each other—the way birds never do in real life, like their sonar was off. And they start thumping into each other and falling down onto my dinner plate, sort of knocked out or unconscious until the table was covered with doves, steeped in doves. I mean, there were doves up to my chin.

"I stopped breathing. I swear I did. And then I moaned and passed out, according to Margaux. Later on, I figured out what it was about."

"What?" I asked.

"It wasn't really about my sadness for her, or missing her," she says. "I just felt bad. I felt really bad about making it—about being bigger than Mom. But I've gotten over that."

———

The first time she contacted me in Virginia—shortly after the Oscars, maybe around the time she had the vision of the doves at the Fungi Palace—she said she was calling to say she was sorry. Her voice was quavering and uncertain. She sounded very small, like she was almost not there. She wanted to know how I was.

"I'm okay," I said.

"I feel bad about what happened," she said.

"Jesus," I said. "You left me for dead."

"No, I didn't," she said. "I mean, there wasn't anything I could do. I went for help. I sent help, didn't I?"

"According to the police report, the rescue team was alerted by another driver on the road."

"That's not what I mean," she said.

She didn't say anything for a long time, just put a stick of chewing gum into her mouth and softened it with a few big chews. I spoke next and changed the subject to something easy and light. And after that, it hadn't come up again. For one thing, I didn't feel like pressing it. I didn't want to push her away. I knew that someday she'd stop calling. And I knew that someday she'd stop sending bizarre postcards from the road, and stop sending shockingly huge floral arrangements on my birthday, or when I had a baby, or right before Christmas on the anniversary of the accident. Eventually she would stop feeling bad. Eventually she would move on. She had to. "Movie stars," as Myrna had said, "make the worst friends." But I was okay with that too. It was fun just to have known Allegra, to have been with her, to have tasted a little of that thing she had, whatever it was—that joy, that insouciance, that tendency to forget.

———

The Mission Inn is a gorgeous, rambling "national landmark" of a hotel in a Spanish baroque design, with fountains and arches and tile roofs and bougainvillea all around. It was built by a prosperous entrepreneur, Frank Miller, first as a home, then as a hotel, at the turn of the last century.

"Tom Swimmer asked about you the other day," Allegra says at the Inn, where we stop for another snack or meal or something. She had driven there without one slipup or wrong turn, but then people always drive around their hometowns in an efficient unconscious way. "I was over at his place getting some stuff I left there," she says. "Yo came with me. He was helping me with the boxes. And I was mostly just talking with Tom. He's so sweet."

"Yeah, he is."

We're sitting in a courtyard, eating a couple of Cobb salads—half of the ingredients of which I don't believe are actually macrobiotic, but I don't bother to mention this to you-know-who.

"I don't think he's gotten over you," she says, "or whatever happened."

"Oh, please."

"Really." She puts down her fork.

"Allegra, there were pictures of you all over his den. It looked like a shrine."

"Really?" Her face seems disbelieving, but I suspect she's playing dumb. Then she scratches her neck. "Tom is really sweet," she says finally.

"Yeah, he is."

"I don't think he's that happy doing TV. He has to work all the time. He's working constantly. He's up early, home late . . ."

I look around at the old hotel. I'm getting tired of talking about Tom, and Spanish architecture always seems so mysterious.

"Isn't this what San Simeon looks like?" I ask Allegra.

"Yeah," she says. "It's where Orson Welles got all his ideas."

"Hearst, you mean."

"Oh yeah," she says. "They've become the same person in my mind."

I can hear a fountain running somewhere—the sound of water trickling, the soft murmur of voices beyond the courtyard. And off in the distance, I heard the *thrung* of a diving board and the sound of somebody splashing in a pool.

The waitress comes and puts a bill facedown on the table. She stares at Allegra like she's seeing a ghost or a monster—someone so impossibly famous that she's now become scary.

I reach for the bill, to pick it up first, and Allegra seems startled. "Oh, no!" she says. "Let me pay."

She twists around in her chair to grab her silver calfskin pouch draped over the back. She digs into the bag with one hand and pulls out a striped wallet. When she opens it and sees there isn't any cash, she pulls out a green Conglom Visa card.

"Oh God," she says, "This is Margaux's. I've had it for so long and I keep forgetting to give it back."

I'll choose not to consider how Allegra came into possession of that Conglom card. Or ponder what it had bought. Every star is born of a conspiracy of sorts.

———

"Tom's nice," I say later, in the car. "But I never really pictured you guys together for long, never imagined it lasting. You know? There's something a little beleaguered about him."

"Kind of downbeat."

"Yeah."

"I know what you mean. Comedians are like that. Kind of depressing."

"Yeah," I said. "And there's something else."

"What?"

"I don't want to sound mean."

"What?"

"His hair."

"What about it?"

"You ever seen it wet?"

"Wet?" Allegra starts to smile. "You're bad. You're so bad."

We are laughing, and we are smiling, and the sky is growing dark by the time we get to an undefined, unsettled part of the desert between Ludlow and Bagdad on Highway 40, the road that will lead us, finally, back to Needles. The wind is cold. The top is closed. The headlights of the Jaguar are low and point forward—twin lights, parallel beams, dissolving into the black desert night.

A truck is in the distance. Allegra doesn't seem to notice.

"Who was your first movie star?" she asks. "The one you really fell for."

"That's so personal."

Allegra laughs.

"Living or dead?"

"What's the difference?" Allegra says. "The first."

"Gable."

"Yeah," she says, nodding her head. "Good choice. Nice mouth."

"And you?"

"Tallulah Bankhead," she says.

"Really? She's so amazing."

"In *Lifeboat*."

"When she gives her mink coat away."

"She should have made more movies."

"Yeah."

"Her father was the Speaker of the House. Did you know that?"

"I know. Amazing. Everything about her is amazing. So raunchy—"

"So alive."

"So *fuck you*."

Allegra bends her head down and squeezes her eyes shut again, to try to stop laughing. Then she pulls the car to the side of the road, and she doesn't do a particularly good job of it. But the road is empty. The desert is empty. It's flat and empty and cold and looks like it goes on forever.

"I've got an idea," she says.

She's wearing a big sweater coat with the tag still on it. I reach in the backseat and face the big bag of new clothes that she's given me, and I take out four sweaters and put them on, one over the other. I put on a baggy pair of cashmere sweats too, over my jeans.

And then we walk and walk as far as we can. We go for fifteen or twenty minutes—a mile, I'm not sure. It feels almost like we have a destination, because we are in the middle of nowhere and walking a straight line. Pretty soon the cold doesn't bother us. The cold seems very far away, like all the stars in the sky.

And then, darling, we scream. And we scream and scream and scream.

ACE IN THE HOLE

Dark Media Drama. Kirk Douglas stars as a corrupt journalist who builds a journalistic circus around a poor bloke trapped in the title hole. Billy Wilder wrote and produced and directed this comment on modern media, but it's so bitter and heartless, not to mention cruel, that the audience fled in droves. Eventually, the title was changed (to *The Big Carnival*) to protect the innocent. Paramount. 1951.

ACROSS THE PACIFIC

Inconsequential Silent Drama. Monte Blue—whose name sounds like a kind of smelly cheese—stars as an army officer fighting Filipino guerrillas. Myrna Loy is Roma, an exotic Asian beauty. Written by Darryl Zanuck and directed by Roy Del Ruth. Warner Bros. 1926.

AFTER THE THIN MAN

Detective Comedy. It's sometimes hard to keep all the *Thin Man* movies straight. They blur in the mind and you're left with only the memory of a martini glass, or Asta, or Mrs. Asta, or the master suite's Art Deco bedroom set with the twin beds. This particular installment—#2—is quite lovely. William Powell and Myrna Loy star as the ever-charming, oft-inebriated detectives Nick and Nora Charles. Jimmy Stewart plays a bad guy with a good-guy face. Directed by W. S. "Woody" Van Dyke. MGM. 1936.

AIRPORT 1975

Better to rent *Grand Hotel*—the inspiration for this epic disaster—than be reduced to watching this unfathomably bad sequel. One feels sorry for Charlton Heston and Myrna Loy, who were trotted out, along with Gloria Swanson, to play cardboard cutouts of their screen personas. One wishes they'd had the dignity and restraint to stay home. Universal. 1974.

ALOMA OF THE SOUTH SEAS

Fizzy Tropical Tonic. Hard to know whether the winsome Dorothy Lamour is the star of this picture, or her flimsy sarong, or the rumbling volcano. Jon Hall costars. Directed by Alfred Santell. Paramount. 1941.

AMARCORD

Comedy/Memoir/Fantasy. Federico Fellini's scathing and loving remembrance of a small-town childhood in Fascist Italy. Vivid, hilarious, imaginative, and, aside from the loneliness, completely unbelievable—but if it were believable, it wouldn't be Fellini. FC Produzioni/PECF. 1974.

ANOTHER THIN MAN

Detective Romance/Fabulous Repartee. The third installment of the *Thin Man* series, with Myrna Loy and William Powell—

and the last one with pizzazz. Directed by W. S. "Woody" Van Dyke. MGM. 1939.

ASHES AND DIAMONDS

Mandatory Viewing for All Film Students. On the last day of World War II, a Polish assassin shoots the wrong guy. Technically, that's the storyline, but mostly, the movie's about politics and class, the dual European obsessions. Starring Zbigniew Cybulski, an adorably roguish Polish heartthrob. Directed by Andrzej Wajda. Film Polski. 1958.

L'AVVENTURA

The Beautiful People Go Yachting Around a Volcanic Island. This esoteric mystery is really about love—and its strange pathway to mindlessness and lack of love. Writer/director Michelangelo Antonioni at his finest. He's in touch with the fickleness of humanity and the emptiness of desire. Monica Vitti is magnificent, and so is everything else. If you can't get into this movie but like missing-persons mysteries, try *Picnic at Hanging Rock* or *Laura*. Cino del Duca/PCE/Lyre. 1960.

BABES IN BAGDAD

Unfunny, Verging on Camp. Exotic harem girls (of a certain age) go on strike. Starring Paulette Goddard, who retired a couple of years later, and Gypsy Rose Lee. United Artists. 1952.

BARBARELLA

Sci-Fi Sex Farce. Despite the talents of contributing screenwriter Terry Southern—he wrote *Dr. Strangelove* and *Easy Rider*—this futuristic Western is deeply shallow and dull. Jane

Fonda hadn't yet learned how to act, but her pointy bras and big hair compensate. Directed by Roger Vadim. Marianne Productions/Dino de Laurentiis Cinematografica/Paramount. 1968.

BEING THERE

A perfectly perfect movie. A comedy that's black and blue and slapstick and everything else; filmed largely at Biltmore, the Vanderbilt estate in Asheville, North Carolina. Peter Sellers stars as Chance, the illiterate gardener who is given shelter by a dying billionaire and rises to national prominence. Shirley MacLaine is adorable and riveting as the billionaire's wife. Melvyn Douglas (in one of his last roles) is the billionaire. Jack Warden plays the U.S. president. Directed by Hal Ashby. Lorimar/Northstar/CIP. 1979.

BEN-HUR

Huge, larger-than-life religious epic—sometimes, in the right light, also a comedy—that almost bankrupted MGM, until the returns started gushing in. The incomparable Charlton Heston was the studio's fourth choice (after Rock Hudson, Marlon Brando, and Burt Lancaster) to star as the brawny and heroic Judah Ben-Hur. But he's tops. Directed by William Wyler. 1959.

BEYOND THE ROCKS

Valentino Vehicle. Rudolph plays an English lord opposite Gloria Swanson, in a silent film (Valentino's twenty-fourth movie out of thirty-two) that, regrettably, has been lost: No negatives or prints are known to exist. Directed by Sam Wood. Famous Players–Lasky/Paramount. 1922.

THE BIRDS

Ornithological Horror in the Spirit of Edgar Allan Poe. People are obsessed with this movie, and too much has been written about it already. For those of us who were already suspicious of birds, it sealed the deal. Starring Tippi Hedren and Rod Taylor, neither of whom figured out how to persuasively look upward with great dread. Directed by Alfred Hitchcock. Universal. 1963.

THE BISHOP'S WIFE

Gushy Inspirational. If it weren't for the very dry charms of Cary Grant and David Niven (who really doesn't act so much as exude wit), this movie would have sunk from sheer wetness. Loretta Young is magnificently misty-eyed. Complaints aside, it holds up quite splendidly. Directed by Henry Koster. RKO/Samuel Goldwyn. 1947.

BLOWUP

Psychological Thriller/Zen Koan. Vanessa Redgrave is the tall, lanky Antonioni girl who's an accomplice to a murder witnessed only by a camera. David Hemmings is the passive hero, a 1960s fashion photographer with white bellbottoms and a Nikon that he follows Redgrave around with. Jane Birkin is a teenager who wants to be a model and wrestles with him on the ground. Haunting, fabulous, influential (everybody wanted bellbottoms and a Nikon afterward). Directed (and cowritten) by Michelangelo Antonioni. MGM/Carlo Ponti. 1966.

BULLITT

Legendary Chase Movie. Steve McQueen plays Steve McQueen—this time as an undercover police lieutenant in

San Francisco. He drives a green Mustang Fastback up and down steep hills and around winding interchanges, some of which, lamentably, don't exist anymore. This movie is so legendary, there are websites devoted to the Mustang alone. Directed by Peter Yates. Warner Bros./Solar Productions. 1968.

CAIN AND MABEL

Awkward Comedy-Drama/Musical. Clark Gable is a brawny prizefighter who falls in love with Marion Davies, who shows off her comic talents as a Broadway dancer. They are pretty great together, but the musical numbers are strange. No matter. You won't be able to rent it anyway. Directed by Lloyd Bacon. Cosmopolitan Pictures/Warner Bros. 1936.

THE CALL OF THE WILD

Dog and Snow Movie That Produced a Love Child. Clark Gable plays a macho, probably sex-starved Yukon prospector. Loretta Young plays a luscious young widow. A blizzard on location in Alaska brought these two stars together, and nine months later, Young had a baby in secret—and then raised her as her "adopted" daughter, Judy. Directed by William Wellman. Twentieth Century. 1935.

CAPTAINS COURAGEOUS

Multi-Tissue Weeper/Classic. A spoiled rich boy falls off a cruise ship and is rescued by a boat of Portuguese fishermen. Spencer Tracy plays the gruff God-fearing peasant whom the boy, played by Freddie Bartholomew, comes to adore. When Tracy dies, it's Oscar time. You're still crying fifteen minutes later. Directed by Victor Fleming. MGM. 1937.

CASABLANCA

War Romance. It's as beautiful as a starry night sky and almost as perfect. Humphrey Bogart plays Rick, a tough, embittered romantic who runs a saloon in North Africa. Ingrid Bergman is luminescent and completely believable as the woman who broke his heart. Claude Rains plays a French captain who sets the tone of the film with a dark yet jolly cynicism (a kind of trench humor). Everybody else is a winner—Peter Lorre, Sydney Greenstreet—except the heinous Paul Henreid, of course. Directed by Michael Curtiz. Warner Bros. 1942.

CITIZEN KANE

Fictional Biopic. Orson Welles brought a unique vision to moviemaking—an imprint that's mannered and yet defies imitation. He plays himself in *Citizen Kane* as much as he plays the publishing tycoon Charles Foster Kane a.k.a. William Randolph Hearst, and watching him is dreadful fun. RKO/ Mercury Productions. 1941.

COME TO THE STABLE

Spiritual Kitsch Classic. If this movie doesn't make you want to become a Roman Catholic, nothing will. Loretta Young and Celeste Holm are two nuns with buttery faces determined to build a children's hospital in staid New England. Based on a story by Clare Boothe Luce. Directed by Henry Koster. Twentieth Century Fox. 1949.

THE CONFORMIST

Moody Marxist-Freudian Romance. Gorgeous, rich, unforgettable. This may be Bernardo Bertolucci's best movie. It's about sexual confusion and fear transformed into political passion. Jean-Louis Trintignant plays a repressed Fascist. Dominique Sanda is Anna, the alluring lipstick lesbian who seems to set everything in motion. Mars Film/Marianne Productions/Maran Film. 1970.

DIRTY HARRY

Revenge Fantasy/Cop Thriller. Clint Eastwood plays a cop, Harry Callahan, who's a very cool hothead. He barely winces when he pulls the trigger, which is often. Lots of bullets and sexy shots of his .44 Magnum. Only for the bold. Great one-liners. Directed by Don Siegel. Warner Bros./Malpaso. 1971.

DR. STRANGELOVE OR:
HOW I LEARNED TO STOP WORRYING AND LOVE THE BOMB

Cold-War Comedy. Only Stanley Kubrick could have made a movie this dark and ridiculous and chilly. Peter Sellers in three roles—as the affable American president, a silly RAF captain, and a disturbed foreign-affairs adviser who everybody said was based on Henry Kissinger—warms up the whole thing. Columbia Pictures/Hawk Films. 1964.

EAST OF EDEN

Overwrought Coming-of-Age Drama. James Dean plays a tortured, rebellious kid who's always being unfavorably compared to his goody-goody brother. Their names are Cal and Aron (a short walk from Cain and Abel, if that helps you figure out where the narrative is going). The acting is incredible—Julie Harris is stunningly good and Dean became an overnight sensation—but the movie clunks along and you find yourself wincing more than Clint Eastwood in *Dirty Harry.* Directed by Elia Kazan. Warner Bros. 1955.

EASY RIDER

Stoner Biker Flick. Please don't attempt to watch this cultural artifact now—the agony will be too great and you might need to hurl objects at the screen. The world has moved on, mostly for the better. But hey, man, once upon a time our parents hung on its every word. Directed by Dennis Hopper. Columbia Pictures/Pando/Raybert Productions. 1969.

THE ECLIPSE

Bitter, Modern Romance. Monica Vitti ends one affair and begins another—and plays with a kind of riveting subtlety an anguished yet remote Antonioni heroine. It should be boring, but it's not—that's how it always is with Antonioni. Dreamy costar Alain Delon helps too. Directed by Michelangelo Antonioni. Cineriz/Interopa Film/Paris Film. 1962.

THE ENGLISH PATIENT

Bridges of Madison County with wings. It's a story too complicated and unique to parboil here. (It will sound as if I made it up.) But Juliette Binoche plays a nurse who is taking care of an Austrian count with a charred body. Ralph Fiennes is the burn victim. Kristin Scott Thomas is a selfish adulteress who wears a bomber jacket and jodhpurs throughout. The whole movie has the feeling of a lie—but the mood of truth. Directed by Anthony Minghella. Tiger Moth Productions/Miramax. 1996.

EVER SINCE EVE

Forgotten Comedy. This is Marion Davies's last movie, before she retired at age forty to her jigsaw puzzles. She plays a sexy secretary who makes herself look dowdy at work in order to put lecherous execs off the scent. But when her new boss runs into her outside the office—when she's not wearing the thick glasses and frumpola wardrobe—he falls for her. A romp ensues. Directed by Lloyd Bacon. Cosmopolitan Pictures/First National/Warner Bros. 1937.

THE FARMER'S DAUGHTER

Political Comedy. Loretta Young plays an earnest, honest, gung-ho Swedish farm girl who heads off for life in the big city, in the role that won her a Best Actress Oscar. She winds up a maid in the house of a prominent politician (played by the very attractive, very single Joseph Cotten). Just when she's proven herself indispensable to the family, she begins to express her political views—and runs for office herself. Funny, and somehow convincing. Directed by H. C. Potter. RKO. 1947.

GIANT

Oilman vs. Cattleman Epic. Very long family saga set in Texas. James Dean plays an upstart oilman who seems to be acting in a different movie from everybody else, mostly due to an overwrought style and self-indulgence. Rock Hudson brings in a decent performance as an old-fashioned heterosexual cattleman. Elizabeth Taylor plays the refined Virginia belle whom Hudson drags back to the ranch to marry. Directed by George Stevens. Warner Bros. 1956.

GIRLS ABOUT TOWN

Big-Hearted Comedy. Kay Francis stars as a gold digger who finds true love in the big city. Joel McCrea is so young he's almost unrecognizable. Hard to find on video. Directed by George Cukor. Paramount. 1931.

GONE WITH THE WIND

Civil War Gothic. Vivien Leigh is the belle of all southern belles—with so many adoring men to chose from she can't really focus properly on Confederate officer/entrepreneur Clark Gable, the only gent who's got her number. An all-star cast, unforgettable film moments, Hollywood in all its glory. Directed by Victor Fleming (and, uncredited, George Cukor and Sam Wood). MGM/Selznick International. 1939.

GRAND HOTEL

Golden Age Masterpiece. People say this movie's a dinosaur, but the performances are still lovely, brilliant, absolutely ace. And they make you forget the ridiculous rushed narrative. Greta Garbo plays the melancholy dancer Grusinskaya. John Barrymore is a painfully well-adjusted European aristocrat who keeps losing at cards—and turns to theft. Wallace Beery plays an awful prewar German capitalist, the sort of bore you always find in first-class seating on airplanes. Joan Crawford is a secretary so thin, so unspeakably lovely and tremulous, that she gives Garbo a run for her money. There have been attempts at remakes—and rank TV spin-offs like *The Love Boat*—but nothing comes close to the streamlined elegance of *Grand Hotel,* now, then, or ever. Directed by Edmund Goulding. MGM. 1932.

THE GREAT ESCAPE

POW-Camp Adventure. This is what *Pearl Harbor* could have been: an all-male, all-star cast; a wicked script; a great director (John Sturges) who really knows how to deliver soaring visual moments. Steve McQueen plays a POW who plans an escape from a Nazi prison camp—along with James Garner, Richard Attenborough, Charles Bronson, James Coburn, David McCallum, and a few others. The music is great, and for sure cinematic excitement, McQueen's getaway on a motorcycle rivals the *Bullitt* chase scene and *E.T.*'s flying bicycles. United Artists/Mirisch Company. 1963.

THE GREATEST SHOW ON EARTH

Big-Top Drama. Cecil B. De Mille tries to turn circus life into a grand unfolding epic (complete with train crash) but makes it look creepy and tired instead—like a David Lynch movie without the good music. De Mille won a sympathy/frequent-flier-points Oscar for Best Picture anyway and made *The Ten Commandments* four years later, his last movie. Starring Charlton Heston, Jimmy Stewart, Betty Hutton, Cornel Wilde, Dorothy Lamour, and Gloria Grahame. Paramount. 1952.

THE GRIFTERS

Darkness at Its Most Bleak and Unspeakable. Anjelica Huston is a liar, a thief—a relentless con artist who raises her son, John Cusack, in the timeless grifter tradition. Annette Bening is the grifter girl of Cusack's dreams, but he winds up with Mom in the end anyway. Only for the bold. Based on a Jim Thompson novel. Directed by Stephen Frears. Palace Films/Cineplex Odeon/Miramax. 1990.

HER JUNGLE LOVE

Tropical Romance. Ray Milland is an aviator with the luck to crash into a jungle where Dorothy Lamour—at her sweetest— is living with Gaga, a chimp, and Meewa, a tiger cub. There's also a volcano, of course, and, if I remember rightly, an earthquake. Hugely popular. Directed by George Archainbaud. Paramount. 1938.

HOFFMAN

Hilarious Movie You'll Never See. Peter Sellers at his most silly and perverted. Friends complain they can't find this movie anywhere—and I do wonder if some loathsome film-rights sadist is getting strange joy by cheating the world out of seeing this fine 113 minutes of comic filmmaking. Sellers plays Benjamin Hoffman, a lonely man who blackmails his timid typist (the splendid Sinéad Cusack, a.k.a. Mrs. Jeremy Irons) into spending a weekend with him. In spite of his underhandedness and the high creep factor ("Are you moved, Miss Smith, by my maleness?"), you wind up rooting for Hoffman in the end. Not to mention crying with laughter. If you find yourself terribly frustrated in your attempts to rent this picture, rent *There's a Girl in My Soup* instead. Directed by Alvin Rakoff. Associated British Films/American Continental Films. 1970.

THE HURRICANE

Love Among the Glistening Fronds. John Ford directed the hurricane—which should have won a technical achievement Oscar on its own—in this Paul Gauguin fantasy flick. When the wicked winds come, and the driving rain, Dorothy Lamour clings to the trunk of a palm tree in a very long, and possibly Freudian, cinematic climax. Samuel Goldwyn/United Artists. 1937.

THE JUNGLE PRINCESS

Tropical Sensation. This is Dorothy Lamour's first real role (after two bit parts) and first time out playing a Tarzan-type girl who can tame all the jungle creatures (Liamu, the tiger, and Bogo, the chimp). She tames Ray Milland too, a British hunter who is rescued by Dottie in the most appealing way. If you've forgotten why youth and innocence are so magical, and fleeting, see how Dorothy moves in her sarong and smiles at the chimp. Directed by Wilhelm Thiele. Paramount. 1936.

KHARTOUM

Splashy Battles and British Glory. This is the tale of how General Charles George Gordon finally died at Khartoum—after a long and valiant career as a British officer, a governor of the equatorial provinces of central Africa, then governor general in various British colonies around the globe. The battles are sensational, the cast unsurpassable—Charlton Heston (as General Gordon), Laurence Olivier, and Ralph Richardson. Academics loved the accuracy of the film but critics decried it as dull. I saw it as a boy and then scurried to the corner bookseller for Lytton Strachey's account of Gordon's life in *Eminent Victorians*. Directed by Basil Dearden. Cinerama/United Artists. 1966.

KING FOR A NIGHT

Rank—and Fortunately Unrentable. It's too bad that an actress with such a sweet face and profoundly memorable name as Helen Twelvetrees should have wasted herself on movies with no shelf life. In this forgotten moral saga, a minister's son becomes a boxer and goes to the electric chair for a murder that his sister committed. Directed by Kurt Neumann. Universal. 1933.

THE LADY EVE

Con Artist Comedy with Verbal Banter and Slapstick. Barbara Stanwyck is a con girl who, with her cardsharp father (played by Charles Coburn), cruises a passenger ship looking for an easy mark. They spy Henry Fonda, the rather nerdy heir to a brewery fortune (he's been up or down the Amazon for the past few years, studying snakes), and decide to take him for a ride. Fonda falls for Stanwyck, then sadly grows wise to her con, then falls for her again when she shows up at his family's estate pretending to be a British aristocrat. Lots of pratfalls, but even those who hate slapstick love this picture. Directed by Preston Sturges. Paramount. 1941.

THE LAST EMPEROR

Unimaginably Beautiful Epic About China's Last Imperial Ruler. It ran 160 minutes when it was first released in 1987, but after the movie won Best Picture and heaps of acclaim, Bernardo Bertolucci came out with a director's cut that was an hour longer. The acting (Peter O'Toole, Joan Chen, John Lone), the sets, the costumes, the music, the photography by Vittorio Storaro . . . it's all so splendid you can't quite fathom it. And the longest producing credit in history: Columbia Pictures/Yanco/Tao Films/Recorded Pictures Company/Screenframe/AAA Productions/Soprofilms.

LAST TANGO IN PARIS

Meditation on Mortality, Among Other Things. When this movie came out, everybody winced and complained about how old and fat Marlon Brando was—how unsexy for a movie that seemed to be all about sex. In hindsight, of course, he's a veritable stud. (And only forty-eight.) Lovely, potent acting, and hilarious dialogue that's cynical without being depressing. Directed by Bernardo Bertolucci. Les Productions Artistes Associés/Produzioni Europee Associati/United Artists. 1972.

LAURA

Sophisticated Mystery with Famous Title Song. It's vaguely Allegra-esque, in that the central figure, the eponymous Laura (played by Gene Tierney), is absent for most of the picture. Clifton Webb is scary as the urbane bad guy. Dana Andrews is handsome, but doesn't seem smart enough to have solved the mystery. On the edge of being film noir. Directed by Otto Preminger. Twentieth Century Fox. 1944.

LIFEBOAT

Survivor at Sea. Tallulah Bankhead is the only one you'll remember afterward—her smoker's voice, her selfishness, her fur coat that she gives away in a moment of humanity, her heavy diamond bracelet as it falls into the deep. She plays a spoiled high-society journalist who, like most of the others in the lifeboat, has survived a U-boat attack on a passenger ship during World War II. (It's war-effort propaganda.) Directed by Alfred Hitchcock. Twentieth Century Fox. 1944.

LOCAL HERO

Relocation Fantasy. An American oil executive is sent to a small seaside village in Scotland to discreetly bring together a big offshore refinery deal. He falls in love with the village, the villagers, the quiet shore. And unlike Dorothy in Oz, he doesn't come to discover that there's no place like home: He comes to discover that there's no place like Scotland. With Burt Lancaster and Peter Riegert; written and directed by Bill Forsyth. Enigma Films/Goldcrest Films. 1983.

LOVE STARVED (A.K.A. YOUNG BRIDE, A.K.A. VENEER)

Helen Twelvetrees Melodrama. You know a movie's a stinker when its name is changed twice. Clementine has a strange obsession with Twelvetrees, an actress who, like a hibiscus blossom, seems to have lasted only a day before withering. This movie is so forgotten, and possibly nonexistent, along with poor Helen (who killed herself in 1958), that I couldn't even find the plot described in *Halliwell's Film and Video Guide*. Directed by William A. Seiter. RKO. 1932.

THE MAGNIFICENT AMBERSONS

Nearly a Masterpiece. This movie is more famous for having been butchered by the studio than for being actually great. We're supposed to take on faith that it *really would have been fabulous* if only poor genius Orson Welles had been left alone. Never mind that the central character, the pampered brat George Amberson Minifer, is played by an actor so weak and incompetent that you keep wanting to step in and redirect all his scenes. RKO/Mercury Productions. 1942.

THE MAGNIFICENT SEVEN

Eastern Western. It's quite funny that a fabulous Western should be inspired by a Japanese samurai movie. But it goes to show you that if you put together a great tale, inspiring music (by Elmer Bernstein), and a cast including Steve McQueen, James Coburn, Charles Bronson, and Eli Wallach, then even

Yul Brynner is utterly convincing as a hired gun. Thoughts of the King of Siam never enter your mind. United Artists/ Mirisch-Alpha. 1960.

THE MALTESE FALCON

The Ultimate Noir Mystery. Fast-paced, timeless, and hasn't lost any of its juice. Hard to believe that this is John Huston's directorial debut—as well as Sydney Greenstreet's first movie role (at age sixty-one). Humphrey Bogart is peerless as cynical Sam Spade, a San Francisco private eye trying to avenge his partner's murder. Mary Astor is birdlike but steely as the noir widow. Peter Lorre and Elisha Cook, Jr.—as Joel Cairo and Wilmer Cook—complete the movie like bookends. Warner Bros. 1941.

MAN WANTED

Kay Francis plays the stylish, overworking editor of *400* magazine, who hires a male secretary with a Harvard degree. This comedy was made at the height of Francis's popularity, when Warner Bros. was pumping out seven of her movies a year. It shows. Directed by William Dieterle. 1932.

MANHATTAN MELODRAMA

Gangster Romance. This is the last movie John Dillinger saw—he had a crush on Myrna Loy—before being gunned down by FBI agents on his way out of a Chicago movie theater. Clark Gable stars as a racketeer whose lifelong pal, William Powell, has become the governor of New York. Myrna Loy starts off as the gangster's girl, then winds up the governor's wife. A bit unbelievable on paper, but somehow

Myrna pulls it off. Directed by W. S. "Woody" Van Dyke. MGM. 1934.

MEAN STREETS

Hoods on the Loose. Martin Scorsese made this low-budget movie about a tight clutch of hoods in New York's Little Italy, and the film world has never been the same. It's inspired, truthful, largely improvised and delightfully plotless—just vignettes, sordid details, hilarious moments. Harvey Keitel is brilliant as the religiously impassioned street kid who wants a quiet, respectable life. Robert De Niro is spellbinding as the sociopath whom Keitel wants to save. Taplin-Perry-Scorsese/Warner Bros. 1973.

MILDRED PIERCE

Noir Fable About Spoiling Your Children. Joan Crawford made an unprecedented comeback in this movie—she was only forty, mind you—playing a driven, ambitious character not unlike herself (complete with wretched daughter). This movie was a sensation and won Crawford a surprising and earned Oscar for Best Actress. Even the hardboiled author, James M. Cain, felt honored to have his remarkable novel realized so beautifully on the screen. Directed by Michael Curtiz. Warner Bros. 1945.

MISTER ROBERTS

War Drama/Comedy. When you go to war, you're supposed to find some action and kill people—not be stuck on a cargo ship in the middle of nowhere. Henry Fonda plays Mister Roberts, the restless officer who winds up tossing the captain's palm tree overboard. James Cagney is the captain. William Powell plays the wise but patient ship's doctor. Jack Lemmon won an Oscar for his portrayal of the neurotic, Mister Roberts–worshiping Ensign Pulver. Directed by John Ford and Mervyn LeRoy. Warner Bros. 1955.

MOMMIE DEAREST
Tattletale Docudrama. Joan Crawford as seen through the eyes of her bitter, browbeaten, and unforgiving (adopted) daughter. (See *Mildred Pierce*.) Faye Dunaway nearly ruined her career playing Crawford in this movie—becoming a laughable cartoon and cult figure all at once—as though Saint Joan were cursing her from the grave. Directed by Frank Perry. Paramount. 1981.

MULHOLLAND DRIVE
Post-Noir Noir. David Lynch's creepy, compelling masterpiece about how Hollywood and dreams of Hollywood corrupt and destroy innocence and authenticity. Naomi Watts gives an unfailingly perfect performance as both the enthusiastic young wannabe and the suicidal never-was. Asymmetrical Productions/Imagine Television/Le Studio Canal/ABC/Universal Focus. 2001.

MY DARLING CLEMENTINE
Moody, Spare Western. Henry Fonda plays Wyatt Earp as a kindly, slightly awkward guy who just wants to clean up Arizona. As Doc Holliday, Victor Mature gives one of his best performances. His tubercular coughing fits are fantastic, along with his gunslinging. Directed by John Ford. Twentieth Century Fox. 1946.

1900

Homage to Communism, Peasant Country Life, and the Nineteenth-Century Novel. This movie isn't everybody's bag—the romance with Communism, for starters. But the cast is full of heavy hitters, and director Bernardo Bertolucci brings his considerable gifts to this grand, serious political epic about the rise of Fascism. A few unique moments alone are worth the price of renting it and the expenditure of 245 minutes, which is how long the movie runs. Robert De Niro (from a landowning family) and Gérard Depardieu (a peasant) embody the political dialectic. Burt Lancaster plays De Niro's grandfather. Donald Sutherland is a bad guy of the bourgeoisie. Artémis Productions/Les Productions Artistes Associés/ Produzioni Europee Associati/Paramount. 1976.

LA NOTTE

Mystery of Despair. Director Michelangelo Antonioni made this film on the heels of *L'Avventura*. It's about a novelist and his wife who discover the hollowness and uncertainty of their marriage, and their lives, over the course of one night in Milan. Marcello Mastroianni, who does shallow and mournful better than anybody, is the novelist. Jeanne Moreau, at her most pouty and alluring, is the discontented wife. Monica Vitti plays a sultry provocateur they bump into at a glamorous party. "I'm sick of both of you," Vitti says to them at the end. But we aren't. Nepi Film/Sofitedip/Silver Films. 1960.

NOW, VOYAGER

Sappy Romance with Lots of Cigarettes. The only good thing about this movie is Bette Davis. As Charlotte, the repressed New England WASP, she's unhappy and fat and her eyebrows are in need of tweezing. As Camille, the mental patient on a cruise, she's spectacularly glamorous and fun. The inexplicable heartthrob Paul Henreid costars. Directed by Irving Rapper. Warner Bros. 1942.

OUR DANCING DAUGHTERS

Gorgeous Jazz-Age Morality Tale. This movie attempts to prove that you can booze it up, dance, flirt, stay out all night, and still wind up okay—if you're honest. Joan Crawford became a big star after she played Diana Medford, a rich girl who lives life to the fullest. She dances on tabletops. She drinks sometimes, too. But she knows when to quit—and settles down with a nice husband. Another girl doesn't—and plunges to her death after one too many cocktails. Directed by Harry Beaumont. Cosmopolitan Pictures/MGM. 1928.

PATTON

Tormented Jackass/Military Hero. This biopic about Gen. George S. Patton was released during the Vietnam War, but the acting, writing, cinematography, music, and inspired directing (by Franklin J. Schaffner) were so extraordinary that even Hollywood couldn't resist loving it. The role George C. Scott was born to play. Twentieth Century Fox. 1970.

PERSONA

Mental-Illness Doppelgänger. Liv Ullmann plays a famous stage actress who has a mysterious emotional breakdown and stops speaking after a performance of *Electra*. She recuperates by the seaside, where her nurse, Bibi Andersson, fills in the long silences with stories from her own life. As the film progresses, Andersson starts to seem as troubled and insecure as her patient—while also beginning to assume Ullmann's persona. Written and directed by Ingmar Bergman. Svensk Filmindustri/United Artists. 1966.

THE PHILADELPHIA STORY

Two Million Memorable Lines. Katharine Hepburn's career was down the chute when she induced Philip Barry to write a play for her. She covered the cost of producing *The Philadelphia Story* on Broadway and took no salary, only a percentage of the profits—canny move, because the play was a huge hit. She bought the screen rights and shrewdly convinced Louis B. Mayer to produce it—and allow her to select the cast and director. Hepburn plays Tracy Lord, the chilly heiress who is poised to marry the wrong fellow. James Stewart is the tabloid reporter assigned to cover her society wedding. Cary Grant is the irrepressible C. K. Dexter Haven, the ex-husband who turns up just in time. Directed by George Cukor. MGM. 1940.

PICNIC AT HANGING ROCK

Creepy True (?) Mystery. In 1900, a group of Australian schoolgirls take a field trip to Hanging Rock, in the nearby wilderness. A handful of them go off to climb the mountain by themselves and never return—only their stockings and shoes are found. Director Peter Weir takes a story widely held to be true (though that's its own enigma), hints at a murky, mystical explanation, and finds a sexual-awakening theme too, but in the end, it's still a mystery and you feel a bit rattled for days afterward. Picnic Productions/Australian Film Commission/Atlantic. 1975.

PLANET OF THE APES

Gorgeous Sci-Fi Adventure. Charlton Heston bares his torso in this fantastic movie about an astronaut who gets tangled up in a time warp and wants to find his way back to Earth. The sad news is, he's already there—and the planet has been taken over by Roddy McDowall, Kim Hunter, and Maurice Evans in the most wonderful ape makeup. Great music and sweeping vistas. Directed by Franklin J. Schaffner, who made *Patton* the following year. Twentieth Century Fox/Apjac. 1968.

IL POSTINO

Romance. A goofy postman delivers mail to Pablo Neruda's island retreat overlooking the blue Mediterranean Sea and becomes inspired to court the town beauty. Massimo Troisi is superb as the mail carrier, but it's hard to believe he could really ride the bike up those hills. Directed by Michael Radford. Buena Vista/Cecchi. 1994.

QUEEN KELLY

Lost and Unfinished—but Still Talked About. Gloria Swanson and her lover/co-producer Joseph Kennedy fired Erich von Stroheim before he was able to finish this movie about a convent girl who goes bad and winds up in white slavery. Swanson, who plays the convent girl, thought Von Stroheim excessive and deranged—not to mention a sexually addicted misogynist. She had the movie recut and released it in Europe only. Various versions exist, but none of them particularly hang together right. United Artists/Gloria Swanson Productions/ Joseph Kennedy. 1929.

RAIN

Morality Play in Pago Pago, Talking Version. In 1932, as talkies were still finding their sea legs, Joan Crawford was assigned to play Sadie Thompson, the prostitute who winds up on a South Seas island waiting for the rain to stop. (Just four years earlier, Gloria Swanson had played Sadie in a hit silent version, *Sadie Thompson.*) Crawford's movie wasn't a huge hit, but she brings something else to the role—modernity, subtlety, and steamy scenes with Walter Huston, who plays a Bible-thumping fundamentalist eventually driven to suicide. Directed by Lewis Milestone. United Artists/Art Cinema Associates. 1932.

RAMONA

Campy American Indian Melodrama. Loretta Young seemed drawn to ridiculous costumes and romances where she could play a passionate good girl. As Ramona, she's a half-breed who takes on greedy white settlers. Hard to find on video. Directed by Henry King. Twentieth Century Fox. 1936.

REBECCA

Anxious Newlywed Thriller. This is Alfred Hitchcock's perfect take on the Daphne Du Maurier novel about a naive girl who marries a rich widower with a fabulous estate on the rugged cliffs of Cornwall. Joan Fontaine plays the socially awkward new bride. Laurence Olivier plays aristocrat Maxim de Winter, who may have killed his first wife. George Sanders is marvelous as the naughty cousin, Jack Favell. But Judith Anderson steals the show as the malevolent housekeeper to end all malevolent housekeepers, Mrs. Danvers. Selznick International Pictures. 1940.

REBEL WITHOUT A CAUSE

Don't-Trust-Anybody-Over-Thirty Message Film. James Dean plays a misunderstood and lonely kid who wanders into trouble with the police because his parents aren't paying attention. Dean ascended to stardom the year this movie was released—and became a cinema hero who made adolescent insecurity seem attractive. Natalie Wood plays a lonely girl. Sal Mineo plays a lonely boy. Directed by Nicholas Ray. Warner Bros. 1955.

RED DESERT

Moody Study of Alienation. It's deeply boring and brilliant at the same time, and the traffic sounds and construction noises are *meant* to be grating. You want to pull your hair out. But it's all for a point. Michelangelo Antonioni is trying to make you feel the way Monica Vitti's depressed character does. Even having an affair with her husband's best friend doesn't help. Film Duemila/Federiz/Franco Riz. 1964.

THE RIGHT STUFF

Astronaut Movie. It's about how the best test pilots in the military were the first men sent into space—as "Spam in a can." It's a good, weird true-life tale, and the book is great, but somehow the movie doesn't hold up. It's like watching a bad cartoon. Sam Shepard plays Chuck Yeager. Ed Harris plays John Glenn. Directed by Philip Kaufman. Ladd Company/Warner Bros. 1983.

RISKY BUSINESS

Teen Party Fantasy/Comedy. Tom Cruise is home alone and unwittingly fills his parents' house with hookers and pimps.

There's a famous love scene on a moving train too. Rebecca De Mornay plays the girl. Written and directed by Paul Brickman. Tisch-Avnet/Geffen Pictures/Warner Bros. 1983.

THE ROAD TO HONG KONG

Adventure/Comedy. Very tired final installment of the once-lively comedy series starring Bob Hope and Bing Crosby and Dorothy Lamour. In this one, Lamour, owing to her unsuitable age (she was forty-eight), has only a small part. Joan Collins is her garish replacement. Directed by Norman Panama. Melnor Pictures/United Artists. 1962.

ROAD TO SINGAPORE

Hope/Crosby/Lamour Road Picture #1. Bob Hope and Bing Crosby play two rich guys who make a pact to abstain from their favorite pastime—women—until they encounter a sensationally sweet Singapore girl played by Dorothy Lamour. Lots of gags, slapstick, and mistaken identities. Directed by Victor Schertzinger. Paramount. 1940.

ROAD TO UTOPIA

Hope/Crosby/Lamour Road Picture #4. Bob Hope and Bing Crosby play a couple of vaudevillians who wind up in the Klondike during the Gold Rush. Gags a-plenty, animals talk, and Dorothy Lamour winds up married to Hope at the end, which seems both unfortunate and unlikely. Isn't Bing better? Directed by Hal Walker. Paramount. 1946.

ROAD TO ZANZIBAR

Hope/Crosby/Lamour Road Picture #2. Set in Africa, this is a spoof of the jungle movies of the previous decade. This time, the guys are con men on the lam. Dorothy Lamour plays Donna Latour, a singer/dancer from Brooklyn who has come to Africa to find her brother. Directed by Victor Schertzinger. Paramount. 1941.

ROMA (A.K.A. FELLINI'S ROMA)

Homage/Memoir/Fantasy. This is Federico Fellini's gorgeous tribute to the city of his dreams and nightmares and everything else. It's about how a place can break your heart and answer your prayers at the same time. There's a papal fashion show that's not to be missed. Les Productions Artistes Associés/Produzioni Europee Associati/Ultra Film/United Artists. 1972.

RYAN'S DAUGHTER

Spare, Windswept Melodrama. It's spare because it's long (206 minutes) and there's room for everything without clutter. David Lean directed this gorgeous, moody tale about loneliness in marriage. When Pauline Kael, the film critic for *The New Yorker,* panned it—in a kind of personal, bitter way—Lean couldn't bring himself to make another picture for eleven years. Robert Mitchum plays a schoolteacher in a small village on the coast of Ireland. Sarah Miles plays Mitchum's unhappy, lovesick wife. Faraway Productions/MGM. 1970.

SADIE THOMPSON

Morality Play in Pago Pago, Silent Version. This is the Gloria Swanson version of the famous W. Somerset Maugham story "Miss Thompson," about a harlot whose past comes back to haunt her. Gloria is stunning. The director, Raoul Walsh, also plays the Marine sergeant who loves Sadie. Lionel Barrymore plays the fire-and-brimstone missionary who is driven mad by her. Gloria Swanson Pictures Corporation/United Artists. 1928.

THE SEVEN SAMURAI

Medieval Adventure. This is Akira Kurosawa's unforgettable and weird classic about sixteenth-century Japanese farmers who hire professional soldiers—samurai—to defend their village from bandits. The battle scenes are unsurpassed. The samurai are perfectly drawn, beautifully portrayed, and you can't help but cry when they start dying off. The Hollywood remake, *The Magnificent Seven,* is good but in a completely different way. Toho/Columbia Pictures. 1954.

THE SHELTERING SKY

Is Our Marriage Okay? If you can imagine an achingly lovely desert romance that combines the directionless despair of *L'Avventura* and the spacy mood of *The English Patient,* with a few bits of John Malkovich being John Malkovich thrown in, you come close to experiencing the essence of this movie (based on the cult novel by Paul Bowles) without having to see it. And if you don't like to strain yourself intellectually, or emotionally, this might be the preferable—not to mention quicker—way to go. Cinematography and acting (with Debra Winger and Malkovich) so beautiful it's scary. Directed by Bernardo Bertolucci. Film Trustees Ltd./Sahara Company/TAO Film/Recorded Pictures Company/Aldrich Group/Warner Bros. 1990.

SHREK

Animated. It's an anti–fairy tale. Shrek is a green ogre who never complains—a far cry from the neurotic, whiny, Woody

Allen–ish cartoon creatures that dominated animation for the last two decades of the twentieth century. DreamWorks SKG. 2001.

SNOW WHITE AND THE SEVEN DWARFS

Animated Fairy Tale. She has the highest voice and the tiniest feet—no wonder she's still so popular in Japan. Has anybody ever noticed that the Seven Dwarfs all look a little like Walt Disney? This was his first feature-length cartoon and everybody told him it wouldn't fly. But it did and still does. Walt Disney Pictures. 1937.

SONG OF THE THIN MAN

Detective Comedy. This is the last installment in the series— William Powell retired in 1955 after making *Mister Roberts,* much to the disappointment of Myrna Loy, who, it seems, would have kept making *Thin Man* movies from her wheelchair. In *Song,* unfortunately, everything has grown stale and the two stars are losing the fight against gravity. Even Myrna seems humorless. Directed by Edward Buzzell. MGM. 1947.

SOYLENT GREEN

Future Shock. Charlton Heston plays a cop in this stylish vision of New York City in 2022. Space is at a premium, along with air-conditioning and strawberry jam. (The hungry hordes live on rations of dry biscuits called Soylent Green, which turn out to be made of people.) Heston befriends an old man, played by Edward G. Robinson (touching and sensitive in his final screen performance), who tells Heston what life was like before all nature was destroyed. Directed by Richard Fleischer. MGM. 1973.

STEALING BEAUTY

Paternity Mystery. Liv Tyler stars as a nineteen-year-old girl who wants to be a poet, lose her virginity, and figure out who her biological father really is. She comes to Italy one summer to visit her dead mother's old bohemian friends and accomplishes all three of her goals. Bernardo Bertolucci made this little film—written by Susan Minot—in the Tuscan countryside after finishing the hugely ambitious *The Sheltering Sky* along with two giant epics set in Asia, and there's a sense here that he hasn't quite adjusted to working without thousands of extras and millions of dollars' worth of costumes. Something's a bit off. Fiction Cinematografica/Recorded Pictures Company/UGC/Fox Searchlight Pictures. 1996.

THE STORY OF ALEXANDER GRAHAM BELL

Silly Biopic. Don Ameche plays the inventor of the telephone. Loretta Young plays the deaf girl he marries. Her costumes are outrageously bad, but, miraculously, Young still looks soulful and luminous. Directed by Irving Cummings. Twentieth Century Fox. 1939.

THE STRANGER

Nazi-Spy Thriller. After the tomatoes were thrown at *Citizen Kane* (1941) and *The Magnificent Ambersons* (1942), Orson Welles set out to make a more ordinary, accessible movie. But maybe he went too far. *The Stranger* is about an escaped Nazi who hides out in a sleepy American college town after the war. Welles plays the cynical, arrogant Nazi, who has disguised himself as a cynical, arrogant university professor. Edward G. Robinson plays the Nazi-hunter who tracks him down. Loretta Young plays Welles's wife. Some great moments—including a hair-raising climax involving a tolling church clock. International Pictures/RKO. 1946.

A STREETCAR NAMED DESIRE

Romantic Notions Bump Up Against Vulgarity. It's hard to imagine a better play, a better movie of a play, or better acting. Marlon Brando is the disgusting young hunk Stanley Kowalski. Vivien Leigh plays the neurotic and fragile and culturally refined Blanche Du Bois. Tennessee Williams wrote it, of course. Directed by Elia Kazan. Warner Bros. 1951.

THE TEN COMMANDMENTS

Swords and Sandals—and Tablets. Charlton Heston is the definitive Moses without one false step, only lots of false facial hair and a very big wig at the end. The all-star cast (including Yul Brynner, Anne Baxter, Judith Anderson, and Vincent Price, to name but a few) is larger-than-life, like the production. For some unknown reason, Edward G. Robinson was allowed to play an ancient Israelite with a heavy New York accent. Directed by Cecil B. De Mille. Paramount. 1956.

THE TERMINATOR

Sci-Fi Comic-Book Adventure. Nobody could ever say that writer/director James Cameron doesn't have a wicked imagination. This movie is full of new gimmicks, new sights, new ideas, and some very new nasty stuff. Arnold Schwarzenegger plays a killer robot in this instant classic. Linda Hamilton plays a macho mom with a gun. Hemdale Film Corporation/Pacific Western/Orion Pictures. 1984.

TEST PILOT

Tortured Macho Men in Love with Myrna Loy. Clark Gable plays a daring aviator who is hooked on cheating death in the air and drinking too much on the ground. Spencer Tracy dies. Myrna Loy cries. A great movie that doesn't deserve obscurity. Directed by Victor Fleming. MGM. 1938.

THE THIN MAN

Detective Comedy. At the last minute, director W. S. "Woody" Van Dyke put William Powell and Myrna Loy together again—they'd thrown some sparks in *Manhattan Melodrama.* It was a stroke of inspired casting. This first *Thin Man* movie was made in less than a month and on the smallest budget possible. But the stars sail through each scene together like an elegant yacht in a good wind. Their banter is famously good. The drinking scenes—the movie was made immediately after Prohibition was lifted—are legendary. MGM. 1934.

THERE'S A GIRL IN MY SOUP

Comedy. Peter Sellers plays a famous TV cook and gourmand—he's supercilious and stuffy. Goldie Hawn plays an adorable airhead with a loutish boyfriend she's trying to make jealous. Sellers picks her up and takes her on the road for a hilarious romp through all the Jet Set hangouts of Europe circa 1969. Directed by Roy Boulting. Ascot Productions/Columbia Pictures. 1970.

TIMES SQUARE LADY

Melodrama. Another forgotten movie of the forgotten Helen Twelvetrees, the actress with the unforgettable name. She costars with Robert Taylor and Virginia Bruce. Directed by George B. Seitz. MGM. 1935.

TOO HOT TO HANDLE

Aviatrix Drama. Myrna Loy shows us what a smart, sophisticated "modern" woman looks like, this time dressed as an airplane pilot. Clark Gable is the fearless newsreel reporter who wants a scoop. Directed by Jack Conway. MGM. 1938.

THE TREASURE OF THE SIERRA MADRE

Depressing Gold-Fever Classic. All John Huston movies are essentially about losers losing—and this one's a beaut. Three prospectors overcome by greed are reduced to lying, stealing, and killing. Humphrey Bogart is the immortal Fred C. Dobbs. Walter Huston (the director's famous father) plays the nimble-tongued Howard. John won two Oscars (for writing and directing), and Dad won Best Supporting Actor, inspiring the predictable heartwarming media stir and stories about a "dynasty." Warner Bros. 1948.

TROPIC HOLIDAY

Hokey Musical Adventure. A Hollywood writer (Ray Milland) is sent to Mexico to soak up the romance. He's engaged to a star but falls for a local beauty, Manuela—played by Dorothy Lamour. Martha Raye sings, and the score is pretty good. Beyond this, I'd be grasping for nice things to say. Directed by Theodore Reed. Paramount. 1938.

TRUE GRIT

Western with an Eye Patch. John Wayne is old and beleaguered and potbellied as the U.S. Marshall Reuben J. "Rooster"

Cogburn—and playing against a fourteen-year-old girl who wants him to avenge her father's death—but he's still John Wayne and that's enough. Directed by Henry Hathaway. Paramount. 1969.

TYPHOON

Jungle Adventure. Dorothy Lamour plays a scantily clad girl who has been a castaway since childhood. She's found by two sailors and you can probably imagine the rest. For some reason, Ray Milland is not in this picture. Directed by Louis King. Paramount. 1940.

THE UNKNOWN

Extremely Weird Silent Movie. This was a vehicle for the talents of Lon Chaney, who was called "the Man of a Thousand Faces." In this picture, he plays a contortionist with a double thumb on one hand who pretends to have no arms. When he falls in love with a sweet girl, played by Joan Crawford, who tells him that she can't stand the touch of a man's hands, he has his arms amputated to make himself honest—and more lovable. Then she changes her mind. No kidding. Directed by Tod Browning. MGM. 1927.

VALLEY OF THE DOLLS

A Starlet's Descent. This is an over-the-top version of the usual Hollywood story—burned by love, a young actress turns to drugs and makes a stunning cluster of bad decisions. With Patty Duke, Barbara Parkins, Sharon Tate, and Lee Grant. Judy Garland was supposed to play the part Susan Hayward wound up with, but was, ironically, indisposed. Directed by Mark Robson. Red Lion/Twentieth Century Fox. 1967.

VIE PRIVÉE (A.K.A. A VERY PRIVATE AFFAIR)

Celebrity Fable. Brigitte Bardot stars in this preposterous movie about fame—and how it ruins your life. She's an actress who, like Bardot herself, grows unhappy the more successful she becomes. In the last scene, she tries to evade the media who stalk her by walking on a roof. When the paparazzis' flashbulbs flash, she falls—presumably to her death. Marcello Mastroianni plays her boyfriend—but the two disliked each other in real life, which may be another reason the movie doesn't work. Directed by Louis Malle. Progéfi/Cipra/CCM/MGM. 1961.

VIVA LAS VEGAS

Musical. Elvis Presley plays a race-car driver who arrives in Las Vegas for some fun. He falls in love with Ann-Margret— and did in real life—but then, who wouldn't? Great songs and shimmying. Directed by George Sidney. MGM. 1964.

THE WAY WE WERE

Mixed-Class Romance. An upper-class WASP, played by Robert Redford, wants to become a serious novelist, but he's also given to yachting, cocktail parties, and goofing off. Barbra Streisand is his love interest, a politically radical Jewish girl who can't stand any of Redford's jaded, starchy friends. They marry and move to Hollywood—where Redford sells out by writing for pictures and Streisand defends everybody on the blacklist. Wistful ending. Great title song. Directed by Sydney Pollack. Columbia/Rastar. 1973.

WHAT EVER HAPPENED TO BABY JANE?

Horror Show. This became a cult movie, partly because it's campy, and partly because the powerful performances made people so uncomfortable. Bette Davis plays a deranged former child star, Baby Jane Hudson, who lives in a very darkly lit Hollywood mansion with her long-suffering, co-dependent sister, Blanche, played by Joan Crawford. Directed by Robert Aldrich. Aldrich/Warner Bros. 1962.

THE WILD BUNCH

Big Bloody Western. In the 1960s, when everybody was murmuring "Make Love, Not War," director Sam Peckinpah rose to prominence—almost as if to compensate for all the pacifist sentiment in the air. His cinematic violence is supposed to be art, though. The spurting blood in Peckinpah's film is stylish, even poetic, and the bad guys fall like dancers in a perfectly choreographed ballet. William Holden and Robert Ryan—who both look incredible in their long, slim dungarees—play anachronistic cowboy outlaws in the early twentieth century. With Ben Johnson, Warren Oates, and Ernest Borgnine too. Warner Bros./Seven Arts. 1969.

THE WIZARD OF OZ

Fairy Tale/Musical. Such a classic, and still so alive in our minds, there's nothing more to say except that "Over the Rainbow" is what movies may be all about. Directed by Victor Fleming (along with King Vidor, who did the sepia Kansas scenes). MGM. 1939.

YENTL

Cross-Dressing Musical. If this movie were funnier, and not so melodramatic, it might have been wonderful. Plus, nobody really wanted to see Barbra Streisand—her first time out as a writer-director-producer-star—dressed as a boy. Barwood Films/Ladbroke Investments/MGM. 1983.

ZAZA

Silent. When Gloria Swanson made this movie, she was twenty-four—and gorgeous, unspeakably rich, and acclaimed as the Queen of the Screen and the Best-Dressed Woman in the World. An average of ten thousand fan letters were delivered to Paramount for her each week. In *Zaza,* she plays a tough but honorable French soubrette who falls in love with an aristocrat. When she discovers that he's a husband and father, she gives him up. Until she died, *Zaza* remained one of Swanson's favorite films—not just because it was made during her heyday, or because she adored the director, Allan Dwan, but because it was the "fastest, easiest, most enjoyable picture I ever made." Famous Players–Lasky Corporation/Paramount. 1923.

ACKNOWLEDGMENTS

In the parts of this novel where real actors appear, I've tried to rely on primary sources—accounts that movie stars have given of their own lives—rather than biographies. In some cases, in hopes of capturing her sensibility in her own words, I've taken anecdotes directly from a star's memoir. In particular, I am indebted to *My Side of the Road,* by Dorothy Lamour, *Myrna Loy: Being and Becoming,* by Myrna Loy and James Kotsilibas-Davis, and the magnificent *Swanson on Swanson,* by Gloria Swanson.

My portrait of Loretta Young was drawn from interviews she gave during her lifetime, and from *The Things I Had to Learn,* an as-told-to written by Helen Ferguson, as well as Joan Wester Anderson's *Forever Young.* For Tallulah Bankhead, I leaned on Brendan Gill's *Tallulah* and Denis Brian's *Tallulah, Darling.*

My attempt to capture Marion Davies at the end of her film career was based largely on research I did for an article that appears in *Vanity Fair's Hollywood* ("San Simeon's Child"). Thanks to *The New Yorker* magazine, which originally assigned the piece, I was able to interview biographer Fred Lawrence

Guiles, whose book *Marion Davies* has no equal. Interviews with Davies's living family members, and also with Randolph Hearst and Billie Dove, were enormously helpful.

I was helped tremendously by online movie databases, namely imdb.com and silent-movies.com. A handful of pictorials and reference books guided me, in particular *The Image Makers,* by Richard Lawton and Paul Trent; *Vanity Fair's Hollywood,* edited by Graydon Carter; *Halliwell's Film and Video Guide; The Film Encyclopedia,* by Ephraim Katz; *The Movie Guide,* by James Monaco and the editors of *Baseline;* and two excellent books by Jeanine Basinger, *Silent Stars* and *A Woman's View: How Hollywood Spoke to Women, 1930–1960.* I also want to acknowledge my debt to homefilmfestival.com, a terrific movie-rental service where I found hard-to-rent movies I needed to see—from *Our Dancing Daughters* to *Zabriskie Point.*

In the seven years I was a feature writer for *The Washington Post,* I had many chances to meet and interview film directors and actors—experiences that made all the difference when it came to writing this novel. I profiled Bernardo Bertolucci for the newspaper in 1995, and over the years, I met or interviewed others who are mentioned in this book, including Lena Basquette, Robert De Niro, Clint Eastwood, Katharine Hepburn, Charlton Heston, and Peter O'Toole, who told me about how a seagull is pecked to death if you tie a piece of red string to its leg. As a young reporter covering the Kennedy Center Honors, I enjoyed a gossipy evening with director Billy Wilder, who shared the rumors about Greta Garbo that circulated in Hollywood during her heyday.

My friends Geraldine Brooks and Michael Kohn read the manuscript in early drafts and offered invaluable suggestions large and small. My cousin Leslee Peyton Sherrill made me laugh, talked me off a few ledges, and always seemed to know my characters better than I did. My uncle Steve Sherrill was a tour guide, raconteur, jazzman, and hotel-o-phile whose enthusiasm so often inspired me. Flip Brophy is a fabulous agent and even better friend. Elsa Walsh had last-minute suggestions that made all the difference. My husband, Bill Powers, has been creative, funny, brutal, patient, generous, tirelessly loyal—and pretended to enjoy having a starlet around the house during most of our marriage.

There are so many people to thank at Random House. Benjamin Dreyer, Sarah D'Imperio, Laura Goldin, Sunshine Lucas, and Beth Thomas helped everything move smoothly through what can be—for so many authors—a difficult process. Ann Godoff, my editor, is somebody I've come to think of as, if not divine, then very near its threshold.

Last but not least, I'd like to express my gratitude to *Esquire,* where "Dream Girl: The Allegra Coleman Nobody Knows," the germ of this novel, first appeared. Very little of that piece survived the journey to this book, but the essence of Allegra is, as she would put it, unchanging.

ABOUT THE AUTHOR

Martha Sherrill has written for *The Washington Post*, *Esquire*, *Vanity Fair*, and *The New York Times Magazine*, among other publications. Her last book, a work of nonfiction, was *The Buddha from Brooklyn*. She was raised in Los Angeles but doesn't live there anymore.